DATE DUE

KILLER RIFF

Also by Sheryl J. Anderson

Killer Deal
Killer Cocktail
Killer Heels

Sheryl J. Anderson

KILLER RIFF

St. Martin's Minotaur
New York

This is a work of fiction. All of the characters, organizations, and events portrayed in this novel are either products of the author's imagination or are used fictitiously.

www.minotaurbooks.com

Library of Congress Cataloging-in-Publication Data

Anderson, Sheryl J., 1958–
Killer riff / Sheryl J. Anderson.—1st ed.
p. cm.
ISBN-13: 978-0-312-35141-0
ISBN-10: 0-312-35141-0
1. Forrester, Molly (Fictitious character)—Fiction.
2. Women journalists—Fiction. 3. Sound recording executives and producers—Crimes against—Fiction. 4. Music trade—Fiction.
5. Single women—New York (State)—New York—Fiction.
6. Manhattan (New York, N.Y.)—Fiction. I. Title.

PS3551.N3947K555 2007
813'.54—dc22 2007035211

First Edition: November 2007

10 9 8 7 6 5 4 3 2 1

To my parents,
Alden & June Anderson,
for everything, for always

Acknowledgments

Inspiration comes from such wonderful places:

Thanks to my uncle, Donald McLean, whose tale about "Hot Heels" planted the seed of this story several Christmases ago. And further thanks to Uncle Donald and Aunt Diana, Uncle Bud and Aunt Connie, and my parents, for passing along their love of music, especially jazz.

Thanks to our dear friend Ann Abraham for the rockin' title (and the wicked air guitar performed while pitching it), as well as for the great pictures and the world-class margaritas.

Thanks to my Bunco group, who provide more inspiration than they know (especially on those nights when we're actually a Talko group!).

Thanks to my colleagues and students at Act One, who keep me on my toes, spiritually and artistically.

My dad, an incomparable father, friend, mentor, and inspiration, passed away while I was writing *Killer Riff,* so I want to give special thanks to all the people who were so gracious to my family during a very difficult time—our beautiful extended family, our loving congregations in California and Virginia, and all our amazing friends.

Special thanks to our marvelous editor Kelley Ragland, for

her infinite patience, to her splendid assistant, Matt Martz, and the rest of the team at St. Martin's, and to our terrific agent Andy Zack.

And love to the usual suspects . . .

KILLER RIFF

1

"I can't balance my diet, so how am I supposed to balance my life?"

Tricia nodded sympathetically. "Everything you've been hoping for. For it to all happen at the same time—it's just criminal!"

Coming from anyone else—in fact, coming from my other best friend, who was also at the table—it would have sounded snarky at the very least. More probably, it would have sounded like a righteous put-down. But coming from Tricia Vincent, it was a sincere and heartfelt expression of how fate can take something that should be glorious and turn it into a major kick in the teeth.

Cassady Lynch pushed a glass of champagne across the table to me. "I thought we were here to celebrate."

"That was before I had two things to be happy about." Two things that clashed with each other with all the vigor of freight trains colliding at top speed. On the one hand, I had the professional promotion I'd been dreaming of. On the other, the romantic redemption I'd been yearning for. But since professional issues were responsible for derailing the romance to begin with, I felt smacked by an Olympian dose of irony, with no clear vision of how—or if—I could make this work.

2

Things had been much more promising earlier in the afternoon as I'd stood nervously in my editor's office, listening to her proclaim, "Molly, I'm going to make you happy, and it just kills me."

Gotta give the boss lady this: You always know where you stand with her. Usually that place is akin to the crumbling lip of a rumbling volcano, but there's never any question it's exactly where Eileen wants you to be. So she gets points for honesty, if nothing else. The problem is, from that point, it can be pretty tricky to see where she's headed, and even though I should know better by now, I always try to figure that out. For the most part, it's an exercise in futility, but it's the only regular exercise I get.

On this particular occasion, looking ahead was especially tempting because Henry Kwon was somehow part of the equation. He was slouched on the couch in Eileen's office. I couldn't tell if that was an expression of how relaxed he was about what was happening or how impossible it is to sit properly on that ridiculously unyielding piece of furniture. Even so, he looked great—he always looks great—and he was smiling. What could that mean? I looked him in the eye, and his smile grew.

Having a handsome man smile at you is rarely a bad thing. But this particular handsome man was also the associate publisher of our magazine, so the potential reasons for his smile were all the more intriguing. And the fact that he was flat-out gorgeous didn't hurt. Especially since I had been painfully single for seven and a half weeks and deeply missed having someone gorgeous smile at me.

Pushing that distraction from my mind, I did my best to concentrate on decoding what Eileen and Henry were up to. Even though I've been out of school more years than I care to admit, I still feel as though I've been summoned to the principal's office when I have to go into Eileen's lair. So even though Eileen was suspiciously proclaiming that she was going to make me happy, my perpetually fluctuating self-worth and guilty conscience were conspiring to make me nervous. That annoyed me, because I don't like letting Eileen get to me. I particularly didn't want Henry to think of me as anything but cool and controlled.

I tried to dismiss the feeling that I'd done something wrong and focus on the positive sheen to Henry's smile. Eileen was too savvy to have pulled him into something political between the two of us, so this had to be substantial. It had to be about something pretty darn good, too, if even Eileen was forced to admit it would make me happy. Were they moving my advice column to a different position in the magazine? Expanding it? Or was I being traded to another magazine for a copy editor and an assistant to be named later?

"The Publisher was very impressed with the article you wrote about Garth Henderson's murder," Henry said smoothly.

I nodded, remembering the huge bouquet of flowers The Publisher had sent me after I'd helped nab Garth's killer. Although I had wondered if part of the grandness of the arrangement was because I'd sent Eileen flying across a densely populated hotel ballroom in the process. The Publisher, after all, is known for his sense of humor. "I appreciated the flowers very much," I said.

Eileen grimaced as though bracing herself to taste something foul. "So he wants you to do it again."

It took me a moment. "A follow-up? An article on the trial?"

"No," Henry said, "not that specific. But we do want you to focus on feature articles from now on."

I actually considered fainting. Millions of microscopic helium balloons launched themselves in my head, trying to push off the top of my skull, and my hands tingled and sweated simultaneously.

"Features?" I repeated, knowing it didn't sound bright but that it beat standing there gaping in silence.

"We've been discussing new ways to increase the profile of the magazine, and including more substantial editorial content is absolutely key. The investigative articles you've done are exactly the kind of thing we're looking for. So we want that to be your new focus, and we'll use it as a springboard for further growth of the entire publication." Henry's smile grew. "No pressure."

And no pressure just because this was what I'd always wanted, because this was a dream coming true, because I knew I could really make something of this break.

"Thank you," I said, wishing I could be eloquent and charming, but caught so completely by surprise that two words were all I felt able to string together. I'd been working toward this for such a long time, trying to move into feature writing, grabbing chances when they came my way and proving myself, but never getting the bump. In the last few weeks, I'd actually been quietly checking out opportunities at other magazines because I figured I was never going to be released from my existence as an advice columnist while I was working for Eileen. She's not the sort to recognize and nurture potential; she's more the crush-or-curry school of management, specializing in picking favorites, usually attractive young men, and whipping everyone else with delight and regularity.

Small wonder it was killing her to give me this break. Or, more correctly, to sit there and watch Henry give it to me and not be able to do anything about it but scowl. I knew part of her unhappiness was because of her aforementioned aversion to making me happy, but there was more at stake here, too.

She'd been brought in to "put teeth" in the magazine. If The Publisher and Henry felt that wasn't happening fast enough and that they had to get involved in the process, perhaps Eileen was spending some time standing on that volcano lip herself.

"There is a catch," she said with a crinkle of her little nose that was sharp enough to burst my bubble. I kept smiling. How bad could the catch be if it was part of becoming a feature writer?

Henry frowned, one of those polite frowns bosses use to soften a blow. My stomach gave a lurch like the one you get on the first dip on a roller coaster, the one that's the tease for that huge first drop. "This isn't my usual style," Henry explained, "but we have your first subject, already approved by The Publisher and Eileen."

My breath came back with a happy puff. "That's fine," I said, immediately feeling better because I couldn't imagine an article they'd come up with that I wouldn't be willing to write.

"And he's dead, just the way you like them. Sadly for you, though, he got there all on his own. No conspiracy, no mystery. Nothing to solve, just an article to write," Eileen said with enough precision that I knew I was being warned as much as I was being informed.

I understood why she was concerned, given my track record of digging into a story where everyone thought there were no unanswered questions and winding up in the middle of a homicide investigation. She didn't approve, even though I always met my other deadlines; had I fallen on my face with one story, I have no doubt she would have taken great delight in sending me packing. But I'd worked hard and been fortunate, other than losing my boyfriend. Now, here at last was the step up I'd been striving for the whole time. Whoever this person had been, I would dive in and do a great article to prove The Publisher's faith in me—and Eileen's inability to erode it—had been for the best.

"It's not all about him," Henry said, cutting a look at Eileen. They'd already discussed this, and not altogether happily. I wondered which was upsetting her more, the choice of subject or my promotion. Henry continued, "It's about his daughter keeping his legacy, that sort of angle. Right?"

Eileen gave him the kind of smile you give the dentist after he's shoved the X-ray film as far back in your mouth as it will go. "Right."

Henry's marvelously dark eyes swung back to me. "My sister went to college with Olivia Elliott. Russell Elliott's daughter."

I nodded in recognition. Russell Elliott, a renowned rock-and-roll producer who had started out as the manager of one of my favorite bands, had died three weeks before, alone in his Riverside Drive apartment with music on the stereo and a highball glass in his hand. While the print media politely conveyed the medical examiner's finding that it was an accidental overdose of prescription medication mixed with alcohol, the Internet and tabloids feasted on the similarities between Russell's death and that of the lead singer of the aforementioned band. Message boards blazed with theories about suicide, old affairs, demons from the past, and other uncomfortable things it has to be tough to hear when you're mourning the loss of your father.

Olivia had attempted to drown out the rumors by throwing a monumental postfuneral bash that had been attended by a blinding array of rock royalty. It hadn't quelled the loose talk, but it had put a pretty gloss on it; people were whispering now instead of proclaiming.

"As you can imagine, she's pretty shattered. She's also unhappy with what's been written about her dad since he died.

And I get her point. I don't know how familiar you are with Russell's work—"

"I had a poster of Subject to Change on my bedroom wall in high school," I admitted.

Henry laughed in understanding. "I spent my entire junior year trying to get my hair to look like Micah's."

Micah Crowley had been the dark, brooding, and intensely sexy lead singer of Subject to Change Without Notice, a blues-based rock band that ripped through the chatter of the hair bands in the late 1980s, helping pave the way for grunge and roots rock. Russell Elliott had been Micah's best friend in college and became the band's manager. Depending on which stories you believed, Russell was largely to thank for guiding the band's artistic development or Russell was mainly responsible for the infamous fights with producers, session musicians, and record executives that were part of the band's history. Toward the end, Russell had begun producing the albums—again, either because he was shaping and protecting their vision or because no one else wanted to put up with the drama. But no matter how it was told, the story ended the same way: Micah Crowley overdosed in 1997, and the band fell apart.

After Micah's death, Russell had become guardian of both the band's music and Micah's family. He'd also developed a solid reputation as an innovative producer who didn't throw temper tantrums anymore—either because he'd cleaned up his act or because it had actually been Micah throwing them—and who'd launched several successful acts in the last couple of years on his own label. His most recent star was Jordan Crowley, one of Micah's sons.

"Are you sure the poster wasn't on your ceiling?" Eileen said with a sniff in my direction.

"Did you like them, or were you too old for such foolishness by then?" Henry asked her. My admiration for him doubled on the spot as she blinked slowly, searching for a response.

"I'm more classically oriented," she replied. I wanted to ask if she meant Beethoven or disco but decided not to push my luck in the middle of such a crucial conversation.

"I'm glad you bring a familiarity with the band to the piece," Henry continued to me. "Thing is, Olivia feels all the press surrounding her dad's death has been about how he took care of Claire and Adam, and now Jordan, after Micah's death. That he's viewed as part of Micah's legend, so his own larger contributions to the music industry have gotten short shrift. My sister mentioned it to me in passing, but I see an intriguing story there. And coming from the daughter's point of view, it's perfect for *Zeitgeist*. And for your first assignment as a full-time feature writer."

Squealing with glee on the inside, I strove to be polished and professional on the outside. "Thank you, Henry. Eileen. I can't tell you how much I appreciate this opportunity," I said.

"Personally, I think it's overdue," Henry said, standing. Eileen glared at him so hard, it made her roots show, but he ignored her. "Morgan in Legal will talk to you about the new contract, pay structure, all that." I'd been so thrilled about getting my dream job that I hadn't even thought about it meaning a raise, too. *Suh-weet.* He held out a business card. "Here are Olivia's numbers. She's expecting your call, keep me apprised."

We had a brief diploma-exchange tangle as I tried to both take the card and shake his hand, but he smiled at the right moment and made me feel much calmer. "Thank you," I said, looking him right in the eye and trying to convey my gratitude and excitement. "Sadly, words escape me."

Henry laughed warmly. "Just make sure they're back by

deadline. Congratulations, Molly." He nodded at Eileen. "Have fun replacement shopping."

I'd intended to follow him out of the office, but that pulled me up short. "Replacement shopping?"

Henry paused in the doorway. "Your column. We're going to keep you too busy for you to stay with it."

I was surprised by the sharpness of the sting as the news pierced my spinning brain. Of course I had to give up my column. That was a good thing. I'd been eager to move beyond dispensing advice to the distraught, obsessive, and lovelorn for a long time. Still, I found myself feeling possessive and even a little sad. I'd created "You Can Tell Me," and it was odd to think of handing it over to some unknown party. Unless they'd already figured out that part. "Do you have someone in mind?"

Henry shook his head, gesturing to Eileen. She pursed her lips and turned to me. "I'm still absorbing this happy news, so I haven't considered its repercussions."

"I'd like to open it up to magazine staffers, if you think that's feasible," Henry suggested. "We should be doing more promoting from within."

Eileen's lips unpursed and curled into a smile. "Oh yes. Let's make it a contest. Our own little *American Idol.* Post some letters and have people answer them. Best answer gets the job."

Henry wasn't going to let her get away with being sarcastic. He opened his arms in a grand gesture. "I love it. Great idea."

Eileen's nostrils flared. "You're not serious. Can you imagine the dreck they'll produce?" She wiggled her French-tipped fingers in the direction of the bull pen outside her office door, where most of the junior editorial staff sat. "Who could we even trust to screen the responses?"

"No one but you," Henry replied. I wasn't sure which was more entertaining, Eileen's discomfort or Henry's pleasure in it. This was a whole new take on Eileen's position in the organization, and I found it fascinating.

"It's Molly's column," she protested with the annoyance of a big sister who's been asked to baby-sit on a Friday night.

"So you and Molly can screen them together, then the three of us will sit down and make the final selection. How's that sound?"

"Great," I said quickly.

Eileen smiled jaggedly. "I look forward to it."

"It'll be a party," Henry said with a smile and a wink as he walked out of the office.

I started to follow him, but Eileen had another idea. "Molly," she said with a thick coating of ice.

I turned around and launched a preemptive attack. "Eileen, I really can't begin to tell you how much I appreciate this. I know we've had our differences, but I also know that you're going to be very pleased by what I bring to the magazine from this new vantage point."

Startled, Eileen took a moment before responding. "Isn't that sweet. I just want to make sure we understand each other."

"About?"

"About how this really changes nothing."

"Except what I'm doing."

"Yes, but you're still doing it for me."

She rose to walk around her desk and get closer to me. It wasn't going to lead to a congratulatory hug, I knew that much. For a flickering moment, I had thought this promotion might encourage a better relationship with my boss because I'd be doing what I was supposed to be doing, not pushing to do something more. But I could tell by the way her petite shoulders squared as she advanced on me that this was only going to fan the flames. She'd been working hard to keep me in my place, wherever she perceived it to be, but now Henry had lifted me out of it. Was her new hobby going to become trying to trip me up so Henry would withdraw the promotion? It sounded paranoid, but working for Eileen for any extended period brings that out in people.

"I'm sure you're going to do good work. And I simply won't publish it if it isn't," she said as she stopped in front of me. "Just remember, The Publisher giveth, but the editor taketh away."

"That won't be necessary," I assured her. I thought about hugging her just to see what she'd do but decided not to start off my new gig by pushing my luck. Besides, I was pretty sure her head would explode, and that wouldn't be pleasant for anyone.

Eileen tilted her head to the side, like a cat deciding whether to play with a mouse or eat it. With an exasperated sigh, she said, "Write a sample question for your column and give it to me. I'll write a memo to the staff about the process of being named your heir."

"Thank you," I said, backing toward the door.

Her lips twitched in the vicinity of a smile. "I had no idea you and Henry were so close."

"We're not," I said, hoping that she wasn't suggesting what I was sure she was suggesting.

"So this brilliant idea leapt into his head all by itself."

"You'd have to ask him," I said, certain she already had and hoping she'd been more graceful with him than she was being with me.

"Fine. Be coy, even though it doesn't suit you."

"Eileen," I ventured, emboldened by the glorious news, "maybe he just thinks I'm a good writer."

"Of course, how silly of me," she oozed. "Merit."

"Isn't that how you got your job?" I asked.

I meant it as a point of perspective, but I could tell it struck a deep and dissonant chord. Eileen's carefully plucked eyebrows knotted together, and she pointed to her office door. "Weren't you leaving?"

I hustled out the door and into the office bull pen, wondering what key point of Eileen's past I had tripped over as her door slammed behind me.

"That went well."

Skyler Christopher was Eileen's current assistant, a job that turns over so often, there should be a turnstile by the desk. A sloe-eyed brunette prone to tight sweaters and tighter skirts, she'd been a startling choice, given Eileen's track record of selecting gay men and dowdy women to guard her office door. Then the grapevine reported that Skyler's grandparents were pals of The Publisher. Eileen doesn't like anyone sharing her spotlight, but she also doesn't miss a chance to be political. Skyler struck me as too smart to last long in her current position, but she was fun to have around in the meantime.

"She's very happy for me," I said.

"I can tell. Congratulations, by the way."

"Thanks."

"So who's going to get your column?" She said it casually, her eyes never leaving her monitor, but I could hear the steely purpose under the question. Three weeks on the job and already looking for her next move. Who could blame her?

"Whoever writes the best response to a sample question. Unlock that inner Ann Landers and go for it," I said, and her eyes swung up to meet mine for just a moment. We exchanged smiles, and I headed back to my desk to start spreading the news.

I was tempted to e-mail everyone so there wouldn't be a question about who got called first. But that was quickly supplanted by the desire to call my boyfriend. And it wasn't until my hand was actually on the phone that I remembered I couldn't call my boyfriend because he wasn't exactly my boyfriend anymore. Mainly because of stories like the one Henry had liked so much.

Kyle Edwards, the man about whom I continued to be absolutely nuts, is an NYPD homicide detective. As supportive and understanding as he tried to be, my attraction to dangerous stories had led to an impasse in our relationship. He'd decided we needed to take a break, and I certainly felt broken. Since the split began, we'd talked only a couple of times; in the last three weeks, we hadn't talked at all, which I tried to ascribe to our individual schedules, even though I knew our individual stubbornness was really to blame.

So I went back to pre-Kyle mode and called my best friends to tell them. Tricia was with a client, but when I explained to her assistant that I had big news and Tricia should call me when she got a chance, her assistant put me on hold and Tricia picked up immediately.

"What big news?" she asked cheerily.

"It can wait. Take care of your client."

"It can wait, but I can't. Besides, they're trying to decide on linen colors, and I may not be able to get back to you until sometime next week." Tricia Vincent is an event planner, the key to her success being that you feel as if you're getting great personal advice from that one friend whose own style and look you secretly covet, "I'm trying to convince them that gray napkins will look dirty, not elegant, and it may take awhile. Tell me."

So I told her about my promotion and delighted in her gasp of pleasure. "*Yes!* Are you jumping up and down right this very minute?"

"Actually, no. Wrong shoes."

"Fine, I'll jump for you. And I'll meet you for champagne at the place of your choosing at six p.m. Unless you and Cassady have another plan in mind."

"I haven't talked to her yet."

"How flattering. I'm sure it was just my turn to get called first, but I'll pretend it was a deliberate choice. Let me know what she says about six o'clock." Tricia blew kisses into the phone and went back to her napkin dilemma.

It's become something of a game over the years, this issue of who gets called first when something important happens or even when something inconsequential but emotionally resonant occurs. But underneath is the exquisitely comforting knowledge that the three of us have a bond that can withstand anything. So far.

As I reached for my phone to call Cassady, it rang. Expecting it to be her being psychic, I snatched it up and said breezily, "Hello there."

"Molly, it's Ben Lipscomb, and everything's okay." Despite Ben's quick reassurance, there was still time for my heart to stop for a moment as my mind raced through all the terrible reasons Kyle's partner might call me out of the blue. Emergency rooms or worse headed the list, but I didn't get much past them before his disclaimer sank in.

"Nice to hear your voice, Ben," I said genuinely. Ben is a big man who's intimidating and imposing in the field but gentle and charming at the core. I suddenly realized I missed him, not just because he was Kyle's partner, but because he was a good guy and you can never have enough of them in your life. "What's up?" I continued, trying not to sound breathless.

"I just wanted to call and check on you."

"Really?"

" 'Cause that's what people do when they care about other people. They call and they check on them."

It was less a rebuke than an instruction, but I still winced. "I have called."

"Not lately."

"Who's keeping track?"

"Who's admitting to it or who's pretending not to? Just because I'm the one calling to check in doesn't mean I'm the only one thinking about you."

I found myself grinning at the unmasking of Ben Lipscomb, decorated homicide detective, as Ben Lipscomb, old-fashioned matchmaker. "Ben, what are you up to?"

"Molly, when you do what I do for a living, you see way too many people whose lives go wrong because of bad decisions. So I try to make a point of getting the people around me to make good decisions while they can."

I had a sudden vision of willowy blondes—Naomi Watts and Uma Thurman, to be exact—dressed in Badgley Mischka cocktail dresses with navel-baring necklines advancing on Kyle like panthers stalking prey. Was Ben trying to tell me someone else had entered the picture? "While they can?" I repeated as a request for clarification.

"Wasting time on pride is stupid, if I may be frank."

I started to protest that pride wasn't the issue here, but the words wouldn't come out, probably because they weren't true. Kyle and I hadn't broken up solely because of pride, but it was a large part of the equation. In our painfully few recent conversations, all we'd done was acknowledge the impasse, not even beginning to see a way around or through it. The crux was, he worried about my getting hurt while writing about a crime, and I couldn't see that as anything but a demand to choose between him and my job.

My job. What elegant timing. Getting back together with Kyle wasn't going to be any easier since one of the first things I'd have to tell him would be that I was a full-fledged feature writer now, which would fan the flames under all his worries. However, thinking optimistically, it might be fine. Russell Elliott hadn't been murdered, so there wasn't going to be any danger involved in this assignment. Which would give me the opportunity to show Kyle I could juggle my job and his concerns. Let him get used to the idea that he didn't have to fear for my safety and buy us time to get everything back on track.

The conversation was going to be a touchy one, but suddenly I couldn't wait to have it. "Does he want me to call him?"

"Clearly he doesn't know what he wants or I wouldn't have to be looking after him like this."

If he'd been in the room with me, I would've hugged Ben Lipscomb. "If I call him, will he call me back?"

"That's my plan."

"You're a wonderful person, Ben."

"Yeah, and aren't many of us, so we have to stick up for each other."

"I appreciate it."

"You do know that this conversation never happened."

"Even though I'm very glad it did."

"Hope I see you soon, Molly."

"Me too."

I hung up and grinned at the phone. A promotion and an indication that Kyle would be open to getting back together. It was turning out to be a pretty darn spectacular day. But as I started to dial Kyle's number, my excitement did a nice little tuck and roll and transformed into anxiety. What was I going to say? How was I going to start? Was it going to look as if I were calling today because of the new job? How many wrong ways could he take that? Confronting those questions made my stomach flip again, so I dialed Cassady instead.

"It's about damn time," was her response to my news. Cassady's a lawyer, and I always appreciate her incisive take on things.

"The job or the call from Ben?"

"Both. Your stars are aligning, sweetheart, and you better take advantage."

"I know, but I can't exactly call Kyle and say, 'Just wanted to let you know I got the job you were dreading when we were together. Wanna come back?' "

"Then don't say that."

"Thank you, Counselor."

"What's wrong with calling him to let him know you've been thinking of him, then just allowing the job news to work its way into conversation in due course? Besides, this is a murderless story. Doesn't that solve a lot of problems right there?"

"I hope so."

"Call him."

"It's not that simple."

"Of course it is."

"How many times have you called an ex just to say you were thinking of them?"

"I never think of my exes."

"Comforting."

"Yes, but I come from the scorched-earth school of dating, while you are one of those irritating girls who can be taken home to Mother when things are going well and remembered fondly after they tank."

"Do I apologize at this point?"

"Not to me. But you could always run a mea culpa past Detective Edwards."

"Wait. It's not all my fault."

"No, but there's this fascinating concept we call 'contributory negligence' that might apply."

I had no worthy response. It was easy to say that my relationship with Kyle winding up on the rocks wasn't all my fault, but it was impossible to say I wasn't partly to blame.

"I'll take your silence as an admission that you're at least going to think about it. Nothing wrong with a little show of vulnerability, Molly. I happen to think Kyle struggles with your lack of it, so he might respond to a quick flash here."

"Maybe." I did need to think it through, though, rehearse it in my head a bit. This conversation was too important to improvise.

"Don't start thinking," Cassady said presciently. "You'll talk yourself out of it, and that would be a huge mistake."

"Did Ben call you?"

"No, but he should have. Great minds and all that."

"Could we move on for the moment? Will you join Tricia and me for a little celebration this evening?"

"Only if you've called Kyle by the time I see you."

I hesitated, trying to manufacture a plausible excuse, but Cassady cleared her throat impatiently. "I promise."

"That wasn't so hard."

"That wasn't calling him."

"That won't be hard either."

"Says the woman who's never done it."

"Show me the way. The Bubble Lounge at six."

"Bring Aaron, too," I added. Aaron was a droll physics professor who was demonstrating impressive longevity in the role of Cassady's boyfriend. It can be difficult to integrate new men into our circle, but Aaron had slid into the dynamics with ease and bemusement.

"I believe he has a seminar, but I'll ask, just to show you care. Will you be bringing Kyle?"

"Pace yourself. And me," I requested before exchanging good-byes and hanging up.

I left my hand on the phone, as though breaking the connection would let what resolve I'd summoned while talking to Cassady drain away. Was I making this all too hard? Was it really as simple as calling Kyle and saying, "I miss you and I'd like to see you"? But that wasn't simple at all—if, in fact, that was even the question to ask. Had years of writing an advice column in a women's magazine taught me nothing?

Dear Molly,

Why are the most important questions in life the hardest ones to ask? Like "Am I happy?" and "Is this really what I want out of life?" and "Do you still love me?" If I hesitate to ask these questions, is it because I'm afraid of the answer or because I already know the answer? Is it better to have called and asked than never to have called at all?

Signed
Reach Out and Touch No One

Framing my problem as someone else's letter always gave me clarity and perspective, and this time was no different. I wasn't being proud, I was being a coward. If I was really that afraid of Kyle rejecting me, then it was better to get it out in the open and get it over with. Yank the Band-Aid off instead of peeling it back bit by painful bit. I took a deep breath, lifted the receiver, and began to punch in his number.

"Sorry, am I interrupting?"

My finger hovered over the last digit, and I plunked the receiver back down, embarrassed by the accompanying sense of relief. I smiled at Dorrie Pendleton, the editorial assistant who fidgeted before me, frowning nervously. Dorrie did everything nervously, but she also did it dependably and well. She even dressed dependably and well, just this side of tweeds and sensible shoes, which made her stand out in our pool of burgeoning fashionistas, but she seemed oblivious to the contrast. "What can I do for you, Dorrie?"

"Is it true that staffers are going to be given an opportunity to submit work for consideration for replacing you on 'You Can Tell Me'? Not that anyone would really replace you, but—"

Impressed by how efficiently the rumor mill was operating, I held up my hand. "I appreciate that, but I'm sure one of you will prove quite capable of filling my kate spades. Eileen's going to circulate a memo about the process."

Dorrie perched in the chair beside me, leaning forward to create the illusion of intimacy. She had to be just as aware as I was of the number of our colleagues who were suddenly easing back in their chairs to catch a snippet of our conversation. "Your column sets this magazine apart. It's crucial to maintain its integrity and insight."

"Thank you." I smiled, bracing myself for the pitch for herself as leading candidate.

"And I'm so relieved that the rumors about Eileen forcing you out turned out to be wrong."

My smile locked into something that felt more like a grimace. "Yeah, me too," I managed out of one side of my mouth. Hearing my private paranoia voiced as office gossip was unsettling, even in light of this afternoon's events. Had talk about my leaving the column because of my new position been misunderstood, or had Eileen really been trying to get rid of me? Either way, why was I the last to know?

"You're an inspiration," Dorrie continued, but her adulation was making me uncomfortable now, and I started edging out of my seat.

"Thanks again, and good luck in the competition," I said as I stood up, even though I wasn't sure I knew where I was headed.

"No. Thank you," Dorrie said, and she quickly slipped back to her desk, leaving me to stand awkwardly beside mine and realize that at least four people had dropped the subterfuge of working while eavesdropping and were staring directly at me. I considered blowing them a big kiss, but despite not being known for discretion, I thought I'd give it a try; I grabbed my cell phone and headed for the elevator.

There's nothing like not wanting to confront one problem in your life to make you willing to confront another. I'd barely stepped out into the constant rumble of Lexington Avenue before I'd flipped open my phone and speed-dialed Kyle. I had no idea what I was going to say, but I was determined to say it.

He answered on the second ring, before I had a chance to change my mind. "Hey," he said, and my knees wobbled and my eyes dampened with the sudden sharpness of missing him.

"Hey," I replied with all the eloquence I could muster. "Am I interrupting?"

"No. How are you?"

"Miserable," I said without thinking.

"Good."

"What?"

" 'Cause I am, too."

"Sounds like something we should talk about," I said, resisting the impulse to shout over the blood rushing in my ears.

"Good idea. What are you doing tonight?"

Anything you suggest, I thought, but I swallowed hard and said, "I'm meeting Tricia and Cassady for drinks at six. Care to join us?"

"No. No offense to them, but I just want to see you." I was about to break a cardinal rule and offer to cancel with them, but he continued, "Where are you meeting them? I can meet you somewhere near there afterwards."

"The Bubble Lounge."

"Champagne before dinner? Why? What happened?"

That was the downside of being involved with a detective, but hesitating now would only make it worse. "I got promoted. They're making me a feature writer. My first article is about this woman Olivia Elliott, who's trying to protect her late father's legacy. It's not about his death, he just happened to die, and now she's trying to make sure he gets remembered properly," I overexplained, wanting it perfectly clear that this was a homicide-free assignment and nothing to worry about.

There was enough of a pause for sweat to bead along my spine before he said, "Russell Elliott the music guy?"

"Yes."

"I loved Subject to Change Without Notice."

"Yeah, me too."

"That's great."

"Our similar taste in music?"

"Your new job."

"Is it?"

"Isn't it?"

"I hope so."

"Then it will be."

"Thank you."

"Okay, count me in for the champagne. But I'd like dinner to be just the two of us."

"Absolutely," I said, wondering if my hands would have stopped trembling by then.

"See you there."

"Yes."

"I'm glad you called."

"Me too."

I stood on the sidewalk, catching my breath and blessing Ben Lipscomb at the same time. The tiny helium balloons returned, and I felt as if I could float all the way to Central Park with one decent gust of wind. I had to do something with all the adrenaline that was coursing through me or I was apt to start grabbing strangers as they walked by and hugging them, inviting them to dance, and otherwise making a fool of myself. Determined to channel my energy a bit more productively, I fished Olivia Elliott's business card out of my pocket. I considered calling her office number but decided it would be simpler to leave a message on her cell phone than to explain myself to a receptionist.

"Olivia Elliott."

Her voice had the dusky richness of a jazz DJ and caught me by surprise. I hadn't expected her to answer, so it took me a moment to frame my response. "Ms. Elliott, my name is Molly Forrester, and I'm a writer for *Zeitgeist* magazine. Henry Kwon talked to you—"

"Yes, yes, and Henry spoke highly of you. I'm so pleased you'll be doing the article about my dad."

"Thank you. I was—am—a fan of his, especially his work with Subject to Change."

"Very kind. Though I need you to understand from the outset that I'm not interested in participating in an article that will be yet another rehash of Dad's so-called glory days."

By the end of the sentence, all silkiness was gone from her voice, replaced by a sharp, bitter edge. I waited a respectful moment before replying. "Henry and I discussed your concern that his contributions to contemporary music are being overlooked, so I thought we could focus on your role in ensuring your father is remembered properly."

"And I can't really do that until he's buried properly, can I?"

"I'm not sure I follow."

"Ms. Forrester, I assumed Henry had chosen you for this article because of your body of work. I thought you'd be more attuned to the central issue here."

"And that issue is?"

"No one seems to care that my dad was murdered."

2

"*Maybe she's just hoping* her father was murdered," Cassady suggested, pushing my still-untouched champagne glass closer to my hand. The whole point in coming to the Bubble Lounge, a bar that specializes in champagne, was to be celebratory, but apprehension was letting a little helium out of the balloons, as it were.

Tricia shivered. "What an awful thought."

"If it's between believing he was murdered and believing he committed suicide . . ." Cassady shrugged. Tricia considered that a moment, then nodded in agreement.

Not a theory I'd broached with Olivia on the phone. What I'd done was take a deep breath and say, "It was my understanding your father's death was accidental."

"That would be a *mis*understanding, then. An all-too-common one, which is why I want it cleared up. You'll discuss that in the article, won't you?"

I could hear the train whistles screeching, yet I said, "When would you be free to meet with me?"

"I have patients in the morning. . . . Are you free for lunch tomorrow?"

Patients. It took me a moment to remember that the papers had described Olivia as a therapist. Interesting choice for someone who'd grown up around the outsize behavior of a band like Subject to Change. "One o'clock?" I suggested.

"Let's make it twelve-thirty. The Grill Room at the Four Seasons? I'll get us a table."

A very old school, pro-establishment choice that struck me as odd. But maybe she was consciously separating herself from the wilder world in which she'd grown up. I agreed to meet her there, making a mental note to check with Henry about the expense account that went with my new job. She had thanked me for calling before she hung up. It had impressed me, but I still felt as though the heat of her anger had scorched my ear. Even now I considered putting my champagne glass against it as a salve.

"So," Cassady continued, drawing out the word deliberately, "what are you going to do?"

"I'm going to have lunch with her."

"Will you try to talk her out of her theory?" Tricia asked.

"Not until I've heard it."

"What if she's right?"

I did my best to sound matter-of-fact and ignore the odd gnawing in the pit of my stomach, especially since I couldn't tell if it was nerves or excitement. "Then it's a bigger story than we thought it was."

We all knew what the next question was and everything that was riding on it, but Cassady voiced it anyway. "What are you going to tell Kyle?"

I checked my watch. Was he late, or was he not coming? "That I'm very glad to see him. I hope you'll do the same."

Tricia gave that little snap of the head that makes her shining hair bounce beautifully yet still conveys total disagreement. "If you really want Kyle back in your life, you have to stop hiding things from him. Especially things that are central to your relationship."

"Tricia," I said lightly, "did I tell you they're looking for someone to take over my column?"

Tricia frowned less lightly. "You're only being mean to me because you know I'm right."

"She's not being mean," Cassady said soothingly, "she's being snippy. But give her time, it's early." She checked her watch. "Earliness being a relative concept."

"Now you're being mean. He'll be here," Tricia said crisply.

And suddenly, he was. Even though I'd been doing my best to watch discreetly as people passed the front window and approached the entrance, Kyle was standing in front of us, breathtaking in his effortless way, running his hand through his hair to absolutely no avail. "Sorry to keep you waiting."

Tricia bounced to her feet and hugged him in greeting, while Cassady rose more elegantly. I stayed planted on the sofa right where I was because I wasn't sure I could stand up. As he hugged both of them, those amazing blue eyes tried to lock on mine, but I wasn't sure I could do that, either. I wasn't sure I could do any of this. I swallowed a sharp urge to cry.

Freed from my friends, Kyle held out his hand to me. I took it and felt as though he were lifting me to my feet. Eye to eye, I was even more flustered and hoped he couldn't feel it through my hand. It's times like these that I want so desperately to be Lana Turner, all cool composure and well-timed gesture. But I'm always June Allyson, all stammers and earnest smiles. I try to comfort myself with the fact that June Allyson usually winds up with the guy at the end. Even if he never gets Lana Turner completely out of his system.

What on earth were we thinking? We, not just I, because he'd agreed to it. Given that we hadn't seen each other for almost two months, how did we think we could meet in a club for a drink and carry it off as if it were a normal after-work rendezvous and not a reunion carrying the weight of everything that had gone unsaid and unresolved in the meantime? Drinks with friends and then what? Dinner? Dessert? Depositions?

Then again, there was a lot to be said for taking this step in the presence of other people, said presence making it all the more important to be polite and restrained and not get all weepy and hyperventilate. Not that I thought Kyle was considering that, but I certainly was.

He, damn him, had the presence of mind to look me in the eye, squeeze my hand gently, and say, "Good to see you."

I smiled. "You too." I kissed him on the cheek, and he pressed his cheek against mine. I thought of Lana Turner and John Garfield in *The Postman Always Rings Twice* and considered throwing him down on the coffee table before God, my friends, and all the patrons of the Bubble Lounge. Instead, I remembered my manners, took a deep breath, and gently guided him to sit next to me on the couch.

"Are you on duty, Kyle, or can we buy you a drink?" Cassady asked, already signaling for the waitress.

"I'm here to celebrate," he said, casting a dubious eye on my kir royale. "But nothing fancy."

Cassady ordered him a glass of Taittinger while Tricia leaned out of her chair to put her hand on his shoulder. "It's so nice to see you, Kyle."

"Good to see all of you, too."

"Isn't it great news?" she said with a nod in my direction.

"Yes, it is. Amazing how people can be slow to recognize how lucky they are to have her in their lives." He looked down to take my hand and squeeze it gently, so he missed the huge eyes both Cassady and Tricia gave that pronouncement. Having an audience for this definitely wasn't such a good idea, because it made me want to jump up and proclaim, "Did you both hear that?"

Again, Cassady got to her feet first. "Excuse me. I can

never remember where the restroom is here." Tricia started to point helpfully, but Cassady arched an eyebrow at her. "Come help me find it, Tricia."

Tricia smiled guiltily, and they swept off, arm in arm. I watched them go because I didn't quite trust myself to look right at him. Especially when he said, "You look great."

I tried to clear the flutter out of my throat before I turned. It wasn't my imagination; his eyes had gotten bluer since the last time I'd seen him. Licking my lips delicately to make sure I wasn't drooling, I said, "You too."

He studied my face for a long moment before saying, "Thanks for calling."

"Thanks for coming."

"Seriously, you been okay?"

I started to shrug and say something noncommittal, then remembered what Cassady had said about vulnerability. And what Jesus had said about the truth. "No. Have you?"

He was the one who shrugged. "No. Serves me right. I wanted time to think. And all I've done is think about you."

I touched my fingertips to his lips, almost expecting him to pixilate away like some hologram I'd created out of desire and frustration. But other than kissing my fingertips, he didn't move, he didn't go away, he was really there, really back.

"I missed you," I said quietly.

He nodded, taking my hand and pressing his lips to the palm. I could have sat there for a century, easily, but then what came next was even more amazing. "I'm sorry," he said with a simplicity that knocked the wind out of me.

I groped for something stunning and memorable to say in response, but all I came up with was, "So am I."

"I'm proud of you. The new gig."

"I don't know."

"You'll do great."

"Olivia Elliott thinks her father was murdered."

"Excuse me?"

I'd said it before I thought it. Or at least before I was aware that I was thinking about saying it. Now I wasn't sure what else to say, though "Oops" seemed like a reasonable option. Instead, I said it again. "She thinks her dad was murdered."

"Why?"

"I want all my cards on the table. I don't want to repeat mistakes."

"Not 'Why are you telling me,' why does she think he was murdered?"

Although it would have been nice to blame the champagne for the sudden rush of blood to my cheeks, I sadly knew better. Guilt can do wonders for a girl's appearance. "I don't know yet, I haven't actually interviewed her. I've just talked to her on the phone and she mentioned it and I thought I should mention it so I didn't look like I was trying to hide anything because I've done that before and it was such a bad idea, but I've learned and I really don't want this to be an issue for us."

His pressure on my hand increased slightly, just enough to make me realize I was going to run out of breath long before I ran out of justifications. Sliding into silence, I leaned back against the couch and tried to slow my heartbeat by sheer force of will. The fact that he then leaned over me, his mouth almost on mine, shot that plan to smithereens.

"We can decide what comes between us, can't we?" he whispered.

"I hope it's a very small list," I whispered back.

"Might come down to nothing."

"Even better."

He leaned in a little more, and his lips brushed mine. Goose bumps sprinted across the back of my neck, and I had to really concentrate to hear what he was saying. "Especially because it was an overdose."

"Say the papers."

"Says the ME."

"Says you."

"Says me. I pulled the file."

"You did?" I asked, forgetting we were supposed to be whispering.

He sat back a bit, eyes moving carefully across my face to determine if I was happy or not. I was trying to decide the same thing. "My cards on the table," he said. "I wanted to know what you might be getting into."

"And the problems it might cause."

He pulled back farther, and I sat up straighter. "Don't get ahead of yourself. Or me."

"I'm not, I just want to understand."

"I want to, too. I don't think I did a very good job with that before. Like you said, why repeat mistakes?"

Forgetting everything I had ever been taught about the classless nature of public displays of affection, I grabbed him and kissed him as hard as I could without leaving permanent marks. Not that permanent marks would be a problem, since I didn't plan to let him go ever again and I was willing to ignore marks of my own making.

It was like that first chocolate egg you grab out of the basket before church Easter morning after giving up chocolate for Lent; you can't wait another minute to remember how sweet and creamy and intoxicating it is, and you can't believe you went so long without it. I was ready to gorge myself on the whole basket when Cassady's voice cut tartly through the buzz.

"I guess we could have fussed with our hair a bit longer."

We pulled apart and pulled ourselves together. Cassady was

giving us a mock scowl, but Tricia was beaming. "This is going even better than I'd hoped," she said, pulling on Cassady's sleeve.

"Are you taking credit for any of this?" Cassady asked her.

"Ladies . . . ," I attempted.

"Only for being supportive and hopeful," Tricia told Cassady.

"I was, too."

"I didn't say you weren't."

"God help me, I've missed all three of you." Kyle helped me to my feet. "Let's go get some dinner."

"We haven't finished our champagne," Cassady pointed out.

"True." Kyle's glass had been quietly deposited on the table while our attention was elsewhere, but now he held it up for a toast and looked at me expectantly. When I hesitated, he was the one who offered, "To new beginnings."

Between the clinking of our glasses and the happy buzz in my ears, I almost didn't hear—maybe tried not to hear—the cell phone ringing. New beginnings were going to be tough if the old problems didn't even let us catch our breath.

With grim resignation, Kyle fished out his phone with his free hand. "Yeah," he answered, voice cool and tight. His eyes closed as he listened, and I could feel all the bubbles in my glass going flat. "Yeah," he said again, and hung up.

I glanced at Cassady and Tricia, but they were fixed on him, hoping that the call was something that could wait. I knew better. His eyes opened again and moved slowly to me. "Ben sends his regards."

"Yeah." I smiled as much as I could. "Tell him I send them back."

"You don't have to go," complained Tricia, ever the optimist.

"Body's cooling as we speak," he said, then shook his head

as she reacted. "Sorry. Kidding. But they did pick up someone we've been looking for, and . . ."

"And we'll see you later," Cassady said helpfully.

"No, you won't," Kyle said politely, "but with any luck, she will." He caught my hand in his for one last moment, then let it slide away as he took a step back.

I wanted to show some modicum of self-control, yet I drifted after him, less following him to the door than being pulled along by his gravitational field.

At the door, he paused, but rather than blowing me a kiss or even winking, he grinned as he walked out the door. "Remember, most MEs know what they're doing."

"Doesn't mean they're perfect," I said, grinning back. It was as refreshing as a good-bye kiss, and I was delighted. Returning to my seat, I could feel how we were going to slide back together, mesh again with our troubles behind us. Right up until the moment Cassady popped me in the bicep.

"You told him?"

"Tricia said to be honest with him," I said, rubbing my arm.

"Oh, my word, not in the first ten minutes," Tricia protested, moving her bicep out of Cassady's range.

"It's all right. Everything's going to be just fine," I said, which at the time I thoroughly believed.

Cassady shook her head. "Are we to assume that he doesn't agree with Olivia's hypothesis?"

"He does not."

"And are we to assume that it just makes her theory all the more appealing to you?"

"No," I said honestly. As though they'd been rehearsing this moment while in the restroom, Cassady and Tricia linked arms and looked at me expectantly. "I have a job to do, and I'm going to do it," I continued. "And I will be completely frank with you, Kyle, and my editor throughout the entire process." I raised my right hand in a three-finger salute. "And obey the Girl Scout laws."

"You are such lightning bait," Cassady said with a crooked smile, "I'm not sure it's safe to stand next to you, much less go to dinner with you."

Tricia detached herself from Cassady and took my hands in hers. "I believe you can do this. Balance everything. And you know I'll be here for you if you need help."

"I didn't say I was abandoning her," Cassady pointed out. "I said she was dangerous to be around. Which is one of the reasons we love her."

"And I, you," I said. "Now, drink up and let's get some dinner."

We went to Heartbeat and immersed ourselves in great food, wonderful wine, and grand conversation about every topic under the sun. Except Kyle. When Cassady attempted, I parried by asking where her relationship with Aaron was headed, and she withdrew with uncharacteristic speed. Tricia offered her single status for examination, and we proposed a number of possibilities for pursuit, but none of them captured her imagination. So we moved on to broader questions of politics and culture, equally unanswerable, until it was quite late. Sated physically and emotionally, we sauntered off to our separate cabs and headed home.

By the time I was back in my apartment, the caffeine in my Irish coffees was outperforming the Bushmills and I couldn't settle down. I told myself it had nothing to do with the fact that it was after midnight and I hadn't heard from Kyle yet. It was important to take things slowly and not raise false expectations about our slipping back into our old routine as though no time had passed, no feelings had been hurt, and no land mines had been stepped on.

Determined to put my agitation to good use, I changed into my Washington Redskins sleep shirt and sat at my laptop to refresh my knowledge of Russell Elliott, Micah Crowley, and Subject to Change before meeting with Olivia. But as I began surfing, I realized I was missing an important element for my research. Digging through my CD cabinet, I found *Film at Eleven,* the band's third album. The one that was played at almost every party we went to sophomore year of college.

I hadn't listened to it in a long time, but as soon as I heard the opening chords of "Go to War for You," memories pushed to the surface like swimmers coming up for air, and I could smell the sweat and smoke of the crowded off-campus apartments, taste the cheap wine we drank in those days, feel the pulse of the bass line through my back as I leaned against a wall with my lips pressed against Tom Donaldson's ear in a futile attempt to have a conversation. The images and sensations flooded back with a startlingly visceral punch, and I sank to the couch, letting them wash over me until the song was over. With everything he got out of a cup of tea and a cookie, I wondered what Proust would have done with the greatest hits CD from his favorite band. And a couple of Irish coffees.

When the second song started, I made my way back to my laptop. Nearly every one of the fansites featured the same picture of Micah on its home page, taken from a *Rolling Stone* article about the band seeking new direction that had been published only two months before Micah died. Micah shirtless and sweaty onstage at the Meadowlands, his wavy, shoulder-length hair clinging to his neck in damp spirals, one hand on the microphone stand and the other held out to the audience either in blessing or in a request for a moment's quiet. What made the picture so resonant was the look on his face, pleased but perplexed, as though he couldn't be sure how he'd gotten to this place. It was that flash of vulnerability Cassady had been talking about, and fans had responded to the picture ferociously. It graced the cover of the greatest hits CD that was released after Micah's death.

Pictures of Russell were harder to find, but then again, it had never been Russell's job to be center stage. He said in every interview I read that he loved his behind-the-scenes role, that he had no musical ability or aspiration, that his gift was finding the ways to make it easier for Micah to bring his artistic vision to life. I did find one picture from the same *Rolling Stone* article that showed Russell, slight and tailored, leaning forward out of the shadows to whisper into Micah's ear as the band prepared to take the stage. They're both smiling mischievously, like little boys enjoying a joke they're not supposed to be old enough to understand. Gray Benedek, the keyboard player, is walking past them with the sour smile of an older brother who knows the joke well and can't believe they find it funny. The rest of the band is obscured by the other three, their expressions unclear.

Subject to Change had recorded six albums and when Micah died, had seemed poised for entry into that rarefied stratosphere where the Stones and U2 reside. There'd been no talk about drugs or any other issues previously, so his death came as a huge surprise; I could picture Carl Davenport walking into the bull pen at *Youth & Beauty,* the magazine where I was indentured as an editorial assistant, and announcing the news in a hushed, cracked voice. Carl, the photography editor, had a TV in his office, and he let us all cluster before it as CNN ran the short-on-details story with the soon-to-be-iconic picture of Micah floating over the anchor's shoulder. Everyone in the room had a story about seeing the band in concert or hearing one of their songs on the radio at an auspicious moment in their lives. A fleeting moment of unity in a pop culture that had only gotten increasingly fragmented since then. It was shocking to realize it had been almost ten years.

I found a few articles from after Micah's death that had floated the possibility of the band staying together, but before too long, Russell and Gray held a press conference to say that since Micah had been the soul of Subject to Change, they would not continue without him. Jeff Ford joined Downward Spiral, replacing their drummer who had died in a tour bus accident. The bass player, Rob Kenilworth, dropped off the grid and was rumored to be living the high life somewhere in the South Pacific. David Washington, the guitarist, wound up starting a jazz quintet that had won the *DownBeat* readers poll for best electric jazz group the last two years. Gray Benedek had started a couple of different rock bands, but none of them had lasted more than two albums, and he was currently more in demand as a producer than as a musician.

Gray and Russell had put together a memorial concert to mark the fifth anniversary of Micah's death; it was a benefit for Women Against Oppression, a human rights group Claire Crowley, Micah's widow, had embraced after his death. The concert also served as the musical debut of Adam, Claire and Micah's son, who at twenty-three was given the daunting task of filling in for his father as vocalist on several of the band's biggest hits. People had been struck by how much he looked and sounded like his dad, and Russell had announced that he'd be producing Adam's first album. I found a picture of Adam backstage that night, looking stunned but happy. A young woman clung to his arm; the caption identified her as Olivia Elliott.

I took a second look at the picture, trying to reconcile the lanky, jeans-clad girl gazing adoringly at Adam with the crisp, mature professional in the Escada suit I'd seen in the coverage of her memorial for her father. We all change in five years, but the transformation here was startling; it was hard to see that it was the same person. As I studied the picture, I was struck by the body language, the implied intimacy in the way their bodies were touching. I wondered if there'd been something between her and Adam Crowley. He'd be easy to fall for, I reasoned, with his father's knockout sexuality combined with a hint of gentleness. Vulnerability, Cassady again would say.

As I moved my attention back to Olivia, I had the sense of having seen the picture before. I typed in a new search and brought up articles on Russell's funeral. There it was: a picture of the mature Olivia standing in a very similar, seemingly intimate pose with Micah's other son and Russell's last star, Jordan Crowley.

Adam and Jordan were half-brothers. While Adam's mother was Micah's wife, Jordan's mother was Bonnie Carson, whose résumé as girlfriend to the stars was much more stellar than her résumé as backup singer. There was significant tabloid and fan hysteria after Bonnie revealed Jordan's paternity when Jordan was eight years old and Adam was eleven, including speculation about whether Micah would leave Claire, with whom he'd supposedly been having difficulties. But while he acknowledged Jordan as his son and gave the boy his last name, Micah didn't leave his wife. In public, at least, Micah and Claire remained together and gracious, welcoming Jordan and Bonnie into their family circle.

Olivia, whose mother had died when she was only seven, and her father had been part of the circle, too. I was beginning to think the interview with Olivia should focus on her front-row seat for some intriguing family dynamics rather than her father's legacy when the phone rang.

"First ring," Kyle said quietly when I answered. "You're working."

"After midnight," I replied. "So are you."

"We're wrapping up, but I think I should go home."

It wasn't until I felt the pang that I realized how deeply I'd been hoping he'd come by, even if he didn't stay all night. I was like a junkie falling off the wagon; now that I'd had one taste, I had to figure out how to get my hands on more. But some lingering shred of decorum prevailed, and I said, "Okay."

"It's not, but it is better this way." We considered that statement a moment before he added, "Not as much fun, but better."

"If it's not as much fun, how can it be better?"

"Broccoli's good for you."

"Are you saying our relationship is a vegetable?"

"This is why I have to go home. I can't keep up."

"I'm sorry, I'll be quiet."

"No, you won't be. Which is perfect. But I'm beat. And you have work to do."

"Work can wait."

"So can we."

"Speak for yourself."

He didn't say anything for a moment, and I was afraid he'd hung up. Then he said, his voice huskier than usual, "It was really good to see you."

"It'd be even better to see you again."

"I'll call you in the morning."

"You better."

"You bet."

"Good night, Mr. Townshend."

"Good night, Mr. Daltry," he said with an approving laugh, and hung up.

As tempting as it was to now put the Who's *Face Dances* on

the CD player and sing "You Better You Bet" at the top of my lungs, I knew that could easily lead to my playing air guitar on the coffee table at three a.m., and I needed to attempt to settle down so I could get a good night's sleep before meeting Olivia. So I swapped out *Film at Eleven* and put on *The Good Fight,* Subject to Change's fourth album, the one with the uncharacteristic power ballads that gave them three *Billboard* number ones. I drifted off in front of the laptop with Micah Crowley singing about love, betrayal, and girls with long hair and longer legs.

"Long-Haired Girls" was still running through my head the next day as I got ready to meet Olivia Elliott in the flesh. Rocking out in front of the bathroom mirror, singing into the handle of my hairbrush as if I were fourteen again, I remembered that although I'd broken the news about Olivia's suspicions to Kyle, I hadn't told Eileen. But I rationalized that while I'd told Kyle to keep him from being upset because I'd kept it from him, Eileen was already upset with me and I didn't need to nudge that thermometer up any further. Certainly not until I knew whether there was any basis for Olivia's concerns.

Figuring I was better off lying low until I knew more, I stayed home to continue my research, increasing my fascination with the circumstances in which Olivia had grown up. The Crowleys and the Elliotts seemed inseparable, and after Micah's death, Russell had stepped in to manage the estate and the careers of Adam and Jordan. Russell was the one who spoke to the press and dealt with the business matters. Claire dedicated herself to charity work, and Bonnie experimented with a variety of endeavors; she was painting now. They sounded like one big happy family.

So where did the discordant note of murder come from? I knew all the happy press didn't mean things had always been sunny, but I was still struggling to imagine what had occurred to put the idea into Olivia's head and not into the medical examiner's.

Olivia was already at the table by the time I got to the Grill Room and neither rose nor offered her hand as the hostess walked me up. She thanked the hostess and looked at the chair, waiting for me to deposit myself in it. "Please, sit down, Ms. Forrester."

She was more delicate in person than in photographs, a porcelain-skinned blonde with a long neck, willowy hands, and fine features. Her hair was pulled back into a simple ponytail, emphasizing the patrician oval of her face. She looked far more at home in this grand setting, with its huge windows, towering indoor trees, and blue-blood clientele, than I felt. We were the same age, but she exuded a more mature air. I couldn't tell if it was a product of her profession or her money.

"It's a pleasure to meet you, Ms. Elliott," I said as I sat down.

"Don't you want to reserve that judgment until you've talked with me for more than a few minutes?" she asked breezily, tenting her long fingers under her chin.

Was I being analyzed or tested? I decided to play along. "No, because if I change my mind in five minutes, it will still have been a pleasure to meet you, but not much fun getting to know you." I unfurled my napkin, rerouting it into my lap.

Olivia permitted me to see a flash of brilliant white, perfectly straight teeth. "Excellent point."

"I wasn't planning on this interview being adversarial, were you?" I asked.

"Not at all," she said, "I just like people to appreciate the weight of what they say."

"Occupational hazard of being a therapist?"

"I think of it more as a requirement of being an intelligent human being."

"Do you mean what you say when you suggest your father was murdered?"

This time, the smile was genuine, but sad. "Unfortunately, yes."

"Have you shared your concern with the authorities?"

She nodded. "I've been told there's no evidence to support my assertion. But all that means is, they aren't looking hard enough."

"What do you think they should be looking for?"

"Claire Crowley's fingerprints. She killed my father."

3

I had to give her credit: Olivia Elliott seemed fully appreciative of the weight of what she had said, even giving me a delicate scrunch of the nose and mouth so I'd understand how terribly awkward she knew all this was for everyone involved.

But where she was cool and unflappable, I was decidedly flapped. I paused a moment, expecting the entire restaurant to fall silent and a few stuffed shirts to explode. But everyone kept talking and cell phones kept ringing and Olivia kept smiling as I made sure I understood exactly what she was saying.

"You think Claire Crowley killed your father," I said, dropping my voice a few decibels and hoping she'd follow suit.

"I know she did," she said firmly but a little more quietly.

"Even though his death was accidental." I'd thought that her belief in a murder scenario might have grown out of her refusal to believe he'd overdosed, but if she was presenting me with a suspect, she'd given the matter rather specific thought. I wondered if there was some emotional component to what had happened for which Olivia held Claire responsible—for instance, that Russell had been depressed and Claire had noticed but not brought it to anyone's attention.

But again, I was a step behind. Olivia had something much more literal in mind. "An accident? That just shows you what people in this city will do for Claire. She's wrapped herself so tightly in Micah's shadow that people think they love her just because they used to love him. She's rehabilitated herself and gone from home-wrecking, coke-sniffing queen bitch to St. Claire, rescuer of the oppressed. She Who Must Be Fawned Over."

The waiter stepped up to ask us for our order, and I deferred to Olivia. I wasn't sure how she was going to eat or that I even wanted to. But she readily ordered the crabcakes and an iced tea, and I nodded; it would give me something to look at besides her blazing eyes.

"Aren't you going to ask me, 'Why Claire'?" Olivia prompted as soon as the waiter withdrew.

"There are actually a few other questions that should come first," I said diplomatically. There was a pressing need to proceed with caution here: Not only did I want to keep this assignment from vaporizing and taking my new job with it, but Olivia was connected to Henry on a personal level, too, which meant the article going south could wreak havoc I hadn't even considered.

"Such as?"

"What makes you think he was murdered, when there's no supporting evidence?"

That actually made her take a deep breath and slow down for a moment. "My father had some issues with prescription drugs back in the day, but he was long past that. Years past that."

Sympathy corkscrewed through my chest as I realized the fragile ground on which she stood. "Just because he hadn't used in a long time . . . ," I began gently.

"My father was clean," she insisted, her jaw clenching.

"Which is why the medical examiner ruled it an accident."

Her slender fist came down on the table hard enough to get

us sidelong looks from the tables on either side of us. "You're not listening to me. He didn't have any pills in the apartment. How could he accidentally take something that wasn't there to take?"

Her anguish was understandable, but I needed to keep what facts I knew in full view. "You weren't living with your father."

"No."

"So he could have had pills and you wouldn't—might not have known."

"I turned the place upside down after he died," she said fiercely, eyes sparkling with anger or tears, I couldn't be sure which. "There was nothing. Nothing."

"Maybe he took it all, so there was nothing to find."

"Why are you so sure I'm wrong?"

I hesitated, and she picked up on it immediately, her fingers picking in agitation at the pattern in the tablecloth. If she went *Spellbound* on me and started drawing ski tracks with her fork, I wasn't sure what I'd do. But the fact that I was thinking about Gregory Peck instead of answering her question probably meant she had a point. Was I sure she was wrong? Was I hoping she was wrong? Did I want her to be wrong so my own life stayed less complicated? No. I wanted to get the story right, tell what happened and not what she hoped or wished or feared happened. "It's not that I'm sure you're wrong, I'm just not sure you're right."

She'd teased a tiny thread out of the tablecloth and now rolled it between her fingertips. "Yet."

"Fair enough."

"Journalism is all about parsing out what people say and twisting it to suit the story you want to tell, isn't it."

"As opposed to therapy, which is parsing out what people say and twisting it to suit the story you think they should be telling."

She sat back in her chair, looking me over analytically. "How long were you in therapy?"

"What makes you think I was?"

"You have a pretty strong opinion about it."

"Does that mean you were a journalist at some point?"

She smiled sourly. "No, but I've been dealing with them most of my life and I know how they play."

"From what I've read, the press has dealt with your family's immediate circle pretty nicely."

"They should've just left us the hell alone."

Tell that to your publicists, I thought, but then again, her father had handled everyone's publicity. So I said, "They'll swarm all over you if you start announcing your dad was murdered."

"It doesn't matter now. Everything's already ruined. I meant before, when there was still a chance for things to work out."

"For whom?"

She took a long time to answer that one. "Any of us."

"And that chance is gone now?" I asked gently.

"My dad's gone," she said with the raspy force of someone determined not to cry.

"And you blame Claire Crowley."

She nodded quickly, eyes opening wider to contain the tears. "Now she's in control."

"Of what?"

"The money. The music publishing, the master tapes, everything. My dad had majority control, but now she does."

"But, assuming she did kill him, why now?"

"I don't know. I was hoping you'd help me figure that out."

Which was why I was standing in the middle of Russell Elliott's elegant home an hour later. The apartment was one-half of the entire fifth floor of a magnificent old building on Riverside Drive. You could see up to the Boat Basin from one end and past the end of Riverside Park from the other. The Crowley apartment was the other half of the floor and, in the cab on the way there, Olivia had told me about running back and forth between the two apartments with Adam when they were children, as though it were all one big house—bigger than the house I'd grown up in, certainly—with musicians, actors, models, artists, and other assorted luminaries coming and going at all hours. People still came after Micah died, as Russell grew in reputation as a producer and Claire got more involved with her charity work and a clothing line; it had still been one of the great rock salons. With Russell gone, would they all still come around?

Olivia gave me the guided tour of the warmly appointed apartment. We now stood in what Olivia called the study, a huge room with a spectacular view of the river, filled with low-slung burgundy leather furniture, coolly shaded lamps, glowing hardwood floors, and impressive stacks of electronics. Everything was tidy and sparkling, very much one of those "a place for everything and everything in its place" sorts of rooms, so it struck me as odd that a small mixing board sat on the floor in front of a stereo cabinet that was otherwise so neatly organized that there wasn't a single dangling cord to be seen.

I pointed to the board. "Was your dad working on something?"

Olivia looked at the board with dull enmity. "He was always working on something."

"What was he working on that night, do you know?"

Olivia looked up at me with a sour frown. Of course she knew, and she was about to tell me when a second thought occurred to her and, instead, she said, "No."

The very fact that she didn't want to tell me about it made it essential for me to know. "I don't believe you."

Olivia shrugged, but I didn't buy the dismissive act. She cared, but she didn't want to admit it. So whatever her dad had been working on had to be important, maybe even related to why she thought he was dead. I tried to imagine a piece of music that could be that monumentally important to anyone and my heart raced when I thought of it. Trying to keep my voice casual, I said, "So the Hotel Tapes are real?"

Crimson flooded Olivia's face, as though I'd walked in and found her doing something illegal and/or immoral. "What makes you say that?"

"You want me to help you, but you're hiding this from me, so it's either huge or secret or both. And the Hotel Tapes would qualify as both."

Rock legend held that Micah had been a compulsive taper. Never sure when a few moments of improv on the guitar or piano might blossom into a hit song, he'd had tape recorders running all the time. Gray Benedek had said in an interview right after Micah died that the best music any of them had ever made was on those tapes. Which set up a howling demand for the tapes to be released. Russell had issued a terse statement that the number and quality of the recordings had been grandly overstated, but the rumors about tapes being found and cleaned up for release bobbed to the surface with seasonal regularity.

"Your dad was working on the Hotel Tapes, wasn't he." I could feel my pulse in the base of my throat, but I wasn't sure if the surge in adrenaline was from discovering a legend was real or finding something someone might have been willing to kill for.

Olivia bobbed her head, as though something were keeping her from committing to an actual nod. "It was his secret hobby. As technology got better, he'd go back and fiddle with them, convinced he could clean them up enough for release."

"How many are there?"

"There were supposed to be twelve, but Micah lost one of them somewhere along the line."

"How long are they?"

"Like two hours each."

Twenty-two hours of unreleased Micah Crowley. I was salivating, and I was only a fan. If I'd been in a position to do something with the tapes or make money off them, would I be willing to kill for them?

I didn't get a chance to think about that too long because Claire Crowley descended upon us at that moment, catching us completely by surprise, and it was hard to keep your focus on something else when Claire Crowley stormed into a room.

"What the hell are you doing in here? With a stranger, no less!" Claire demanded.

Momentarily taken aback by Claire's vehemence, Olivia collected herself and turned the tables as best she could by asking why and how Claire could come barging in unannounced.

Claire held up a ring of keys. "We looked out for each other, your father and I. I thought I heard someone over here, and I wanted to make sure it wasn't an intruder," she said with a cold glance to me.

The fact that she had her own key didn't surprise Olivia, though it gave me pause. Opportunity is always one of the first things you look at in a murder, and having your own key to someone's place creates all kinds of opportunities. And cuts down on telltale signs of forced entry and other forensic footholds.

"This is Molly," Olivia said, striving for decorum. "She's writing an article about Dad."

Claire, having acknowledged me as fully as she was going to, kept the frigid intensity of her glare focused on Olivia. "You self-serving little bitch," she growled, fists clenched and blood pressure skyrocketing. Even with her face contorted by anger, Claire was amazing, lovelier in person than she was in press photos. Although she had to be close to fifty, she didn't seem that far removed from the dewy young woman on the cover of Subject to Change's first album, *Juiced*. I knew more than one guy in high school who picked up the CD just because of the picture, which showed a shirtless Micah standing behind Claire—she, covered only by her long strawberry blond hair and Micah's hands, eating a peach out of her juice-stained hands. Micah claimed it was an homage to the Allman Brothers and to T. S. Eliot before them. But more plainly, it was an homage to the fact that sex sells. So did the album, which went gold in three months.

"Self-serving?" Olivia exclaimed in the upper register between incredulity and offense.

"This isn't about your father," Claire spat. "It's about your pathetic need to be the center of attention. Grow up, little girl, and stop wiping your tears all over the front page of every damn tabloid in town."

It occurred to me to protest that *Zeitgeist* was not a tabloid, but it also occurred to me that remaining quiet would increase my chances of staying out of trouble and allow me to continue to observe from this intimate vantage point.

"Why do you care?" Olivia asked icily.

"You're family, Olivia," Claire replied with a viciousness that would make me run away from home at the earliest possible moment.

"Oh, of course."

"And the boys will get dragged into it—"

"Screw the boys!"

"That was always your goal, wasn't it."

She might as well have slapped Olivia across the face. Clearly, this was hugely sensitive territory I'd have to explore more fully. Silent for only a moment, Olivia flushed with a combination of embarrassment and the effort to respond with equal viciousness. Claire didn't give her the chance, turning to me to ask, "And why exactly are you here, again?"

I didn't want to get in the middle, as sorry as I suddenly felt for Olivia; I'd need to interview Claire at some juncture, and alienating her now would only cause problems then. Right now, spinning the point of view might help everyone. "Molly Forrester, *Zeitgeist* magazine. I'm doing an article on Olivia's perspective on growing up around the band now that her father's gone."

Olivia threw me a grateful glance, while Claire regarded me with suspicion. "Won't that be entertaining," she said flatly.

"I'd like to speak with you when it's convenient, Mrs. Crowley. For background, context."

Claire looked back at Olivia, and I could almost see Olivia melting into a small child under the heat of the gaze. "Excellent idea."

"Do you keep your own calendar?"

"Now that Dad's dead," Olivia said quietly but with an unmistakable bite.

"You want to understand her in context?" Claire asked. "Come to the show tonight. Everyone will be there."

Olivia sucked in a sharp breath, then plastered on a smile. "That's a terrific idea."

Surprise flickered over Claire's face. Had she expected Olivia to protest or just not expected Olivia would be able to smile after the harshness of their exchange? Whichever it was, it didn't linger. "Jordan's playing at Mars Hall tonight. We'd like you to be our guest."

Jordan Crowley live? Me a guest? I tried to remain the cool professional and not shiver into the ardent fan. "I didn't think Jordan played clubs anymore."

"He doesn't usually, but he's struggling a bit with the new album," Claire said. "We thought getting in front of a live audience might inspire him."

" 'We'?" I asked.

"Russell and I. We planned this date before Russell died."

"Are you managing Jordan now?"

"No, no, nothing so formal. Advising more, trying to help fill the void now that Russell's gone."

Olivia's smile tightened. "It takes a village to raise a rock star."

It also took guts or class or both to raise a rock star whom your dead husband fathered with another woman while you were still married to him. Claire Crowley certainly wasn't coming across as a warm and nurturing woman—though perhaps I wasn't meeting her under the most flattering of circumstances—but she'd found a way to include her husband's illegitimate child and the child's mother into her innermost circle. It might have been a stunt, but it was an impressive, long-lived one. When Bonnie and Jordan first surfaced, Claire issued an elegant statement about forgiveness and understanding and wanting to strengthen the family, not break it apart. In her position, I think I might have been issuing a statement about castration and smacking faces and yanking hair out by the roots.

Even after Micah's death, Claire, Bonnie, and the boys were reported to stay close. Things may have been—must have been—rocky behind closed doors, but in public, Micah's clan was one big happy family, with Russell as the wise uncle who oversaw their problems and their musical careers. Could something have tipped the idyllic balance and, as Olivia suggested, driven Claire to the breaking point?

"I've never seen Jordan live," I said, struck by how odd the term sounded when standing in a room where a man had died. Maybe been murdered. "I'd love to come," I said, making sure to direct the response to both of them.

"That pleases me," Claire said politely. "We'll leave your name at the door. What was it again?" She knew, but if she needed to mark her territory, I could play along. I repeated it for her, and she nodded, her arm sweeping in the direction of the front door, like a Realtor who had decided I couldn't afford the property she was showing and it was better to move along before anyone's time was wasted any further.

Olivia frowned at her. "We're not ready to leave."

Claire bounced her key ring in her hand. "What else are you going to do?"

Olivia made a high, unhappy sound in her throat. "This is my home," she managed.

"You couldn't be here when your father needed you, but you can be here now? How convenient. For you," Claire shot back.

"Don't you blame me," Olivia said, on the verge of losing control. I stepped forward instinctively, realizing a split second later that I was concerned she was going to accuse Claire too early, before a persuasive case could be made. Guess Olivia was getting to me after all.

"You're the therapist, sweetheart," Claire said, mockingly maternal. "You're well versed in how often people blame someone else because they can't handle their own guilt."

I could feel the knowledge radiating off Claire like heat. Claire knew that Olivia suspected her. A quick glance to Olivia showed she was unexpectedly pale and quiet. Was this her first brush with Claire's awareness? How close to the bone was Claire cutting? And what did Olivia have to feel guilty about? She was so vehement about her dad being clean, maybe he had had a problem that she hadn't been willing to recognize. But did that make her suspicions of Claire any less valid? Or was this really just a case of everyone pointing fingers at everyone else because no one could accept the fact that Russell had killed himself, intentionally or accidentally?

"Please leave," Olivia said in a voice I hadn't heard yet—small, young, and tired.

Claire bounced her ring in her hand again, weighing her decision and not the keys. She looked at me, and I tried to concentrate, for the article to come and for my own peace of mind, on how vibrantly green her eyes were, not how cold they seemed. "Has she told you about finding her father?"

I started to answer that she hadn't had a chance, but I stopped, wondering why I was feeling pressed to defend Olivia. Just because she was the first one to point a finger didn't mean she was right. She might even be wrong that it was murder. But she'd raised Claire's hackles, which raised my suspicions.

"Please leave," Olivia repeated with increased urgency.

Suddenly, Claire held out her arms to Olivia and, when Olivia didn't respond, swept her into a large yet perfunctory hug. "Don't be late tonight."

In response, Olivia stared at the floor and said nothing while Claire's heels punctuated her anger all the way out the front door. Once the door rasped closed, Olivia looked at me expectantly. I wasn't sure how I was supposed to react, so I tried not to, which thrust the burden of comment back on her. After a few moments, she said, "Would you like a water? Coffee? I should've asked earlier."

"No, thank you." She seemed smaller than when we'd first

met, as though interacting with Claire had made her shrink down into herself, like an anemone recoiling from a brush with a barracuda. I wanted to turn our conversation back to the tapes, but first I had to ask, "What should I know about your finding your father's body?"

"I didn't find his body, I found *him,*" Olivia said grimly. "He was still breathing when I got here, so Claire says it's my fault he died. That I should've gotten help for him more quickly than I did."

"What do you think?" I asked, self-conscious that I was sounding like a therapist and treading on her toes.

"I couldn't think. He'd called me and asked me to come over, but he was sounding crazy. He'd been drinking. So when I first came in, I thought he'd just passed out. I figured I'd just tidy up, sit with him, talk to him when he woke up." She gestured to an armchair with a deep seat and a long matching footstool, almost like a two-piece chaise longue, and I understood this was where her father had been sitting when she'd found him.

The end table beside the chair was a heavy disk of hammered brass resting on a column of monkeywood. It was Thai; I'd seen them when I was growing up, in the home of friends whose parents had been stationed at the embassy there. There was a circular stain on the brass, just about where you'd put a glass if you were sitting in the chair. I rubbed at it with my finger, but the stain didn't lift. The circle was so perfect, it had to have been the same glass, night after night. A ritual.

There were also four scratches marking the corners of a rectangle on the table. The scratches were brighter than the ring. Newer. An ashtray? No, something bigger. But I didn't want to get distracted, I needed to get the story out of Olivia. "Your father drank."

Her nostrils flared in irritation. "I never said he didn't. I said he didn't do pills."

"Okay. Did he drink heavily?"

"Not so much anymore. Said he was getting too old for the hangovers. But every once in a while . . ." She shrugged. "Don't we all?"

"What happened to make you think this was different?"

"His breathing started to sound funny. I tried to wake him up, but I couldn't. So I called."

"Nine-one-one."

"No. Adam."

"Adam Crowley?"

She bobbed her head in agitated assent. "He's my . . . This is going to sound stupid, but he's like my brother."

"Has he ever been anything else to you?" I asked, remembering Claire's slam about "screwing the boys."

Her head snapped up, and she looked at me with narrowed eyes. "Claire's a bitch, and you can't believe half of what she says."

"That's not an answer."

"No, we've never been anything else."

I couldn't tell if the anger in her voice was specific to that statement or about the whole situation, but I decided to press on. "Okay, so what happened when you called him?"

"He was finishing up rehearsal for this play. He told me he'd be right over, but he was coming from the Upper East Side."

"He didn't tell you to call 911?"

"You don't understand, I didn't want anyone to see my dad that way."

"Unconscious?"

"Messed up."

I started to express my objection to that line of thinking, but she cut me off. "Anyway, while I was waiting, Dad's breathing got more distressed and I got scared, so I called 911 anyway."

"But they didn't get here in time?"

She swayed a little as she searched for the proper description. "Barely. They did their thing and rushed him in the ambulance, but he stopped breathing once on the way, and by the time he was in the ER . . ." She shuddered at the memory. "They asked me if he'd taken anything, and I said of course not. I didn't know . . ." She made a shooing gesture, but I wasn't sure if it was directed at me or the memories.

"But now you're sure. Why?"

"Because I'm an idiot. Claire came over when she heard the paramedics, but I told her she didn't need to come with us. So she was in here with all kinds of time to clean up and hide evidence and do anything else she needed to do."

I rubbed the circle on the brass table again. "Did she say she cleaned up?"

"Of course not. She claims she went back to her apartment and waited by the phone."

By the phone. I looked at the suggestion of a rectangle on the brass table again. "Where did you go to call Adam?"

Her breath clicked in her throat in irritation at my change in focus. "I didn't go anywhere. I had my cell in my purse."

"What happened to this phone?"

Olivia looked down at where my finger was tapping the brass table and blinked slowly, then looked around the room. "It's . . ." She looked back at the table, perplexed. "I don't know."

"Was it there that night?"

She gazed at the table for a long beat, as though replaying the scene in her mind frame by frame. "No," she replied slowly. "His glass and his headphones. That's all. It didn't even register . . . That's so odd."

If someone had indeed laced Russell's nightly cocktail with a pharmaceutical kicker, it would be logical to remove the phone so he couldn't call for help. But had it been removed before or after Russell called Olivia?

"What did your dad say when he called you?"

She waved her hands dismissively. "He was drunk."

"In vino veritas."

She paused uncomfortably. "I don't remember."

"Then I can't help you."

She walked away from me suddenly, as though that would put distance between her and my question. Perching on the edge of a sofa, she laced her fingers in her lap and was quiet so long that I almost thought she was waiting for me to leave. Finally, she said in a crisp, detached tone, "Everything had turned out to be a lie, and what was most precious to him had been used against him."

That would be hard to hear anyone you care about say, much less your father. And then when it turns out to be the last thing he says to you, ouch. I gave her a moment before asking, "Do you know what he was talking about?"

"Guess," she said unhappily.

"You."

She gave me a withering look, thinking I was making fun of her, then looked away when she realized I was serious. Watching her face, I could see her censoring the answer until there was almost nothing left. "His work."

"How could that have been used against him?"

"I don't know. It didn't make any sense to me. But I know it has something to do with Claire. Everything has something to do with Claire. She's been his work since Micah died. I mean, Dad took care of her, got her back on her feet emotionally, watched over her in every possible way."

"Then why would you suspect her of having something to do with his death?"

"I think she came to resent it. Him. That more and more over the years, people talked about how important Dad was, not how important she was. And after Adam's career tanked, Claire blamed that whole thing on Dad, and things eroded from there."

"I thought Adam decided to quit performing." After he wowed everyone at the memorial concert for Micah, Adam had recorded an album under Russell's tutelage. My recollection was that it had been successful. I owned it, though truth be told, I hadn't played it in ages. But I did remember reading about Adam giving up his music and moving on to other pursuits, and I hadn't heard anything about him in a couple of years.

Olivia managed a smile. "That was Dad's magic, putting everything in the best possible light. Adam's album was actually pretty strong, but when everyone's expecting the Second Coming, anything else is a disappointment."

"It hasn't hurt Jordan." Jordan's album had come out eighteen months ago, torn up the charts, and was still getting decent airplay. It was eerie how much he sounded like Micah, as both a singer and a writer. Even more so than Adam. Jordan had captured those of us old enough to remember and adore his father, as well as the teenagers who embraced him as the next rock legend. Critics and the public were clamoring for his new album.

"Which drives Claire crazy. That the 'other son' is the one to inherit Micah's crown. Something else she blamed on Dad."

"Because he produced the album."

"Because he treated Adam and Jordan the same."

Claire struck me as the kind of mother who could turn

tigress and devour anyone who threatened her young, but I needed to fill in some of the gaps in my knowledge of this intriguing group before I could decide whether there was something to Olivia's theory or not. And how the tapes fit in.

"Who has the tapes?" I asked.

"I do."

"Where?"

"I don't see how that's relevant."

"Fine. But you know they're safe, secure."

Olivia rose, hands clamped to her sides. "You think the tapes have something to do with this?"

"I don't know what I think yet. That's why I'm asking so many questions." I smiled, wanting to end our first encounter on a somewhat positive note, to ensure there would be a second. "I need to go back to the office, but I would like to continue our conversation."

"Of course. I'll see you tonight, make sure you meet the right people."

"Thank you."

Olivia let out a long breath, as though we'd crossed a finish line. "Thank you. For listening. I wasn't sure you would."

I nodded. "I'd suggest you be cautious about discussing this with anyone else."

"And spoil your exclusive?"

"I'm more concerned about how it would play on *Page Six*." Every gossip column in the city would have orgasms over Olivia accusing Claire, and it just wasn't smart.

"Point taken."

I still wasn't convinced any of this was a motive for murder, but I was intrigued. Out in the hallway, staring at the call button for the elevator, I wondered about the strain of living in the public eye, with paparazzi charting your every move, mood, misstep. It had to take a thick skin, and a skin that thick would get hard to shed over time, might even become your regular coat. Combine that with the ballistic power of artistic egos, and small wonder relationships went sour, marriages faltered, and families got weird.

I was in the middle of trying to figure out what I'd be like if I'd grown up with rock stars when a slender hand grabbed my upper arm with viselike strength. I came close to literally jumping out of my shoes, but that didn't faze Claire in the least.

"You do understand that she only sees her side of the story," she said darkly.

"Pretty common affliction," I said, trying to ease my arm away from her. But she wasn't going to let go until she'd had her full say. I hoped I'd still have use of my fingers at that point.

"Olivia has a particularly flexible relationship with the truth," Claire continued urgently. "Her grief over what's happened makes it even more difficult. I don't want you to take her fantasies and present them as fact. She's a very troubled girl, and she should be allowed to come to terms with her responsibility in private with the help of the people who love her."

" 'Responsibility'?" I asked, no longer caring that my arm was numb. It wasn't just Olivia's imagination or guilty conscience.

Claire released me abruptly. At first I thought she was being coy, then I realized she'd genuinely said something she hadn't intended to say. I was willing to bet that was a historic event. "Poor choice of words on my part."

Still, it gave me an opening I couldn't resist pushing at a little harder. "Unless you think Olivia had something to do with Russell's death."

Claire ran her tongue over her top teeth, pushing out her pursed lips even farther. She was waiting for me to continue or, better yet, to change the subject, but I wasn't about to let her off that easily. Finally, she said, "His death was an accident."

"Not a universally held opinion."

"The official decision."

"What do you think?"

"What exactly is your article about?" she said, putting on the practiced smile of a public person.

I'd gotten as much as I was going to get at the moment. "Olivia as gatekeeper of her father's legacy."

The last thing I expected from Claire Crowley at that moment was laughter, especially the throaty laugh of the bitterly amused. Before I could ask her what was so funny, the doorway at the other end of the hall opened, framing Olivia. Claire saw her but made no effort to quell her laughter. Olivia stepped out in the hallway, but Claire turned back to me and said, "We should talk. So our lawyers don't have to," and walked back into her apartment without another look at Olivia or me. As soon as Claire's door closed, Olivia withdrew and closed her door. I was left standing in the hallway, rubbing the hairs on the back of my neck and wondering exactly what I'd thought was wrong with being an advice columnist.

4

"*You can't go alone.*"

"Thank you for being worried about my safety."

"Oh. That too."

"Excuse me?"

"Okay, I admit it. I love Jordan Crowley, and you're denying me the opportunity to see him up close, all sweaty and artistic and magnificent."

It was nearly déjà vu. We were in my bedroom, with Cassady going through my closet with the precision of a U.S. Marine on a search-and-destroy mission, Tricia sitting on my bed clutching a pillow to her chest and proclaiming her affection for a rock star, and me standing in front of the dresser and wondering if I wouldn't just be better off shaving my head since I'm never happy with my hair. For a moment, we were suitemates in college again, and it was rather gratifying that those days didn't seem out of reach. At least completely.

"You need to bring along someone who's really into him and can give you a genuine reaction to meeting him in the flesh for the first time," Tricia continued. She twirled a lock of hair around one finger and smiled at me beseechingly.

"You meet celebrities all the time," I said. The events she

planned were often star-studded and brushed her up against many hot personalities of the moment.

"The ones I meet aren't necessarily the ones I crave," she replied, letting her smile slide into wicked territory.

"I'm not really going because of Jordan. I'm going to try and understand Olivia better." They both looked at me with large, intent eyes until I added, "And figure out if she really thinks Claire killed Russell or if she wants to cause trouble for Claire for some other reason."

"Perhaps because Claire harbors a suspicion or two about Olivia?" Cassady frowned deeply at one of my favorite pairs of black slacks, then shoved them dismissively back into the closet.

"What's wrong with those?"

"Nothing. If you're staying home," she answered, continuing her search.

"If Olivia accuses Claire, and Claire accuses Olivia, don't they cancel each other out?" Tricia asked.

"You trying to cancel out my article?" I asked.

"No, but you're at such a delicate place with Kyle, I'd hate to see it founder for no good reason."

"'It' being the article or the relationship?"

"Either."

"You notice she's not taking Kyle with her tonight," Cassady said, draping an ice-blue silk tee across the pile of clothes at the foot of the bed.

"That would be mixing pleasure with business," I protested lamely.

"Which is which at this stage?" Tricia asked sweetly.

"More to the point," Cassady said, perching on the bed beside her, "it would be mixing someone who believes this was murder"—pointing to me—"with someone who doesn't." She gestured vaguely in the direction of the front door to indicate Kyle.

I'd already told Kyle that I was going to the concert as part of my research for the article, and we'd left it at that. I had tried to maintain the same lilting, intimate tone with him that I'd employed in our morning phone call before I'd met with Olivia, even though my concern about where this article was going to lead had sharpened considerably. He hadn't expressed any interest in the concert or any concern about my going alone; I suspected he was giving me time to sort through whatever facts Olivia would be able to offer and then come around to his way of thinking, that Russell's death had been accidental. I was going to need a lot more than Olivia and Claire pointing fingers at each other to persuade him differently. And I was going to have to find out more about the tapes.

"It's much simpler than you're making it. Claire Crowley asked me to come, and it didn't seem appropriate to ask to bring a guest. I'd love to have you both there, believe me."

"Thanks for the thought," Cassady said, "but I'm seeing Aaron tonight for the first time in three days, and that will be hotter than any Crowley in concert, save perhaps Micah returned from the grave."

I shivered. "That's such a disturbing mix of images, I can't possibly respond."

"Wow. Not having seen him for three days and you're so excited," Tricia said with a theatrical sigh. "Imagine if you hadn't seen him for three weeks. Or maybe even six!"

Cassady looked at her askance. "We said we weren't going to pry."

"*You* said we weren't," Tricia corrected.

"What's there to pry about?" I asked, slipping into a black tiered jersey skirt.

"The next time you and Kyle are getting together," Cassady said, stretching out on the bed, hands behind her head, ankles crossed carefully beside, not on, my pile of potential outfits.

Tricia stretched out beside her, mimicking her pose. "And any relevant details."

"I'd love to share, but I have work to do," I said, starting to pull on a teal boatneck blouse.

"Not in that, you don't," Tricia said, sitting back up with a disgusting lack of effort, pulling the blouse out of my hands, and floating back down.

"Kyle and I are talking again. Isn't that enough for the moment?" I asked.

"Is it?" Cassady asked. "Try the peach one."

I obediently picked up the peach blouse and slid into the crisp cotton while I tried to decide if the fact that Kyle and I were talking again *was* enough. Much as I missed him, I was acutely aware of the fact that we hadn't addressed our problem, much less fixed it, so the slower we took things, the better our odds of successfully getting back together. I was also acutely aware that such intellectual sandbagging could hold back the emotional floodwaters for only so long. Especially when I could still feel my lips humming from his kiss.

"It's not enough. I can tell," Tricia said with authority.

"How?" I asked.

"You're buttoning your blouse wrong."

I persuaded my friends to table the discussion about Kyle, since it was making me increasingly nervous, so I could concentrate on my approach for the concert, not that it was anxiety-free. This would be an ideal opportunity to get a feel for the dynamics of the inner circle and see if any of the rest of them were supporters of the theory that Russell had died by someone else's hand. Not that I was planning on using the question as an icebreaker, but I hoped I'd be able to pick up some undercurrent along the way.

I needn't have worried.

Walking up to the entrance of Mars Hall, I took in the throng of fans waiting to get in and allowed myself a moment's thrill at being on the right side of the velvet rope for a change. I knew that the few people who even noticed me were more inclined to be thinking "I wonder who she thinks she is" than "I wonder who she is," but it was still cool to walk up to the heavily muscled gentleman girded with the all-powerful clipboard and say, "Hi, I'm a guest of Claire Crowley. Molly Forrester."

My head barely came up to his mammoth shoulder, even though Cassady had persuaded me to wear my four-inch Max Studio black ankle straps with the little satin bows, mainly because Tricia had talked me out of the jersey skirt and into the one leather skirt I own, given to me by a former fashion editor at the magazine because I'd let her niece interview me for a school project. It was a tad shorter than I was used to, but I had vowed not to tug on it once during the course of the evening.

The doorman looked down at me with a frown. "Holly who?"

I repeated my name for him, my buzz from being on the right side of the rope quickly dissipating as the first few people in line snickered with each other, figuring I was trying to bluff my way inside. Had Claire changed her mind or just forgotten? What was the most polite way to proceed with a guy who had no doubt heard many more inventive reasons why "no, really, my name should be on the list" than I could possibly come up with in the ninety seconds I had left before he got impatient with me? He was at least polite enough to look at the list again, but he was shaking his head as a voice said, "It's cool, she's with me."

It was a beautiful voice, low and resonant, and its owner was pretty hot, too. It took me a moment to recognize him because he was wearing his black hair shorter, the curls cropped into waves, and his face was a little thinner, his cheekbones more prominent. But there was no question about the dazzling green eyes and the full-lipped mouth. "Adam Crowley," I said. Squeals from the women in line confirmed it.

"No, pretty sure *I'm* Adam Crowley. Which makes *you* Molly Forrester." His lopsided smile was slightly pained, as though being charming didn't come easily to him, which I doubted was the case.

It was hard not to smile back as I shook his hand. "If you insist."

"Let's give it a try, see how it goes." He thanked the doorman and pushed open the door for me. The women in line called his name, several reaching out for him. He waved to them politely and scooped his hand around my back, hurrying me inside.

"I don't mean to take you from your fans," I apologized as the door closed behind us.

"Just because someone screams your name doesn't mean they love you," he said wryly. He made a point of giving me the once-over. "Though you probably haven't been in that kind of relationship."

"You're very kind."

"Only occasionally." He cocked his head to the side as though considering pursuing that line of thought further, then seemed to change his mind. "We're back here," he said, jerking his thumb over his shoulder, then turning and walking in that direction.

I fell in beside him. "I appreciate your coming out to meet me," I said as we walked through the back of the theater, the darkened interior already crackling with the energy of employees hurrying to prepare for the doors to open. It was a large open-floor plan, with an old proscenium stage on the front wall and tall gilt mirrors along the back. There was table seating on the floor and an upstairs balcony on the three sides facing the stage. The decor was minimalist, just this side of sawdust on the floor and cowboys at the bar; brass sconces on the wall and accents on the balcony railings were the only noticeable efforts at glitzing up the place.

"My mother wanted to make sure you were properly escorted. Does that mean you're someone deserving of special treatment or someone she doesn't trust?"

I laughed, hoping it didn't sound nervous. Or adolescent, given that a shrill little teenage girl in my head was screaming, *Adam Crowley! I can't believe it, Micah Crowley's son Adam is talking to me!* I cleared my throat and tried to clear my head. "I just met her, I'd hope it wasn't a matter of trust."

"So you're a new girlfriend of Jordan's, not an old one or a stalker."

"None of the above," I said, stopping just as he was about to lead me through an unmarked door flanked by two men who made the giant out front look undernourished. "Maybe you were supposed to pick up someone else."

He made a face that was probably supposed to look sheepish, but the green eyes were too amused to pull it off. "I just assumed—I get sent to the front door to pick up a beautiful woman, you must be connected with Jordan in some way."

"I'm here with Olivia, actually."

"One of her patients?"

"Hardly."

"She's one of yours?"

"Colder."

His smile grew more relaxed, and he backed through the door, cocking his head again as I followed him. "You can't be a friend of hers," he said as he led me down the hallway decorated with posters of performances at the theater that formed a crash course in rock history: Jagger, Byrne, Verlaine, Johansen, Hynde, Springsteen, Cobain . . .

"Why couldn't I be a friend of hers?"

"Because I've met both of them and they're not lovely or interesting."

Now I cocked my head at him. "She speaks highly of you."

"Either she's lying or you are."

"Would you feel better if I said she didn't talk about you at all?"

"I'd know we were getting closer to the truth," he said, his smile dimming slightly. We turned a corner into a new hallway densely populated with roadies trying to get work done and assorted hangers-on who were hanging. Adam turned so he was facing forward and tucked my elbow into his hand. "Stick with me, you'll have a much better time." Steering me expertly through the crowded hallway, responding with a smile to the people who called out his name in varying levels of excitement as we walked by, he moved me quickly through the throng.

I was fascinated that people responded to him so strongly, even though he hadn't recorded anything in a long time, and had said on more than one occasion that he was done performing. Of course, he was putting on quite a show for me, and I wondered if that was just his way, to be "on" all the time. Or maybe it had something to do with the real tenor of his relationship with Olivia, which could be an interesting aspect of the article. Especially if Olivia and his mother had genuine reasons for suspecting each other in Russell's death.

"I would like to talk to you, somewhere quieter than here," I said.

"Great. Let's go." He stopped, pulling back on my elbow as though to turn us around so we could go back to the entrance.

"Later. Right now I have work to do."

"C'mon, Olivia can be difficult, but work? Give the kid a break." He propelled us to a door with a printed sign that read JORDAN CROWLEY. As he raised his hand to knock, the door swung open and a striking but very unhappy man strode out. Tall and thin, with exquisitely sharp cheekbones and thick, shoulder-length black hair shot through with silver. My breath caught in my throat and stayed there—fortunately, because it kept me from shrieking his name or babbling about how huge a crush I'd had on him when I was a teenager.

Dancing awkwardly around us, he forced a polite smile. "Excuse me."

"Gray, you leaving?" Adam asked.

Gray Benedek's hazel eyes went cold, even though his smile never faltered. "Buddy, I don't even know why I came."

"Let me talk to her," Adam began.

"I'm sure you've got better things to do." Gray tipped his head in acknowledgment of my stammering, starry-eyed presence and hurried down the hall.

It wasn't until he was out of my line of sight that I could breathe again. As impressed as I was to be standing next to Adam Crowley, he wasn't a superstar idol from my formative years, when I'd all but glue on headphones and listen to one album over and over again while gazing at the band's picture and memorizing every word, every bit of phrasing, on every song. "Was that Gray Benedek?" I asked, trying to force the squeak out of my voice.

"Yeah. Sorry, I should've introduced you," Adam said, looking back over his shoulder to spot Gray.

"Some other time," I assured him. Sometime when I was prepared not to drool. I needed to be professional now. As my mother had told me when I got invited to an embassy formal while in college, "Pretend you do this all the time."

Once Adam knocked successfully, the door opened, revealing Claire Crowley, dazzling in a swirling vintage Indian cotton dress, something she might have worn when Micah was starting out. And looked just as good in it now as then. She smiled at her son, but he didn't return it. "What's wrong with Gray?" he asked.

"Nothing," Claire said, "he just had to go." She turned to me quickly, giving me the same smile. "Molly, thank you for joining us."

"My pleasure," I said as she drew Adam and me into the room. It was a classic dressing room, with several lighted mirrors and stools at the left wall. The rest of the space was dominated by two large and slightly bedraggled sofas and a big circular table loaded with iced beverages ranging from water to wine, fruit platters and baskets, and a huge tray of sandwiches and baked goods.

Scanning the faces of the people in the room, I spotted Olivia in the corner of the far sofa, arms folded over her chest as though she'd just finished arguing with someone. Her face brightened when she saw me, and she stood. "This is the reporter I was telling you about," she told the room in general.

Adam let go of my elbow. "Reporter?" he repeated with mock distaste. At least I hoped it was mock.

Olivia tapped the shoulder of the man sitting on a stool with his back to everyone else, hunched over a guitar. He eased the stool around but didn't straighten up. Even from the odd angle, I was struck by the similarities between Jordan and Adam Crowley. Both looked more and more like their father as they got older, especially the penetrating eyes and sharp cheekbones. Their mothers looked so different, I would have expected Micah's features to be altered, softened in each of them, but there was little disparity and no question that they were brothers.

Jordan's hair was longer, a mass of curls that dropped to near his shoulders. Maybe a shade or two lighter than his half-brother's, but not much. The same mesmerizing green eyes, the full lips in the fine-boned face. I thought of the old Dan Fogelberg and Tim Weisberg album *Twin Sons of Different Mothers.* Here it was in the flesh. The most notable difference between the two was the bearing; even as Jordan uncurled from his guitar and stood, there was a slight hunch to his posture, a diffidence in his smile that seemed out of keeping with his rock star status. He waved to me in greeting, even though I was only six feet away, as Olivia explained who I was.

"Hope you like the show," he said, grabbing a water bottle off the makeup counter.

"Of course she will," said a slight woman in an impressively tight pair of 7 for All Mankind boot-cut jeans and red Anne Klein platform pumps as she stepped forward to shake my hand. "I'm Bonnie, Jordan's mom."

After the entrancing similarities between the two sons, the differences between the two mothers were startling. Bonnie was more petite than I had realized from pictures, her hand seeming fragile in mine, her brown eyes huge in her delicate face. The skintight mesh pullover showed there wasn't an ounce of fat on her frame. Her hair was chopped close to her head and streaked with even amounts of red and blond so I couldn't quite detect the original color, and she'd spiked it lightly. She and Claire were about the same age, but Claire appeared to be accepting the fact a little more gracefully than Bonnie was.

"It's great you're doing an article on Ollie," Jordan said, throwing his arm around Olivia's neck. "She's the best. Like the sister we don't think we ever had, right, dude?"

A look of pain snapped between Adam and Olivia, then Adam nodded tightly. "You got it, bro."

"And we all miss Russell like hell, y'know," Jordan continued to me. "Just not the same. I'm gonna dedicate a song to him tonight." He moved away from Olivia, shaking the water bottle as if it were a percussion instrument and humming, too low for me to pick out what the song was.

"Do you think that's wise?" Claire asked coolly.

"It's brilliant," he responded with a grin.

Olivia glanced uncomfortably at Claire before speaking. "Please, Jordan, it'll make people sad."

Jordan shook his head, still keeping time. "It shouldn't, it should make them angry. Pissed that a great guy like that would think that his life had no meaning anymore, that he had no option but to—"

A sob escaped Olivia. Jordan stopped, pulling her to him awkwardly. Everyone else looked somewhere else, and I got the distinct impression that tact was not Jordan's strong suit.

The stage manager knocked as he opened the door to let Mr. Crowley know that he'd be going on in fifteen minutes. Adam said, "He's still warming up," and eased the stage manager back out of the room, leaning against the door so no one else could come in.

"Blood pumping now, Jordan?" Adam asked bitterly.

"Adam," Bonnie said in a tone that would have been more appropriate had she been his mother.

Adam's mother said nothing, just walked over to disengage Olivia from Jordan's embrace. She took Olivia over to Adam as Jordan leaned back against the mirror, drumming his fingers on the water bottle and glaring at the ceiling. Bonnie went to him, stroking his arm, but he didn't react at all. The stage manager didn't belong out front, he belonged back here directing the emotional traffic.

Claire gave me a stern smile. "Why don't the three of you go take your seats while Jordan finishes preparing." It was a command, not a suggestion, and I followed Olivia and Adam out into the hall, wishing I could be a fly on the wall as the remaining three continued their argument or circled the cauldron or whatever they were going to do.

Whatever they did do, it worked. Fifteen minutes later, when Jordan hit the stage, Olivia was still sniffling, but Jordan was on fire. He played with power and passion and sang the same way. His voice, like Adam's, was reminiscent of Micah's, but his had a melancholy tone that deepened occasionally into something anguished. I'd liked his album very much (me and half a million other people), but I never would have guessed how much more compelling he would be live. We were at a reserved table, front and center, and more than once, I felt as though Jordan could see beyond the stage lights and was looking right at us. It was thrilling.

I was so enthralled, I didn't realize Adam had leaned toward me until his lips were against my ear. He explained that the drummer, bass player, and keyboardist were "friends from other bands," bands I didn't know very well. I nodded, but Adam didn't sit back, his lips still at my ear. I waited for him to say something else, and when he didn't, I turned to look at him. He didn't move, so we were suddenly nose to nose. Amused that I was startled, he smiled and sat back. I wasn't sure what game he was playing, but I could tell I was going to have to watch him.

Moments later, I turned away and was lost in the music again. The other musicians kept up with Jordan but never tried to claim the stage from him. It was his show, and he was masterful. So much so that it took over an hour for me to realize he hadn't played a single new song. Songs from his album, a handful of interesting covers, and even an old Subject to Change song, but nothing new. Under cover of a guitar solo, I leaned over to whisper to Adam, purposely pressing my lips against his ear, "I thought he was getting ready to do a new album."

Adam grinned, but his eyes stayed on his half-brother. "Yeah, he is."

"Why isn't he playing anything from it?"

Adam's grin took a sour turn. "Maybe it sucks."

On his other side, Olivia lightly slapped Adam on the arm. "Stop it," she hissed, looking around nervously as though anyone could hear our hushed conversation over the wailing of Jordan's guitar.

Adam shrugged. "Yeah, he's only six months late, I'm sure it's all gold."

I sat back as Olivia smacked Adam once again. The sibling dynamic between the two of them fascinated me, especially in light of Claire's comments about Olivia's feelings for both being far from sisterly. I could imagine emotions ebbing and flowing as they'd grown up, close quarters in an already rarefied environment. Adam's and Jordan's feelings for each other must have fluctuated over the years, too, especially as they were competing for Micah's attention and then for his crown.

Had Russell ever favored one over the other? Adam had been pushed out into the spotlight early—raw in emotion and experience—and not gained the traction people had expected. Had Russell expected more? Too much? And then moved on to Jordan, whose initial impression was that he could be every bit as big as his father, maybe even more so—as long as his second album followed up well? If Jordan was petering out, too, had the pressure of creating the next Micah overwhelmed Russell? Was this a case not of murder, but of artistic despair? But how did that jibe with Russell telling Olivia that his work was being used against him?

As the applause for the last song died down, Jordan stepped forward on the stage. "These guys are great," he said, sweeping his arm at the band, "but I'd like to have someone really special come up and join me now. My brother, Adam."

Shouts and whoops rang out over the thunderous applause, and people craned in their seats or stood to see where Jordan was pointing. Adam sat stock still in his seat, looking less than pleased. Olivia nudged him, whispering, "Go," urgently. After a long moment, Adam rose and walked to the stage stairs, the applause swelling as people spotted him.

Jordan bumped the microphone stand with his hip, leaning into it as he watched Adam approach. "He didn't know I was going to do this, but I knew I could count on him to be a good sport and play along."

The diehard fans screamed, knowing where Jordan was headed even before he played the opening riff. "Play Along" was the monster hit off Subject to Change's final album, released after Micah's death, an anthemic rock song about trying desperately to keep a relationship together even when you know it's over.

Adam stood onstage a moment, hands on hips, looking at Jordan with an unreadable expression. Jordan grinned and played the riff again. I actually thought Adam might turn around and leave the stage, but he smiled, not without effort, and took the seat in front of the grand piano that the keyboard player had graciously vacated.

The brothers locked eyes and tore into the song. Within three bars, the entire audience was on its feet, cheering and, when the lyrics began, joining in: "Been at this game so long, I can play it in my sleep, / But how to beat a score I don't even want to keep . . ." Jordan worked his way over to the piano so he and Adam were within arm's length as they played, challenging each other, goading each other, driving the song as if it were a physical object to be pushed from one point to another. It was electrifying.

When the song ended, Jordan embraced Adam, practically pulling him off the bench, as the crowd managed to scream and clap even louder. Adam returned the embrace, and Olivia burst into happy tears beside me. "They haven't played together for such a long time," she shouted over the din. "This is so wonderful."

Jordan let go of Adam and turned to the crowd, still on its feet. The cheering gave no indication of dissipating, so he pitched his voice to cut through the noise. Adam sat back down at the piano. "We're missing a couple of really important people tonight, people who should still be here." Beside me, Olivia caught her breath. Onstage, Adam tensed, too, as Jordan continued, "This next song is for the two men who raised us—as long as they could."

Jordan played the opening riff, and Olivia's wailing "No" sailed above the crowd noise like a descant. Some people cheered, but others caught themselves as they identified the song. Adam sat frozen at the piano as Jordan sang, "Valium and Jack, / Nothing back, / Nothing to hold on to, / To break my fall . . ." He looked to Adam, surprised he wasn't playing.

Adam walked off the stage.

The crowd, moments ago rocking along in cheerful abandon, grew uncertainly quiet. Olivia sank into her chair, staring at Jordan with great pain. I sat down, too, looking around for Claire and Bonnie, but I didn't see them at any of the other front tables. They were probably backstage somewhere, and I could only guess at how they might be responding.

"Valium and Jack" was the other hit single from the final album, but its virtues as a piece of music were inseparable from its legacy as Micah's epitaph. Popular legend had it that this was the precise cocktail on which Micah had OD'd. Why on earth was Jordan feeding the rumor mill the notion that Russell had done the same thing? Was he trying to link the deaths in people's minds? And if he was, was he being sensationalistic or was he trying to make a statement about what he thought really happened to Russell? Or was he trying to cover it up?

Adam hurried up to the table, dodging the outstretched hands of people at other tables. "Let's go," he said, pulling Olivia to her feet. They both seemed to assume I would follow, so I did, glancing back up at the stage as we left to see Jordan watching Adam carefully but never missing a beat of the song.

I'd expected Adam to leave the theater, but he led us backstage. He had a mission in mind, and for some reason thought Olivia and I should be part of it. I could still hear Jordan's singing, muffled and distorted by the walls between us. The audience was hushed.

Claire was in the hallway outside Jordan's dressing room, waiting for Adam. She started to speak, but he didn't give her the chance, stepping into her, close and furious. "Don't."

"You don't even know what I'm going to say."

"Unpredictability is not one of your charms, Mother."

"You shouldn't have left the stage."

"Why should I associate myself with his infantile need to be the center of the universe?"

"People enjoyed seeing you play again."

Adam reacted in disbelief, but Olivia was the one who spoke. "You told him to do this, didn't you. You want people to think this is what happened to my father. To cover your tracks. You bitch."

Claire Crowley looked as though she were preparing to slap Olivia until she remembered that I was standing there. Adam looked as if he'd be happy if the roof caved in at any point in the next ten minutes. I hadn't even known Russell

Elliott, and the emotional toll of the evening was apparent to me; I didn't know how the rest of them were still upright and coherent.

"Molly," Claire said, placing her hand on my arm instead of cracking it across Olivia's flushed face, "could I ask you to see Olivia home? She'd be more comfortable there, don't you agree?" She gave my arm a squeeze; I couldn't be sure if this one was meant to be encouraging or threatening.

"I'm leaving, but I'm not going home," Olivia announced before I could answer Claire. "C'mon, Molly." She turned with a defiant flourish and started for the stage door.

What would "The Ethicist" recommend in such a situation? I was there at Claire's invitation, but that had been extended only because I was a friend of Olivia's. So which one was actually my hostess, the one I shouldn't offend? But then, my article was about Olivia, so I needed to stick with her, no matter how that might sit with Claire. Besides, if Claire thought I was buying into Olivia's theory that Claire had something to do with Russell's death, she'd be willing to talk to me again just to talk me out of it.

I weighed the odds quickly and said, "Thank you, Mrs. Crowley, it's been quite an evening."

Claire tightened her grasp on my arm, not permitting me to turn away from her. "When can we have lunch?"

"I'll call you and set something up. I'd love to know more about your relationship with Olivia," I said, trying to sound businesslike and polite.

"I'd like it to be tomorrow," she said with the steeliness of a woman accustomed to getting her way.

"I'll call you in the morning," I replied, trying to walk away. Out in the theater, the music stopped and the applause began. Claire turned in response to the sound and let go of my arm.

As quickly as she'd released it, Adam took it and walked me over to where Olivia was waiting impatiently. "I know a great place where the three of us can have a quiet drink and wash this foul taste out of our mouths."

Olivia wrapped herself around Adam's free arm. "Why is everyone being so awful?"

"'Cause they don't know how else to be, Ollie," he said with a quiet sadness.

"Hey, coward! Get back here."

Adam didn't stop, but I looked back over my shoulder to make sure it was, in fact, Jordan who stood just inside the door from the stage, his guitar up on his shoulder as if he were a baseball player leaving the field. Bonnie ran up to him, hand to her throat, eyes wide, as though she were worried an explosion was imminent. She stroked her son's arm, but he didn't react. Claire stood near them, swaying slightly as though vacillating between standing with Jordan and following Adam.

"Adam!"

I couldn't pinpoint the difference in Jordan's tone, but it made Adam stop and turn around. "Good night, Jordan."

Jordan grimaced in disbelief. "You diss me in front of my fans and that's all you've got to say?"

Adam took a deep breath before replying, "Yes."

I admired his restraint. Olivia took a different approach. Bracing herself on Adam, she leaned forward in fury. "You're a soul-sucking pig, Jordan Crowley!"

"You watch your mouth, young lady," Bonnie said sharply.

"I was paying my respects!" Jordan protested.

"You don't respect anything," Adam said, turning his back on Jordan again and escorting Olivia and me out the stage door.

Security, paparazzi, and fans choked the alley. Screams

went up and flashes went off as people recognized Adam. Some yelled for Olivia, too. I just hoped I'd make it down the metal steps to the street without falling, given the height of my heels and the urgency with which Adam was moving us along.

Olivia descended first, and I was about to follow her when the stage door banged open and Jordan flew out. The crowd screamed even louder, but Jordan didn't react to them at all. He lunged straight at Adam, who was still holding my arm, so we both got tangled up as Jordan grabbed Adam by the lapels and shoved him back against the platform railing. I tripped over Adam's feet—or Jordan tripped over mine or some other painful combination—so the three of us crashed into the railing, me between the two of them, Adam behind me. They grappled with each other like Olympic wrestlers, oblivious to the crowd and cameras. Though I struggled mightily to force them apart and escape, I was no match for their fury-fueled adrenaline. Adam grabbed Jordan's shoulders and spun us all around, slamming Jordan into the railing now.

The noise of all the camera shutters firing repeatedly was like all the wings flapping when the birds descend on Tippi Hedren and her friends, and it took every ounce of concentration I had not to scream. What the photographers missed was Adam's question to Jordan as he tried to shove him over the balcony:

"You want to be the next one to go? I can take care of that, too."

5

"*Write the story. Don't* be the story."

Somehow, the only response I could come up with was, "Yes, ma'am." It was early, I was undercaffeinated, and I had a pretty impressive bruise on my rib cage from one of the bounces against the railing. Fresh out of the shower, I was studying the damage in my dresser mirror when I answered the phone, so I was distracted and not fully prepared for the venom at the other end.

"You're supposed to be interviewing Olivia Elliott. Why are you in the *Post,* sandwiched between the Crowley sons?" Eileen exclaimed.

I sighed, partly because of the bruise and partly because, until that moment, I had no idea anyone had actually published a picture.

"Research," I attempted.

"Do you have any idea how this makes the magazine look?"

There had to be a way to spin this that Eileen would approve of, especially since, having already taken a literal hit for the situation, I wasn't interested in taking a figurative one, too. "Like a cool publication whose reporters get invited to all the best parties?"

Eileen made an angry noise in her throat that sounded like

a garbage disposal with too much pasta in it. "Come see me when you drag your overexposed backside into the office. Which better be soon."

"I'm meeting Olivia for breakfast. For the article," I said, knowing that wouldn't make her any happier. And I had to call Claire, too, speaking of unhappy women. But I needed more information before I did that.

"Eat fast. And bring me my ascension-to-the-throne question, too," she demanded, hanging up so forcefully that I thought the reverb might shatter my phone. I slammed my handset down, too, knowing she wouldn't hear it but needing to respond in kind.

As I searched for an outfit in the piles Cassady had left scattered around my room the night before, I reviewed events. Did I have anything I needed to apologize for? Or had I, in pursuit of a thorough background for my article, simply been caught in the wrong place at the wrong time? I preferred the latter, but Eileen seemed to be rooting for the former. One more chance to see me fail.

I'd almost coaxed myself into the comfort of my Banana Republic pinstripe shirtdress when the doorman rang. Danny, the regular doorman, was on vacation, and I couldn't wait for him to come back because Todd, the substitute, took forever to make his point and I really didn't have the patience for it this morning.

"Good morning, Ms. Forrester," Todd began. "How are you this morning?"

"Fine, Todd, how are you?" I asked, hoping he wasn't looking at the *Post*.

"I'm quite well, thank you. There's a gentleman down here who says I don't know him because you stopped dating him, but it's quite important that he see you—"

Even more excruciating. Todd didn't have the paper, but Kyle did. "Thank you, Todd, send him up."

I hung up, shot a brush through my hair, and slapped on my mascara first; if he knocked before I could put on all my makeup, at least my eyelashes wouldn't be invisible, which makes me look as though I'm eight years old and I've been crying.

He knocked just as I was debating eye shadow colors. I wondered what our beauty editor, Marlie, would suggest in a situation like this: keep him waiting or finish painting? I split the difference, pausing long enough to swipe a taupe stripe across both eyelids, then hurrying to the door.

Fortunately, I didn't fling myself out the door and into his arms, but I was considering it, and that must have been evident by my expression.

"It's okay, you can be happy to see me," he said with a grin.

"Hello, Peter," I said with no grin at all.

"You look disappointed. Were you expecting someone else?" His grin broadened. "I told the doorman I was an ex. I won't insinuate that it's a long list, but I can't be the only one on it."

True, Peter Mulcahey was an ex. Specifically, the man I stopped dating when I started dating Kyle. Because we were both journalists, we continued to run into each other, which he enjoyed far more than I did. Tricia believed he went out of his way to seek me out, which was a credible theory, though I did my best to dissuade him. I'd really thought I might've seen the last of him, since the last time we'd crossed paths, he'd gotten shot. Not by me. Not that the thought hadn't occurred to me.

Peter looked good, but he always looked good in that golden glow sort of way, with his bright blond hair and lapis eyes and crooked smile. He came off like Prince Charming, but in my experience thus far, he was more of a chocolate Santa: all shiny and sweet on the outside, hollow on the inside.

"The doorman said you were someone I'd 'stopped dating,'" I said. Perhaps Peter didn't appreciate the sharp distinction between "man I dumped" and "man I stopped dating" that I was making in my head, and given that I still had occasional guilt pangs about not breaking things off with more finesse, that was probably a good thing in the long run. And I really couldn't see him admitting to anyone that he'd ever been dumped. But it was still annoying that it was his misapprehension of his status in my life that had led us to this awkward moment.

"It's the truth." His cool eyes narrowed. "And yet, I surprised you. That means there's someone you've stopped dating more recently than you stopped dating me. Did you finally shake off the cop?"

"Go away, Peter."

His delight was maddening. "You did. Damn, I have great timing. Invite me in."

"I'm on my way out."

He looked me over, starting with my semibrushed hair and moving a bit too slowly down to my bare feet. "Really."

"Peter"—I sighed—"why are you here?"

He held up his copy of the *Post,* offering me my first look at the picture of me, Adam, and Jordan. It looked like a cross between a football tackle and Martha Graham choreography. The headline read: WHO'S COME BETWEEN THEM?

Peter pulled a mock frown. "What exactly is going on here?"

I almost didn't want to know the answer, but still I asked, "What does the caption say?"

Peter read, "'Jordan and Adam Crowley fight over a

woman, or at least around one, after Jordan's sold-out show at Mars Hall last night. Reps for both declined to comment or to identify the woman."

Which meant someone asked Claire what happened and she told them she wasn't going to talk to them. I'd known Peter long enough to be sure that the same approach wasn't going to work with him. Closing the door and ignoring him would only challenge him to pursue whatever he thought the story was with greater vigor. "I'm doing a profile of Olivia Elliott."

Peter held the newspaper close to his face and squinted, pretending to examine the page microscopically. "And where is she, exactly?"

I snatched the paper from him, not sure whether I should shred it on the spot or place it lovingly in my scrapbook. After all, I hadn't done anything wrong, I'd just been standing between two famous semisiblings who had come to blows. And threatened each other's lives. That still sat uneasily. It's problematic to parse a statement that someone spews in the heat of the moment, but I kept coming back to Adam saying, "I can take care of that, too." *Too*. Implying he had previously taken care of something similar. And since the topic at the time had been "the next one to go," it wasn't all that wide a conclusion to jump to Adam saying he'd been a part of someone else "going." Was Olivia looking in the wrong direction by blaming Claire for Russell's death?

I'd never been in this situation before, with this number of people simultaneously pointing fingers at one another and/or themselves over a death. Especially one that had been ruled accidental. Maybe it was all stress bubbling to the surface and hauling up years of emotional baggage with it. But it felt increasingly as though there were more to Russell Elliott's death than met the official eye. Which meant it was a great story. Which meant I had to keep Peter Mulcahey far, far away from it.

So, feeling a little like Granny letting the Big Bad Wolf through the door, I invited him in. For a moment. "Let me grab my shoes and I'll walk out with you," I said, opening the door wider. He took back the newspaper, but he followed me in.

I led him into the living room, discreetly scanning table-tops and hoping I hadn't left too much research in evidence. The cascade of CDs on the coffee table—everything I had by any of the Crowley men—was the most telling material visible, but I hoped it would escape Peter's notice.

"Have a seat," I suggested, pointing at the armchair farthest from the CDs and continuing on to the bedroom. My hope was that I could grab my shoes, handbag, and notebook and have Peter back out in the hallway before he started nosing around. "Just take a second."

"You still haven't painted," he said, not sitting down and surveying the room with a slight frown.

"I keep changing my mind about the color."

"Why don't you like to commit?"

He couldn't have stopped me colder if he'd beaned me with a book from my desk, where he stood now, baldly and boldly poking at the stacks of paper sliding into one another there. I leaned back toward the doorway, thinking about bean-ing him with the kate spade wedge I held in my hand and sorting through the various searing retorts that raced through my mind, ranging from, "Excuse me?" to, "I do so!"

Commitment had not been the issue in our breakup. If anything, he was the one not taking the relationship seriously, and I was already drifting away when I met Kyle. But there was no point in debating; he was fishing for a reaction, and I wasn't going to give it to him. Instead, in a rare moment of restraint, I took a deep breath, put the shoe on my foot, grabbed the rest of my stuff, and strode back into the living room.

"Did you come to analyze me, or did you have something more journalistic in mind?" I asked as I continued past him. One of the advantages of a small apartment is that it doesn't take long to show someone to the door. I opened it and gestured to the hallway. "Let's go."

He strolled past me, smirking. "When I saw the picture, I had to check on you."

"In person."

"I wouldn't have seen the look on your face if I'd called."

He pushed the elevator call button while I locked the door. There was something about him, there had always been something about him, that made me certain he was up to no good. "Let's skip the foreplay, Peter."

"It's one of my strengths," he protested.

"Have you taken a poll?" I asked. "C'mon, what do you want?"

Peter leaned in as though the empty hallway were filled with people and he needed to whisper a state secret. "I heard Adam Crowley's coming into a lot of money."

"How nice for him."

Peter straightened up slightly. "And I was wondering, since you're so close to him, if it had come up."

"I am not close to him."

Peter dangled the paper in front of me again. "Really?"

"Okay, here's some inside info: Adam Crowley already has a lot of money," I said with a sigh, stepping into the elevator.

Peter shook his head. "I hear most of Micah's estate went to Claire, and she keeps everybody on a pretty short leash."

"Quinn has you doing an article on Adam?" Peter wrote for *Need to Know,* Quinn Harriman's relatively new monthly with aspirations that straddled the lad-mag and Manhattan insight genres.

"No, I'm doing an article on Ray Hernandez."

"The club designer?"

Peter nodded. "And Ray says Adam's backing his next venture. Soon as his cash comes in. But Adam's being very mysterious about where that cash is coming from. If he didn't mention a new revenue source, maybe these guys are up to something they shouldn't be."

I sympathized with Peter's zest for looking for a deeper story but was irritated by his casual expectation that someone else would do most of the digging. "Or maybe Ray's playing with you." Peter shook his head doubtfully while I tried to remember: What exactly had Olivia said about Claire controlling the money now that Russell was dead? If Claire was getting more, did Adam think he was getting more, too? Who had the greater need—Claire or Adam? Were Peter and I on intersecting stories? "So?" I asked neutrally.

"I want to figure out if Adam's fronting for someone else or if he's planning a new album and investing his advance."

So far, so good. I was thinking murder, and Peter was thinking finance. The trick was to keep our paths parallel for as long as possible. "I really didn't get that much of a chance to talk to him last night, despite what you think that picture implies. However, in the event that I talk to him again while I'm working on the Olivia piece, I'll see what I can find out."

The elevator doors opened. Peter threw his arm around my shoulders as we walked out into the lobby, proclaiming, "You're better to me than I deserve."

"Got that right," Kyle replied.

Kyle stood in the lobby next to Todd, who was frozen with the phone to his ear, a slightly panicked look on his face. I tried not to imagine the conversation that had preceded

Todd's picking up the phone, though given Kyle's scowl, something about "There's already a gentleman up there" had apparently been mentioned. Kyle reached over and helped Todd hang up the phone.

"Hey, Detective," Peter said with a mockingly perplexed tone. "I thought you guys were . . ." He made a gesture that looked as if he were an umpire calling someone out at home.

Both men looked at me with disconcertingly similar expressions, expectant but still trying to be polite. "I never said that." I didn't know whether to say it defensively to Peter or apologetically to Kyle, and it tumbled out in some faltering, semifalsetto midrange. Kyle and I were never going to get back on proper footing at this rate.

"You didn't correct me," Peter pursued as I tried to picture how far through his right foot I could drive the heel of my shoe before Kyle restrained me. If he'd even try.

There was something slightly absurd about this whole situation. I was, on a purely technical level, a single woman. Aside from the fact that I was still in love with one of these men and could not get the other out of my life, neither one had any right to be quizzing me about what I was doing with my evenings, especially at a point in the morning when I'd had little sleep, zero coffee, and an argument with my boss. My hands planted themselves on my hips of their own accord as I tried to separate my annoyance with Peter's caring from my delight with Kyle's concern from my irritation at being quizzed.

"Not that I particularly owe anyone an explanation for anything, but I was keeping the conversation on business," I said. "Just like now."

"So we're all here for work," Kyle replied.

"We are?" I asked with alarm, given Kyle's field.

"And what's your business?" Peter asked him.

"None of yours," Kyle replied.

Peter gave him a big and completely insincere smile. "I'd forgotten you're funny. How'd I manage that?"

Kyle surprised us both by sticking his hand out to Peter. "Happens to the best of us. Why not to you."

Peter glared at Kyle for a long moment, then shook his hand firmly. "I'd love to stay and play, but I have work to do." He tossed a look back at me. "Let me know what you find out," he said as he walked out of the building.

Todd followed Peter, or retreated from us, or a little of both, then clung to his post at the front door. Kyle and I stood in the middle of the lobby, looking at each other. Not touching, not talking. After our glorious moment of reunion at the Bubble Lounge, I'd hoped our next meeting would be a little more romantic. But it seemed it was our curse that practical matters had the darnedest way of interfering.

"What made him think we'd broken up?" Kyle asked evenly.

Giving up on my romantic fantasy, I clenched my teeth. "Maybe the fact that we had?"

"You told him?"

"Not exactly, but he used the phrase *stopped dating,* and I thought it was about you and me, not about him and me. He and me. Whatever."

Kyle's forehead furrowed quizzically. "We hadn't stopped dating."

"Yes, we had."

"We'd paused."

"Even a TiVo can't pause that long without wearing something down," I said, both bothered and amused by his decision to play semantics at this point. Two could indulge in that. "Why did you tell him you're here 'because of work'?"

"I am."

"I'm work?"

Kyle smiled. "Don't set yourself up like that. I'm investigating a potential assault," he continued quickly, not giving me the chance to react to the first half of the statement before I was surprised by the second.

"What happened?"

"How 'bout you tell me?" Kyle suggested, pulling the folded newspaper page out of his jacket pocket and opening it with a snap. I got the feeling I was going to see a lot of that picture as the day progressed.

"That's not assault."

"Do you fully understand what constitutes assault in the state of New York?" Kyle asked helpfully, turning the paper so he could look at the picture again.

"Are you making fun of me?"

"Not yet."

"I was going to tell you. I'm not hiding anything. I'm not going to hide anything," I said, trying to convey the full weight of the promise I was making.

"From anyone, apparently."

"When did you start reading the *Post*?"

"When a stack of about eighteen copies turned up on my desk this morning."

"You're amused?"

"So far. But I'd really like to hear the whole story. Wanna have breakfast at the Carnegie Deli?"

He looked back at me with calculated timing, so I knew the choice was deliberate. Our first meal together had been breakfast at the Carnegie Deli. Of course, I figured out not long after he sat down that he suspected me of murder and I left without eating, but it was still knee-wateringly sweet of him to offer to take us back to our roots. It's what we really needed if we were going to, as Dorothy Fields suggested, pick ourselves up, dust ourselves off, and start all over again. He was being gracious and open, and I couldn't stand how much I had missed him.

So I had to answer: "I'd love to. But I can't."

He folded the newspaper back up. "Should I take that personally?"

"No, it's work." There was that curse again. "I'm meeting Olivia for breakfast." I reached out for the newspaper, but he slid it back into his jacket pocket. "She's the one who got me into this mess."

"Yeah, but that's one of your charms. You like being in messes."

"I prefer to think of it as straightening messes out."

He nodded, but he dropped his eyes. "That too."

"Could we have lunch together?" I said, not wanting to plead but prepared to do so.

"I'd rather have dinner. We won't be as rushed."

"We do have a lot to talk about."

"That too." His eyes came up again and held me in place while he leaned in and kissed me with appalling restraint. "Let's say Wild Salmon at eight?"

"Wonderful."

He offered me his arm. "Think Todd would mind if I got you a cab myself?"

"He'll live," I assured him.

On the sidewalk, I tried to concentrate on how wonderful it was to be standing with him again, our hands intertwined, our bodies pressed gently together, our eyes locked. He was the one who said, "Why're you having breakfast with her?"

"I'm getting to know her. I have to spend a lot more time with her to write this article."

"Even though her dad's death was accidental." He said it with the finality of a math teacher reminding me of an important theorem right before an exam.

"The article's about her, whatever happened to her dad."

"Okay." He raised his arm without his eyes ever leaving my face, and I heard the throaty rumble of a cab pulling up behind me. "Just be careful." I started to smile, expecting another snarky comment about Adam and Jordan, but he continued quietly, "People in pain get desperate for answers. Don't offer her false hope."

I knew he was right, and as he helped me into the cab, leaning in for a last quick kiss, I knew I should let it go at that. But somehow, I still asked, "So what would it take to get an accidental death investigated as a homicide?"

Lucky for me, he laughed. "Evidence."

"How much?"

"Molly . . ."

"Just so I can tell her, if she gets too worked up."

There was a little truth in that, so he answered, "More than you're going to find, because the man's in the ground and no one thinks he was murdered except his daughter, and she might be wrong. It happens. Leave it alone." He kissed me again, hard, more in punctuation than passion, then closed the door and slapped the hood of the cab, as if I were a prisoner being taken away in a cruiser.

It took me two blocks to realize that the tingling sensation in my chest was not a result of seeing Kyle, but my phone trying to get my attention while I hugged my purse. Realizing I still hadn't called Claire, I dug it out and retrieved the messages. The first was Tricia, laughing so hard about the picture that she could hardly speak. The second was from Cassady, and I expected more of the same, but it was an unexpectedly somber message, asking me to call her when I had the chance.

Laughs could wait. I called Cassady first and was surprised when she answered right away. "Are you okay?" I asked. I'd gotten used to her letting her voice mail do the heavy lifting now that she was so often busy with Aaron or catching up on work because she'd been busy with Aaron.

"I think okay is at least six blocks over from where I am," she said darkly.

"What happened?" Anticipating a comment about the picture, I was puzzled by why it would upset her. I'd expected her to laugh even harder than Tricia.

"He stood me up."

"Aaron?"

"Yes."

This was huge. Cassady's relationship with Aaron had been unfolding sweetly and smoothly; Aaron standing her up was out of character. But that was the lesser of the two hurts. The central issue here was that Ms. Lynch was experiencing something so rare that it might, in fact, be brand new. What man in his right mind would stand her up?

"Has this ever happened to you before?" I asked in disbelief.

"No."

"Has he called this morning?"

"He called last night."

My concern ebbed immediately. "Okay, then, he didn't really stand you up."

"He let me wait for forty-five minutes and then called with an excuse so transparent, you could read the newspaper through it. Nice picture, by the way."

"So clearly not the issue."

"I'm trying to demonstrate I have manners, even in the most difficult circumstances."

"What was his excuse?"

"An emergency with one of his students."

"Okay. Why is that transparent?"

"He's a physics professor, not an obstetrician. What sort of emergency could there have been? An atom split without permission?"

"Now, that would've made the papers before I did. Maybe he's really a member of the Justice League and the world needed saving. They keep that stuff pretty quiet."

"He's cheating on me."

"Cassady, don't."

"It happens."

"Not to you."

"Not often. But it's still possible."

"But not probable. Have you talked to him today?"

"He said he'd call, but he hasn't."

That didn't sound like Aaron, which didn't sound good, but I wasn't about to encourage Cassady to conjure up bitter scenarios. That was my job.

"I'm sure there's a reasonable explanation that might even involve a distressed student. How many times did we go weep on Dean Samson's shoulder at all hours?" I asked, invoking the calm and benevolent dean of students who had guided us through plenty of undergrad crises. "He might be taking you for granted, but I bet he's not cheating on you."

"I could go for a lesser crime," she said with a sadness that meant she was much crazier about Aaron than we'd given her credit for. "Have a great breakfast. Don't let the paparazzi catch you with your mouth full."

"They're not going to be there."

"Yeah, right. Call me later," she said with the beginnings of a lilt, then hung up. She was laughing at my expense, but at least she was laughing, so I'd accomplished something positive. But I couldn't figure out why she thought it was so funny.

Until the cab pulled up in front of Le Parker Meridien and the knot of people milling in front revealed themselves not to be patrons waiting for admittance, but half a dozen photographers. It struck me as an amusing coincidence until I got out of the cab and walked toward the front door. Suddenly, the photographers were between me and the door, snapping away.

I don't like having my picture taken, mainly because I have a gift for closing my eyes and opening my mouth at the precise moment the shutter closes. So strolling down the red carpet while flashes pulse has never figured in my fantasies, and running this gauntlet was certainly not fun. I thought about striding past them with my gaze fixed, Gwyneth Paltrow–like, on some vaguely forward point and a polite smile on my lips. But after about two steps, the absurdity of the situation overwhelmed me, and I stopped, which had the benefit of surprising my new friends, who all paused at least three seconds before returning to their snapping.

"This is a mistake," I said, trying the polite approach for starters. "You don't want to take my picture."

"There's no need for threats, babe," one of them, a burly, bearded guy in a khaki jacket who had apparently seen *The Year of Living Dangerously* at an impressionable age, called out to me.

"Don't call me 'babe,'" I said, struggling to hang on to my polite impulse, "and don't take my picture. I'm not whoever you must think I am."

"You're Jordan Crowley's new babe," he said with deliberate emphasis on the last word.

"Adam's," another photographer, a tall, reedy woman with straight hair hanging down to her belt, corrected him.

"Wrong on both counts," I said firmly. "Thank you anyway."

As I turned away from them, I enjoyed a full two seconds of congratulating myself on handling the incident with aplomb and decorum before I slammed into the chest of the man who had walked up behind me. The cameras whirred into action again as the man slid his arm gallantly along my shoulders.

"They're not bothering you, are they?" Jordan asked.

"Hey, Jordan!" several of them screamed, clustering around us.

Jordan held up a hand to stop them. "Could you all give us a little space? The lady's here to work."

A twinge of panic raced through my stomach. "Oh, please don't—"

"She's going to find out who killed Russell Elliott," Jordan announced, and the cameras whirred even louder in response. "And I'll tell you now—it's the same person who killed my dad."

6

I don't like being left speechless; it makes me feel out of control. I especially don't like it when it happens in front of a crowd of strangers. But Jordan had blindsided me, and I sputtered a moment before coming up with any sort of response.

"That's a new definition of low," I said belatedly, yanking my arm out of his grasp as soon as we were out of the line of fire. No need to add any more drama.

"I'm not sure I understand," Jordan said, looking me right in the eye. He held my gaze long enough to prove his sincerity, then told the hostess at Norma's that we were meeting Olivia. She nodded and led the way deep into the seating area.

Jordan fell in behind her immediately, leaving me to follow him and to figure out why I was so angry. Patrons glanced up, several of them reacting to Jordan with widening eyes and arching brows, but no one made a scene, which was a nice change of pace.

I closed the space between us so I could speak quietly. "You speak cavalierly about the deaths of two men you profess to be close to, and don't understand why that's repulsive?"

"I'm being honest. The same person killed them both. Why lie anymore, now that Olivia's found you to help us prove it?"

We reached the table and the hostess left quickly, avoiding eye contact and probably dialing somebody's tip line on the cell in her pocket. Olivia stood to greet us, twisting her napkin fretfully. "Jordan?" She looked at me unhappily, and I shook my head emphatically, so she turned her frown back to him. "What are you doing here?"

"Mom said you were having breakfast with Molly, and I thought I'd join you. I didn't get to talk to her last night." Jordan sat down and picked up a menu, ignoring the fact that Olivia and I were still standing and Olivia was trying to wish him back out the door.

"She's here to talk to me, Jordan," Olivia said, twisting the napkin so hard that it started to kink back on itself.

"Who tipped the paparazzi? You or your mom?" I asked.

Jordan didn't react, but Olivia did, glancing toward the front door, then flushing and sitting heavily in her chair. She gestured that I should sit, too, before she leaned in toward Jordan. "Can't I do anything without you horning in?"

"It's not like that, Ollie," he assured her, just this side of condescending. "Until now, I thought I was the only one who thought something funky went down with your dad. I'm here to support both of you."

"By raising the possibility that someone killed your father as well?" I asked.

"What?" It came out higher and louder than Olivia intended, and more than one patron looked in our direction. She sank back in her chair and tried to put her kinked-up napkin over her face for a moment in a futile effort to compose herself. Dropping the useless napkin, she snarled at him, "I really hate you sometimes."

"No, you don't," he said confidently.

Olivia covered her face with her hands this time, and I was struck by how much younger she seemed when she was around the Crowleys. The "we all turn twelve when we go home for Christmas" effect, I supposed. I was also struck by how different Jordan was from the moody artist I'd met before the show. Much closer to his charming onstage persona. Maybe it was a function of how he prepared for a show. Or maybe something had happened in the dressing room right before I'd arrived that had dampened his spirits. An argument with Bonnie or Claire? Gray Benedek?

"Do you genuinely believe your father was murdered, or are you creating a press event?" I asked as politely as I could.

"I'm all about truth," he said.

"Which is a lie," Olivia said, snapping her napkin back into her lap.

I tried to remember the old brainteaser about meeting two people, one who speaks only lies and the other who tells only the truth, and having to come up with the one question that will expose which one is which. With the accusations flying thick and fast, I needed to be able to sort fact from nonsense just as quickly. "I have the same question for both of you: Why would someone kill your father?"

"I'm not going to talk about this in front of him," Olivia said crisply. The waiter who had been tentatively approaching our table did a discreet fade back out of harm's way. "In fact, I'd like you to leave, Jordan."

"Ollie, come on," Jordan said with a hint of irritation. "Stop treating me like the enemy. We're on the same side."

"I doubt that very much. I don't remember the last time we were on the same side for even the simplest thing," she sniffed.

"We're victims of the same evil," Jordan insisted, and Olivia frowned suspiciously.

"Let's not be too grand," I warned, sensing the approach of some overblown, metaphorical statement about fame, popular culture, and the artist's sacrifice.

Jordan took Olivia's hand gently in his. "Claire killed both our fathers."

I'm not sure who had the sharper reaction—me, who nearly dropped my water goblet, or Olivia, who gave a sharp, tight giggle of delight. "What are you saying?" I asked.

"Claire Crowley killed my father, and now she's killed Russell, too," Jordan said patiently, as though it were abundantly clear to everyone in Manhattan except me.

Olivia beamed at Jordan as though he had just presented her with roses and champagne. "I had no idea!"

"You already told me you thought Claire killed your dad," I said, feeling a little dizzy.

"Of course, but I didn't know Jordan felt the same way," she said, squeezing Jordan's hands.

Who would've imagined a shared suspicion of murder could be a bonding opportunity? While Olivia and Jordan seemed quite happy, I was a little queasy. Something about Jordan's demeanor wasn't ringing true. Particularly the adoration he was offering Olivia after being so dismissive of her the night before. That had felt painfully real, and this felt like another performance, but whether it was for Olivia's benefit or mine, I couldn't be sure. So I had to ask, "Jordan, what are you up to?"

"You're a very suspicious woman," Jordan said, leaving his hand in Olivia's as he turned to me.

"Kinda comes with the job," I explained. "But then, things do happen that make me even more suspicious than usual. Like you announcing, years after the fact, that you think your father was murdered. And doing it in front of those barracudas out front. You realize it's probably already posted on half a dozen Web sites. More by lunchtime," I said, hoping I would not be in any of the pictures.

"We should check Gawker," Olivia blurted, though she

had the decency to look embarrassed as soon as it was out of her mouth. "I didn't mean that the way it sounded."

There are moments when your professional life flashes before your eyes and you just have to wave good-bye. I pushed back from the table. "I'm sure the two of you can find a magazine that's willing to play along with whatever game you've cooked up, but *Zeitgeist* isn't it," I said, picking up my purse and immediately beginning to work out how I was going to explain this to Henry.

Jordan stood with me, leaning in so the people at other tables couldn't hear, hard as they might try. "My father was going to leave Claire, and that's why she killed him. And Russell, God rest his soul, made the same mistake."

I didn't sit down immediately, because I sensed that was the reaction he was looking for, but I had to lock my knees to stay upright. But before I could say anything in response, Olivia was on her feet, too, and she wasn't giving any thought at all to what the people at other tables were hearing, thinking, or texting to their friends as she hissed, "You're disgusting."

Jordan kept his face turned to me, as though her rage would dissipate if he didn't look at her. "Olivia didn't approve of her father's affair with Claire," he said calmly.

"They didn't have one! Why do you have to make everything worse than it actually is?"

"You're the therapist, sweetie, you tell me."

Olivia snatched her purse off the table and gestured for me. "I'll go with you."

As I looked at her flushed face, the ending of the brainteaser popped into my head: Both the liar and the truth teller will give you the same answer, and you should do the opposite. "Wait, please," I said as gently as possible.

Olivia zipped around to stand between me and Jordan, her

back pointedly to him. "I forgot to warn you that most of what he says is self-serving crap."

"Except when he agrees with you," I said.

She hesitated a split second before nodding in agreement. "That's how you can be sure what I'm saying is the truth. Even Jordan agrees with me."

"Yet you seem a bit at odds on the question of motive," I pointed out, glancing up at Jordan to check his reaction. He was staring intently at the back of her head, perhaps willing her to turn around, perhaps sending her telepathic messages to shut up. Otherwise, his face was blank. Beautiful, but blank.

Whirling on Jordan, Olivia defiantly cocked her chin—which came up to his collarbone—and said with shimmering anger, "It's all about the tapes and you know it."

I expected another glib and inappropriate response from Jordan, but instead, this time his face flushed. "Shut up, Olivia."

"Not this time," she said with a weight that spoke of years of capitulating to him.

"There are no tapes and you know it," he said, his voice dropping in register and volume.

"I've seen them, and I've heard them," Olivia insisted. "They're real, Jordan. And Claire wants to release them and take all the money for herself."

Jordan looked at her for a long, silent moment, debating a difficult question. I couldn't figure out why Olivia's assertion that the murder had been about money was more troubling than about love and/or sex. Then he spoke with an emotion-clogged voice. "I want to hear them."

Now I understood. He was reacting to the existence of the tapes and the possibility of hearing his father, not to Olivia's hypothesis. With all the albums, concert footage, and TV interviews of Micah, there still had to be a bittersweet thrill for his son to realize there was another piece of his father out there, a piece the world hadn't shared yet. That was the surprising rawness in his voice, as though he were holding back tears, even though his expression stayed cool.

What surprised me even more was Olivia's pause before answering. What could she be debating? Of course he should hear the tapes. It was very odd that he hadn't heard them, hadn't even believed they existed, and I looked at her sharply, waiting for her to explain. "I guess that would be okay," she said with a frown.

Before I could offer my opinion, Jordan asked, "Has Adam heard them?"

Olivia shifted away from him slightly, knowing he wasn't going to like the answer. "I think so."

Jordan's smile was ice cold. "Then I better damn well hear them. Now."

"How about this evening?" Olivia suggested. "I have clients to see, and I have to get them and—"

"Where are they?" Jordan interrupted.

Olivia shook her head, looking confident for the first time. "You think I'm going to tell you?"

Jordan's cool smile tightened. "When and where?"

"Meet me at Dad's apartment at six o'clock. You come, too," she told me.

I accepted before Jordan had a chance to voice an objection and hurried Olivia out, leaving Jordan behind us to brood. The paparazzi had dispersed to spread Jordan's new proclamation all over town, so I was able to stand with Olivia while she hailed a cab and ask, "Who else knows you have the tapes?"

"No one," she said, not looking me in the eye.

"Who else suspects you have the tapes?" I pressed.

"Claire. Bonnie. I thought Gray did when he came to the

show last night, but he was just back on his old thing about getting Claire to license one of the band's songs for a commercial. If he thought I had songs that hadn't even been released, he'd be all over me." She smiled quite brightly, enjoying the thought of that kind of power. "But you cannot tell anyone until I decide what I'm going to do with the tapes."

"Did your father leave instructions for you?"

"I know what he wanted done," she replied as a cab slid up to the curb for her. "Thank you so much for being here. I'm sorry about Jordan."

"It's fine." I shrugged.

"No, it's not," she said, getting into the cab, "but he does it anyway. See you tonight."

Which meant, as I stood in Eileen's office, that I had six and a half hours to do some research before I saw Olivia again. And to reassure my editor that I was still in control of my senses and my story. My first line of defense was proving I could meet a deadline and presenting her with my screening letter:

Dear Molly,

Is control really an illusion? Or is it something that only women respect, so whenever men sense it forming, they're compelled to destroy it? Every time I think I'm gaining momentum in my life, a man steps into my path and I have to brake and swerve. Am I driving the wrong road, or should I just keep my foot on the gas?

Signed,
Balancing Act

Eileen looked up from the printed letter to squint at me suspiciously. "I like this." She was sitting behind her desk, her delicate feet balanced on the edge and encased in Bottega

Veneta boots with a lethal heel. I wanted to keep an eye on the heels in case I said anything to upset her and she came across the desk in some Emma Peel–ish effort to impale me.

Trying to keep my heart heel-less, I refrained from commenting on how surprised she sounded and just said, "Thanks very much." Leaning back as far as I could without taking an actual step, I prepared to bolt from her office. I could practically hear my life crashing down around me, like icicles popping off the rain gutters because the house has caught fire, but there was very little I could do about it until the Dragon Lady deigned to release me.

"I was expecting something more girly, about unrequited love and sleeping with people you shouldn't and that sort of thing," Eileen continued. "But this really applies on several levels, so it's an excellent litmus test for the next person to fill your heels."

I sighed. I couldn't help it. Experience is a fine teacher, and I'd worked for Eileen too long not to recognize a setup when I heard one. She was getting ready to hand me something—a diatribe, a reprimand, perhaps my head on a plate.

Sadly, not without cause. The moment Jordan announced to the paparazzi that he believed his father had been murdered, I prayed for some sort of miracle that would roll back the clocks and begin my day again. Perhaps my week.

In the time it had taken me to have breakfast with Olivia and Jordan, his comment about my "investigation" had taken on a life of its own. It was something akin to tossing a pebble in a still lake and watching the ripples spread to mind-boggling size. But in this case, Jordan had lofted a boulder into a shark-infested pool and not only churned up the water, but riled the inhabitants. Between the blogs and Web sites and "entertainment reporters" on a whole range of outlets, it was now being reported as acknowledged fact that Russell and

Micah had been killed by the same individual, and I was tracking down that individual. And I was now flooded with calls from a dozen fellow journalists and two former boyfriends who wanted to know what I knew.

So, Eileen was winding up for her swing at me, and I had no choice but to brace myself and take it. She smiled icily. "Assuming you're still pursuing the profile of Olivia Elliott."

"Absolutely."

"That was your original assignment, wasn't it? I could call and check with Henry to be sure. In case you've forgotten. Or gotten distracted. Or inventive." She put down the hard copy of the test question and stretched her hand out toward her phone.

"I'll call Henry and bring him up-to-date myself, but thanks for offering to help."

"I wasn't being helpful."

"I know, but I was being polite anyway."

Eileen pursed her fake smile into a pucker of distaste. "What on earth have you done, Molly Forrester?"

"I've allowed Jordan Crowley to exercise his First Amendment right to free speech. That's all. I don't believe I can be held responsible for his being a media whore."

Eileen pulled back into her chair. She's hard to surprise, and here I'd done it twice in one morning. Maybe it wasn't such a disastrous day after all. "What are you saying?"

"I don't believe him," I said. "I don't think the same person killed Russell Elliott and Micah Crowley."

"But you do believe they were both murdered?" she asked, her voice inching up into the coppery register of irritation.

"I'm keeping an open mind. Isn't that a journalist's goal?"

"A journalist's goal is to do the story that's been assigned." She tossed the letter on her desk and let her indignation inflate enough to lift her out of her chair. "You must think you have a tremendous amount of luck to press it this hard." She grasped her hips with her spidery hands, but she would have been happier if those hands had been around my throat. "If you tick off Henry, I won't be able to defend you."

"Only because you don't want to."

"Go away very, very quickly," she commanded.

"But the letter works for you?" I asked as I backpedaled out of the room.

"Better than you do!" she spat with satisfaction.

It would buy me a long stretch of peace and quiet to let her have the last word, so I closed the door and bit my lip to keep from responding. It wasn't until I turned around that I realized Skyler was watching me with a big smile. "Did she like the letter?" she asked brightly.

"Does she like anything?"

"It's all relative."

"Distantly related."

"Can you give us any hints about the test question, what you'll be looking for in the answers, what you think are the most important qualities in an advice columnist?" Carlos, one of the editorial assistants, had suddenly appeared at Skyler's desk with PDA in hand, ready to take notes. Behind him, four other assistants were working their way forward with varying degrees of casualness, eager to catch any inside information I was willing to share.

Nice perspective check. A job I was so anxious to be done with, to get past, was something they were all more than ready to fight for. Wanting to move up was admirable, and I needed to make sure I didn't taint their goal with my own agenda. "Answer from the heart," I said. "From what you believe to be true. It's what will make your voice stand out and let people know you really care."

There was a brief pause as they soaked in the insight and

before Skyler started to laugh. I tried to take some comfort in the fact that no one joined her, most of them watching me nervously for a reaction. "Okay, Skyler, share the joke," I said, trying not to sound like a kindergarten teacher.

"Sincerity's not going to get anyone anywhere at this magazine," she said, still amused. "We preach crafting a facade."

"Life is about your choice of facades," countered Irina, a gaunt, intense young woman who always dressed as though it were snowing outside.

Dorrie elbowed Carlos aside to stand right in front of Skyler. "That's terrible," she exclaimed breathlessly. "Just because you sit at that desk, you think you're better than the rest of us, and you're not."

"Did I even mention you?" Skyler asked.

"Stop it," I said, as uncomfortable with the sniping as with asserting my dubious authority to end it.

"The way Molly's been doing the column is perfect. That tone and quality should be maintained," Carlos offered.

"Suck up on your own time, there's work to do," Skyler said dismissively, sounding more ready to take over Eileen's job than mine. Shooing them away from her desk, she turned her back to them and made a great show of getting to work.

They drifted away obediently, though both Carlos and Dorrie looked back over their shoulders upon realizing that I hadn't moved. Instead, I leaned over Skyler's desk and, resisting the impulse to pinch her perfectly upturned nose, said, "You can get over yourself anytime now."

Skyler blinked slowly. "I'm entitled to my opinion."

"And your colleagues are entitled to their dignity."

"Which is why you treat Eileen so well?"

I straightened up, debating whether to confide in her or try to get her fired. While I admired her assertiveness, it was also irritating in this context—namely, that she had a point.

"You're pretty fast with the judgments for somebody who just got here."

"I learn quickly."

"Then learn the right things. And log a little time before you start dispensing attitude."

She sensed a boundary and pulled back, giving a little snap of the head that was half nod, half hair flip. "Thanks for the advice."

"On the other hand, given your gift for cutting through to the heart of the matter, I look forward to your submission."

She looked at me suspiciously, and I knew she was trying to figure out whether she'd damaged her chances. I actually hadn't decided yet. Both of us would have to ponder that while I gave Cassady a quick call, then went to visit the very first rock star I ever met.

Once upon a time, Risa van Doren was the music editor and I was a lifestyle reporter at a teen magazine called *Fresh*. We were roughly the same age, but while I was newly out of college, Risa had just retired from her first career, drumming for a punk girl band called Estrogen. The band had formed in Risa's backyard in San Diego when the members were freshmen in high school. Novelty launched them, talent sustained them. But when the lead singer drove her brand-new Porsche over a cliff and into the Pacific Ocean at the ripe old age of twenty-one, Risa hung up her drumsticks and headed east. "I've decided to fade away rather than burn out," she told me when we first met, though it was hard to imagine Risa fading at all. What she'd done was reinvent herself with admirable efficiency and success. We'd kept in touch after we moved on from the magazine, so I'd given her a call that morning, requesting to meet her and ask a couple of research questions.

It was easy to pick her out at the bar at Boqueria, a noisy but delightful tapas bar in the Flatiron District. She still sported a spiky platinum haircut ten years later, but she claimed it was because she'd bleached her hair so many times that it was damaged at a cellular level and wouldn't grow any other way. Her style of dress had swung from Courtney Love to Annie Lennox now that she was head of A&R for The Vault, an indie label with a small but successful following.

"You look fabulous," I said, sliding onto the stool next to her after we'd hugged.

"Once you're a public person, you learn to be prepared at all times for your picture to be taken. You'll see," she said with a delighted crinkle of her nose.

"The most amazing part of this whole experience is discovering how many of my friends read the tabloids," I said, and sighed.

She shook her head. "Randy Dunn e-mailed me the link to Gawker this morning." Randy was a former associate of ours from *Fresh,* and I sighed again, trying to imagine the snide and snarky messages jostling for space in my e-mail inbox. Risa laughed and patted my knee. "Not to worry, you looked great. And those two boys—what a delicious rock and hard place to be stuck between. Though I hear Adam's a little crazy, so be careful."

"Adam's crazy?"

"This is off the record, right?" I nodded, and she continued, her tone frank and nonjudgmental. "A music journalist I know met him at a concert last year, started dating him, but it got really ugly very quickly. She said he was a little too into the anguished artist thing, mood swings, that whole deal. Not that the girl couldn't use a solid regimen of Zoloft herself, but it definitely got weird." Her eyes narrowed as she smiled. "Was that your research question—which one to date?"

"No, no."

"Don't dismiss the idea so quickly," she said.

"Seriously, I have a hypothetical question that's inspired by meeting them, that's all," I said, feeling my way into the topic gently.

"Okay. Ask away."

"What do you suppose the market is for previously unreleased recordings by someone like Micah Crowley?"

Risa took a deep breath and let it out very slowly. "Don't screw with me."

"What?"

She gripped my hand a little tighter than was comfortable. "Have you heard them?"

"Heard what?" I tap-danced. "I'm just looking for some context—"

"Bullshit. Have you heard the Hotel Tapes?"

One thing I learned from Kyle early on is that most people get themselves into trouble because they answer more than what the question asks. Risa was asking me a simple question, and I didn't need to complicate things or implicate myself by getting into how much I knew about the tapes and when I was hoping to hear them. I just needed to say, "No," and leave it at that, tough as that was for me.

Her grip on my hand eased slightly while she searched my face for some telltale sign of dishonesty. Remarkably, she didn't seem to find one and decided to answer my question. "If the Hotel Tapes are in decent condition, and if they were engineered and packaged properly, we're talking millions of units. Tens of millions of dollars."

Tens of millions of dollars that might wind up in brand-new hands now that Russell Elliott was dead. I nodded to acknowledge the size of what she was saying but still hoping not to tip her off. Olivia and the boys had the right to make the information public when they were ready, but I needed a context in which to understand the value of the tapes. In dollars and in human life. If anything material could ever be worth a human life. But I'd been around enough murders to know that people all too often decide that's the case.

"Let's trade hypotheticals," Risa continued, an unfamiliar gleam in her eye. "The Vault is a small label, but we're all about the artist. Or his family. And if we were entrusted with something like those tapes, we would produce them with the utmost care and respect for the artist, his family, and his legacy." She flashed a twisted smile. "And pay through the nose for the right to do so."

I'd never seen Risa in sales mode, but it was effective. Except that her hand trembled as it lay over mine. She hadn't heard the tapes, wasn't even sure I'd heard them, couldn't even be sure they existed, but her desire for them was palpable. Could someone's desire for them have been so keen that murdering Russell Elliott was a viable step in the plan to get them? Who could have been in the apartment that night long enough to kill Russell, but not long enough to get the tapes? It had to be someone in the inner circle, or selling the tapes would be impossible. Was the intention to get the tapes that night or to put them in play as part of his estate? Were they specifically mentioned in Russell's will? Olivia had them now, but that didn't mean she had any right to keep them. Perhaps the killer was hanging back, waiting for the estate to be administered. But who was it?

To buy myself time to answer that question, I had to make sure Risa didn't get swept up in dreams of major acquisitions. "I honestly don't know anything about the tapes, but if the subject comes up while I'm working the story, I'll keep you informed."

"Do you know how much money Courtney Love made last year, just for selling part of the publishing rights to Kurt's songs? Twenty-five million dollars. I'm not saying Claire

Crowley could get all that for the tapes, but it's a valid point of reference," Risa said, squeezing my hand again.

"You think Claire has the tapes? If they exist?"

Risa snatched back her hand and mockingly bit at the back of her fist. "Stop teasing me. Who has them?"

"I don't know, since—"

She nodded, finishing my sentence for me in exasperation. "Since you don't know that they exist." She shook her head. "People were never sure the Holy Grail existed, either, but they did pretty extraordinary things to try and find it."

She was agreeing it would be motive enough for murder for some. I didn't dare ask any more questions for fear of betraying how much I already knew, so I smiled broadly and asked, "So how is Randy Dunn these days?"

Risa laughed. "Almost as sly as you are." She threw up her hands in surrender. "Okay, moving on. You heard about the office uprising at *Kewl,* didn't you?"

We had a terrific lunch, stealing from each other's plates and dishing back and forth about mutual friends and enemies, while the various people who might feel entitled to the tapes danced into a lineup in the back of my mind. I went back to the office full of gossip and olives, but no closer to a theory.

By four o'clock, Cassady was calling with the results of a question I had asked her: A few discreet lawyer-to-lawyer calls had determined that Russell's estate hadn't been administered yet. "So, whoever killed Russell still has to deal with the fact that the tapes might wind up with someone other than Olivia," I said after thanking her profusely.

"Are you listening to yourself?" she asked tartly.

"Do I sound like I'm coming down with something?" I asked, sniffing reflexively.

"Yeah, a bad case of the 'so it was murder' flu."

She was right. I couldn't pinpoint the moment, but I'd moved from debating whether Russell had been killed to who might have done the killing. "My instincts are telling me . . . ," I attempted.

"Those are the same instincts that told you you'd look good with your hair dyed purple," she countered. "Honey, I'm not trying to slow you down, I'm just trying to keep you honest. I'll leave it to Tricia to try and slow you down. Although I could recommend an excellent flu remedy."

"I can barely bring myself to ask."

"Take one hunky detective and don't call anyone until morning."

"I'm seeing him for dinner."

"Good, then you're not as far gone as I thought you might be. Don't eat too fast."

So as I sank into the leather couch in the Elliott apartment that evening, I was still trying to figure out whether the killer knew who would take possession of the tapes after the reading of the will. Was the killer counting on them going to Olivia and being able to talk her into parting with them or at least releasing them? Or would the will put them in other hands? Or was the killer going to have to take matters into her or his own hands again?

They were thorny enough questions, but compounding their difficulty was Jordan's presence next to me. The give of the couch made me feel as if I were tilting toward him whether I wanted to or not. Fixing me with a penetrating gaze, he smiled slowly. "Feel history approaching?"

I nodded. "It is momentous."

"Damn straight." He stood up as Olivia walked into the room with an ornate wooden box, very medieval looking with brass fittings and detailed carvings on the sides. He seemed to be standing out of respect for what was in the box more than out of respect for Olivia. I started to get up, but the depths to which the sofa had settled made it awkward, and I decided to just stay put for a little longer.

Jordan reached for the box, but Olivia pulled it back, more as a reflex than a statement. "Give me a second," she protested, placing the box on the brass end table and trying to ignore Jordan hovering over her as though he could barely contain himself.

Which he couldn't. The moment she put down the box, he was struggling with the latch to open it. And her whimper of frustration was barely voiced before he exhaled in a loud bark of anger. "What the hell, Ollie?"

And I knew from the look on their faces that the box was empty.

7

In a science class somewhere along the line, I learned that music is stored in a specific, more easily accessed part of the brain than other information (such as which science class I learned it in), which is why they teach children the alphabet and state capitals by putting them in a song. It's probably also the reason a song gets stuck in your head and won't go away for hours at a time. Or that four bars of a song heard in a commercial as you flip past a radio station or as you walk by someone humming can transport you back to a specific moment in time with heart-stopping speed and accuracy. The Pretenders, "2,000 Miles": kissing Mike Tomlinson on his grandmother's front porch on New Year's Eve as it started to snow. Ella Fitzgerald, "Just One of Those Things": learning to fox-trot by standing on my dad's feet as he did the steps. Talking Heads, "Life During Wartime": driving to Cape Cod with Tricia and Cassady on a perfect summer evening, with the top down.

As we stood staring at the empty box, all I could hear was Pink Floyd's "Money," the rhythm of the guitar and bass lines mixing with the clanging cash register and the cascading coins. And the cascading coins were pouring through Olivia's and Jordan's hands then disappearing into thin air.

"You should call the police," I said quietly, feeling a little uncomfortable about being pragmatic at a moment when Olivia looked as if she were about to faint and Jordan as though he were going to throw up.

"We can't," Olivia said with a long exhale.

"Why not?"

"Because then people would know about the tapes."

"People already know. They've been asking me about them, for crying out loud." I pointed to the box. "Besides, you have to know about something to take it."

Olivia shook her head forcefully. "No. Most people hope they exist, but don't know. We need to keep this quiet, or people will be tearing up the city looking for them, it'll be insane."

I looked to Jordan to see if he was going to back me up or at least grab Olivia and shake her, but he was still staring at the empty box with a stunned expression. "But you want people looking for them, don't you?" I pressed. "If these tapes are everything everyone believes them to be, they could be the reason your father's dead, Olivia."

She turned to me as sharply as if I had grabbed her. " 'Everyone?' This is family business."

"A friend of mine said the tapes could be worth seven figures. People have killed for a lot less."

Jordan's head snapped up. "Who've you been talking to about the tapes?"

"No one," I evaded. "People bring them up on their own."

"Who've you been talking to, Ollie?" Jordan pursued.

"You know better than that." Olivia was fighting tears, but she managed to hold his gaze and convince him—us—of her sincerity.

"Olivia, have you seen the tapes since your father died?" I asked, trying to sound helpful and not investigative.

"Yes. I listened to them after his funeral, and then I locked them back up, and . . ." Olivia slammed the lid on the box as though it would contain her emotions, but tears still leaked from the corners of her eyes.

Jordan drummed his fingers on the table in a furious tattoo, then spun and headed out of the room. Olivia didn't move, but I hurried after him. "What are you going to do?"

"I can count on one hand," he said, holding up his hand to illustrate, "the number of people who knew those tapes were real. Which makes it pretty damn clear who took them." He curled his hand into a fist and strode to the front door.

Olivia called his name in anguish and raced past me. As she and I rushed into the hallway behind Jordan, I realized he was shooting straight past the elevator. To Claire's door.

It all raced through my mind in a whirling three seconds. Micah leaves the tapes to Russell and not to Claire; Claire wants them, but Russell says no; they fight, Claire's pushed to the brink, and she kills Russell to have the tapes. It would make sense. Perfect sense. If it had happened six or seven years ago, as the dust from Micah's death settled. But why now?

Jordan didn't share my hesitation, pounding on the door with his fist and hollering for Claire as Olivia ran up to him, yelling his name. Good thing they were the only two families on the floor or someone would be calling the police in another bellow or two.

"Jordan, wait. Think this through," I urged as I caught up with them.

But I didn't get to say anything else, because the front door swung open and Claire stepped out. Jordan opened his mouth to say something angry and ugly, I could tell by the torque of his lips, but before he could even get out the first sound, Claire cracked him across the face with startling force.

It was so sudden and so loud that Olivia and I flinched; Claire got three for the price of one.

Jordan's shoulder lifted a few centimeters, and I started to lunge forward to keep him from hitting her back, but his shoulder rolled back down and he rocked back on his heels, looking at her more in disbelief than in pain.

"You pathetic infant," she spat. "How dare you stomp over the graves of the men who raised you just to get your self-centered face into the news?"

I put my hand on Jordan's back in a gesture meant to placate them both. "I don't think this is a conversation either one of you should have right now," I said, trying to catch Olivia's eye and draw her into my diplomatic effort.

"And who the hell do you think you are?" was Claire's appreciative reply.

"Mrs. Crowley," I attempted, "I'm only trying to help."

"Your career?"

"Mother, stop." Adam walked up behind Claire, a wineglass in his hand. He was the only one in the group who didn't look ready to strangle someone, and I was including myself in that number.

"Adam, stay out of this," she warned.

"Like that's ever been an option in this family." He acknowledged my outsider status with a quick flash of an apologetic smile.

"Somebody nailed your feet to the floor, bro?" Jordan asked. "Last I heard, you were free to go."

"And miss all this fun?" Adam shrugged grandly, but frost was creeping into his voice.

"I'm trying to understand this, Jordan," Claire continued. "Did God pack you so full of talent that there was no room left for manners and good sense? Or have you just chosen to live without them?"

"This isn't about me," Jordan said.

"Wow. Note the date and time." Adam looked at his watch in mock surprise. "This won't happen again soon."

"I happen to believe what I told the 'razzi rats this morning, but right now, you need to listen to Olivia," Jordan insisted.

Claire took a deep breath, steeling herself, and turned to Olivia with the practiced smile of a teacher who isn't going to answer the question because she knows it's going to be ridiculous. "What is it, Olivia?"

"I want back everything you've taken from me," Olivia said quietly but steadily.

Claire seemed surprised. "But everything you have is because of me."

Adam took his mother's arm. "If you're going to flay each other, at least don't do it in the hallway." He eased her out of the doorway and gestured for the three of us to follow them into the apartment.

The Elliott apartment was a cool, muted space, heavy on the earth tones and leather upholstery. In contrast, the Crowley apartment was shockingly bright and airy, with more archways than doorways and bright, vibrant art pulsating on the walls. Adam led our ragtag procession through the tiled entryway, which seemed one central fountain away from a Roman piazza, and into a living room designed to make you gasp at the view of the river. The sofas were tweedy, long and low, emphasizing the spaciousness of the room and facing you toward the windows.

Adam gestured for people to take seats. Olivia obediently slid onto a couch, but Jordan marched to the window, and I stood uneasily as close to the archway as I could. Whatever was about to happen, I wanted to be there to take the whole thing in, but the sense that I was intruding on family business made me restless.

Claire sat in one of the few chairs in the room, an armchair that faced the room, back to the view. Maybe the room wasn't arranged to honor the river as much as the person who sat in that chair. She crossed her legs, folded her hands over her knee, and sat with her back so straight that it made mine hurt. She was poised for action of some kind, but whether it was to be able to slap Jordan again or bolt from the room, I couldn't be sure.

"So . . . ," Adam began, sliding onto the sofa near where I stood, his demeanor as relaxed as his mother's was stiff. "Who wants to dive in and try to explain just what the hell is going on?"

"Your mother robbed me," Olivia said in the same steady voice, but her eyes were on Adam now, not Claire.

Claire continued to look at Olivia steadily, her bottom lip scooping out in an exaggerated expression of sorrow. Her hands parted briefly as she recrossed her legs, then cinched up again around her left knee. "Are you on something?"

Jordan snorted. "Why is that always your question?"

"Because it's usually the answer," Claire said with a crisp sneer. "I've never understood why children who've had their lives handed to them on a silver platter have such a difficult time facing a rather lovely reality."

"I thought maybe you were on something and wanted us to join the party," Jordan said. He stayed at the window with his back to all of us, and I watched with fascination as he and Claire refused to turn to face each other.

"Watch it, Jordan," Adam said, his body still relaxed but his voice sharper.

"C'mon, Adam. I know you'll eat worms if your mother tells you to, but are you really going along with this 'lovely reality' crap?"

Claire softened her pose enough to look at him over her shoulder. "If you hate your life, Jordan, I'm very sorry. But the rest of us don't need to listen to it."

Adam smiled, which should have been a warning. "Unless it's on that new CD that was supposed to drop . . . when?"

Jordan came at him so quickly that I didn't even think about what I was doing, I just stepped in between them as Adam rose from the couch, one hand out in front of me to stop Jordan and the other in back of me to contain Adam. Neither Olivia nor Claire moved, either caught more by surprise than I was, which seemed doubtful, or content to let me become the DMZ, which was more likely.

The brothers pulled themselves up enough that they weren't grappling with each other around me this time, but they were only a heavy breath away from it. I dropped my hands. "I'd really like to join you all for Thanksgiving dinner. It must be magnificent."

"Ms. Forrester, you don't need to be here," Claire said, deigning at this point to rise from her throne.

"Actually, I do," I said. "Not just because I'm the only one who seems interested in preventing a brawl, but because I'm writing a story about Olivia and I'd like to hear your response to her statement."

"All the more reason for you to leave," Claire said, gliding past us back toward the front door. "I'm not going to enable this ridiculous behavior on any level."

"Give me back my tapes and I'll leave you alone," Olivia offered.

"What tapes?" Adam asked.

"The Hotel Tapes."

Adam's breath came out in an explosive grunt, as though Olivia had kicked him in the stomach or even lower. Before he could say anything, Claire turned around and fixed him with a glare so cold that I shivered, standing next to him. And with good cause, because the glare moved to me next. "Did you put her up to this?"

"Me? Up to . . . ?" I wasn't sure what I was being accused of, and I wasn't about to admit to anything that was going to stoke her wrath.

"She's not an interesting enough story by herself, so now you're going to manufacture one for her?"

"First of all," I said as evenly as possible, "Olivia's a great story on her own. But if I wanted to create a story, I'd be putting cocktails and small firearms on the table and setting up a videocamera in the corner. Fortunately, I'm interested in minimizing damage, not documenting it."

"My mother's never had a good relationship with the press," Adam offered.

"As opposed to all the other sterling relationships in her life?" I asked.

Surprisingly, Adam looked pleased, and Claire just seethed. "The Hotel Tapes do not exist," she said slowly, as though this were too difficult a concept for me to easily comprehend. "I burned them when Micah died."

"Liar!" Olivia exclaimed. "I've heard them!"

Claire's eyes didn't move from my face. "The fact that some of the tapes might have survived is a fantasy Russell embraced for years and, apparently, passed down to Olivia. Despite the fact that, if they existed, they would belong to me."

"Double liar! Micah gave them to my father, and my father willed them to me!"

I thought about shifting over to stand between the two women in the room for a while, but I was too stunned by Claire's claim to move. "Why would you burn them? They were priceless."

Disgust swam across Claire's face. "So was everything I lost because he couldn't stay clean or focused . . ." She shifted her glare to Jordan.

"Or faithful?" He said it with the lilt of an old joke, but it was a dagger between the ribs, and Claire struggled not to wince as it hit home. So much of her golden reputation was based on the perception that she had graciously opened her home and her family to Bonnie and Jordan, it was a revelation that Micah's affair continued to pain her all these years later. Sort of like discovering that Mrs. Claus hates the elves.

Claire looked at him for a long moment, working her lips between her teeth, and Jordan waited with a satisfied look for her to say something. Adam stepped around me, and I grabbed at his sleeve, but he patted my hand reassuringly and I let go. Rather than going after Jordan, he touched his mother lightly on the arm, and she shook herself, turning to Olivia. Or, more precisely, on Olivia. "I'm very concerned about you, Olivia."

"Excuse me?" Olivia said, faltering at the sudden shift in focus.

Claire took Olivia's hands in hers in a gesture somewhere between maternal and papal. "I know how devastating it is to lose someone who's been the center of your universe. We've been doing our best to support you, sweetheart, but it's becoming abundantly clear that we aren't able to give you everything you need. You must have a colleague you can sit down with, someone you trust?"

It took a moment for the full hurtfulness of Claire's statement to register with Olivia, who then slid her hands free of Claire's pressing palms. "I am not unbalanced," she said measuredly.

"Of course you're not," Claire said in a patronizing tone designed especially for use on unbalanced people. "It's the stress of the loss. But the sooner you get someone to help you through it, the better off we'll all be."

"All?" I couldn't help but ask.

"Her delusions are going to waste your time and make the rest of us look like fools," Claire said, her tone only a shade less patronizing with me.

"The Hotel Tapes are real," Olivia said, her voice thick with tears.

"No, sweetheart, they're not," Claire replied.

"The tapes are real, and I want them back." Olivia's voice got higher but no stronger as she cast a wild look in my direction for help, but I honestly didn't know what to say. Could this really be a figment of Olivia's imagination? Or did Claire know exactly where the tapes were and was casting doubt on Olivia to throw us all off the scent? And if Claire was in possession of the tapes, had she killed Russell to get them?

Jordan shook his head. "This reeks."

Claire flicked a brittle smile in his direction. "I'm glad you see that, Jordan."

"You're never glad about anything, Claire, which right now seems pretty damn just."

Her mouth twisted, and I swore I could smell gunpowder in the air. Before any sparks could fly and ignite it, I took Jordan's arm, which was inappropriate yet still seemed like the right thing to do. "Time to go." I needed to regroup, and they needed to stop pushing Claire, because it was only going to make her hunker down further. If she did indeed have the tapes. If the tapes existed.

Jordan actually nodded in agreement. "C'mon, Ollie," he said, keeping his arm through mine and heading for the front door.

"I'm not finished," Claire protested, following our unhappy little parade out into the foyer.

"Yes, you are," I said politely. "Olivia's looking for something you said doesn't exist. What more is there to talk about? Other than the fact that you think she needs help. Which I actually think is an excellent idea."

Olivia and Jordan stopped, not liking the sound of that, but I was more caught by Adam's expression. For some reason, he was grinning as he stood behind his mother. I tried to keep my eyes on Claire's face, but it was hard, especially once Adam realized he was distracting me and booted up the wattage on his smile.

Claire immediately dialed back, ready to work me as an ally. "I'm so glad we agree. Do you know someone?"

"Yes, I do. One of the best lawyers in town."

"Lawyer?" Claire exclaimed.

"Thank you very much for seeing us, Mrs. Crowley," I said as Jordan opened the door and hurried Olivia through it. Claire started to sputter, but Adam whispered something to her and she stalked back to the living room.

He dropped a half-bow and made a mocking sweep of his arm as I walked past him. As he started to close the door behind us, it hit me: Adam was the only one in this whole group who wasn't upset. Even his momentary reflexive anger with Jordan had passed. Either he cared less than everyone else—or he knew far more. Spinning around, I caught the door. "It's time for a drink. Would you like to join us?"

He smiled slowly. "Us or you?"

"Us."

"Too bad. So . . . no, thank you. But the other, another time." He jiggled the door gently, and I withdrew my hand, allowing him to close the door. Still smiling.

I continued to mull over exactly what was behind that smile as Olivia, Jordan, and I entered Wild Salmon. Committed as I was to the task at hand, I was mindful of the time and trying to be efficient in my travels. If all went well, I could wrap up my business with Olivia and Jordan and let them go on their way before Kyle arrived. So far, fate was being kind: Cassady was at the bar, waiting for us.

I'd called her from the cab, given her a quick summary of events, and asked her if there was any way she could offer Olivia some advice about the legal ownership of the tapes and how she could protect herself—and get the tapes back—when they popped up on the market. They had to pop up eventually, didn't they? As a family jewel unearthed or a found treasure with a flimsy backstory or even just mysterious bootlegs on the black market? Why else would someone have taken them except to sell them to the millions of fans who still hungered for Micah's work?

Once I'd explained the situation, Cassady was happy to oblige, since the restaurant wasn't far from her last meeting of the day and since I mentioned Jordan was coming along. Which was undoubtedly the reason Tricia was there beside her.

Fortunately, no one had tipped the paparazzi, so we were able to make a reasonably discreet entrance. As we crossed to the bar, I watched people glance up. They'd recognize Jordan, then either pretend not to care and let their eyes continue casually upward to the golden fish dangling from the ceiling or gaze at him raptly for a few moments. How hard was it to be onstage every moment you were in public? What did that do to your perception of where you fit into the scheme of things? And how did it impact people like Olivia and Claire, who lived in that space where the spotlight spilled over? Did it make you long for the dark—or for center stage?

I tried to push away the questions as I spotted Cassady and

Tricia at the bar. Even though both were in business clothes, they looked pretty stellar sitting there, and Jordan hummed appreciatively as we walked up to them. "You have much better taste in lawyers than I do."

"I make a point of surrounding myself with lovely people," I replied.

"And we all enjoy the assignment very much, don't we?" Cassady said, extending her hand to Olivia first and then to Jordan as I made introductions.

"You don't mind, do you, Molly? We're having dinner after this, so I thought I'd tag along," Tricia asked, pretending to talk to me while absorbed in Jordan's shaking her hand.

Jordan answered before I could. "I'm very glad that you did."

"Don't take him too seriously," Olivia warned. "Or he'll shred your heart to ribbons—"

"And you'll weep, but you'll never sleep again," Tricia finished.

"Wow, great lyrics. Who wrote those? Oh, right. I did," Jordan said with a self-deprecating roll of the eyes.

"I loved your album," Tricia pressed on.

"Now, that's something I never get tired of hearing. If you'd like to go into details, I'm all ears."

"Should we start with the first track or my favorite?"

I knew exactly how Tricia felt. The chance to blatantly adore a rock star wasn't a normal part of our daily fare, even though Tricia had plenty of luminaries on her client list. I wanted to squeal with her in delight, but business came first. Luckily, Jordan hadn't impressed Cassady nearly as much, and she was staying focused.

"This flirting is going to be a terrible distraction," she said, "so why don't Olivia and I take a table while you three pose seductively here at the bar?"

She swept Olivia away before I could reply, sarcastically or otherwise. Pleased, Tricia slid back onto her stool and focused again on Jordan. "Your CD is exquisite."

"Thank you. What was your favorite song?"

"'Strip Me Bare,'" she replied without hesitation. "I have it on my iPod."

"Downloaded legally and everything. She's a good girl," I added, more in reaction to Jordan's wolfish grin than to the manic gleam in Tricia's eye. Jordan struck me as the kind who would happily love 'em and leave 'em, and I wasn't going to let him do that to my friend. So I changed the subject to, happily, one that I needed to pursue. "So you'd never heard the tapes, Jordan?"

Tricia tossed me a dirty look, not realizing how noble and protective I was being. "Sorry, are you still working?"

"I'm with you, Tricia," Jordan said with a showy look at his watch. "Do I at least get to order a drink before we go back to the serious stuff?"

"Sorry," I answered, "but I think this thing with the tapes is huge. Assuming they actually exist."

"Claire didn't burn them, if that's what you mean," Jordan said, trying to catch the bartender's eye. "I remember my mom asking her about them after my dad died, and Claire told her she had no claim to them, the usual kind of bullshit between the two of them."

"But if Claire had them then, how did Russell get them, and why is she claiming she burned them?"

The question hung in the air while Jordan ordered a Grey Goose rocks for himself and a Rob Roy for me. "Because if she says she burned them, she doesn't have to admit that she couldn't sweet-talk Russell into giving them to her while they were a couple."

Tricia gasped. "Claire Crowley and Russell Elliott?"

Jordan nodded wearily. "And I gotta tell you, I wouldn't want to be Gray Benedek right now."

I didn't follow. "What? Why Gray Benedek?"

"Because the men Claire Crowley sleeps with die young."

8

Time and I don't have a great relationship. I hate being late, but I usually am. Tasks take me longer than I think they should. I lose track of how long it's been since I've talked to people or written them or checked books out of the library. And let's not even get into the whole aging portion of the discussion (shouldn't there be a period somewhere between Clearasil and Oil of Olay when you and your complexion actually get along?).

But then, every once in a while, Time decides to give me a break and we work together, the pieces of my scattered, overscheduled life fitting together smoothly—for a moment, anyway—and I find myself right where I'm supposed to be, with a moment to take a deep breath and appreciate it. Or at least a moment to take a deep breath and scribble down all the notes I've come up with in the last few hours so that when a very handsome homicide detective walks up to me at a bar, I can give him my undivided attention without worrying that I'm going to forget anything crucial.

"Hey," Kyle said, running his hand along my arm with a comfortable familiarity that thrilled me. "You're early."

"Thank you for not seeming shocked," I said, smiling. I wanted to kiss him, but I had yet to figure out exactly where we were on the "getting back together" spectrum; since I rarely got a second swing at a relationship, I wasn't sure what etiquette dictated in cases such as this.

He didn't lean in to kiss me, either, and I took a moment to wonder if he was wrestling with the same question or if he just didn't want to kiss me. Before I could worry about that too much, he glanced at my glass. "Been here long?"

Half the letters I've answered for the magazine contain the advice "Honesty is crucial in any relationship." But it's paramount when you're dating a detective. All those forensic instincts are on duty even when he's not, and he's apt to pick up on things that mere mortals would miss completely. I followed his glance to my glass; it was half-empty, and the condensation had run down the glass enough to pool around the base, despite the coaster.

I wanted to be truthful, but I was also determined to be as off-duty as he was and not to let work intrude, so I waltzed around the question as best I could. "Tricia and Cassady and some other people I know were here, so I came by to see them first." I wasn't even going to try to explain how I had also rushed them out to go have dinner somewhere else, suggesting that they would be more comfortable in a more out-of-the-way restaurant, mere moments before he arrived. "Would you like a drink?"

He ordered a Manhattan straight up and leaned against the bar next to me. "You look nice."

"Thanks. You too."

"I'm glad we're doing this."

"Complimenting each other?" I teased.

"Talking to each other," he said with such gravity that my chest tightened. My mind went blank as he took my hand, holding it tightly and studying it as though he were looking for trace evidence.

I nodded. "I'm going to do everything I can to make sure we keep talking, that things don't go unsaid. I think if we're willing to work at it, we can be perfectly comfortable being completely open with each other all the time, about everything."

"Whoa," he said softly.

I slammed on the brakes. "Okay, now I'm talking too much."

"No, it's fine. It's just, you're suddenly talking like we're back together."

I felt as though I might slide off my bar stool in an untidy, humiliated heap. The tightness became a lead weight, and I didn't trust myself to pick up my glass because I wasn't sure how much my hand was shaking. "We're not?" I finally croaked out.

Kyle fixed me with his amazing blue eyes and a look that I'm sure has gotten much harder hearts to confess to all manner of crimes. "I was planning on it, but you were the one drawing lines this morning, so I figured you were going to stay elusive for at least another dinner or two." He smiled slyly, and I could feel the color rising in my cheeks as my heart started to pump again.

"Maybe I decided we've already wasted too much time," I said genuinely.

Just as he leaned in to kiss me, the hostess appeared to show us to our table. He kissed me anyway, a light but promising kiss that made it difficult for me to rise from the bar stool without wobbling. As we walked to the table, I was grateful for his hand at the small of my back.

We joked back and forth while we studied the menu, but once the waiter had taken our orders, the jokes faded away. Time for a real conversation. "How've you been?" I asked, half hoping for a detailed description of the misery and longing that had pervaded the days we were apart.

He shrugged. "Working too much. Trying to stay busy so I didn't think about you all the time. You're not easy to be with, but you're hell to be away from."

I felt dizzy again. "Do I say 'thank you'?"

"No, you say you missed me, too."

"I thought I'd already mentioned that."

"It's worth mentioning again."

"I missed you."

"Glad to hear it." He straightened his silverware for the fifth time. "So how's your story going?"

I hadn't expected him to voluntarily turn the conversation back to work, so I hadn't thought out how much detail to offer. How long was it going to take before I could answer a question without weighing all the political ramifications first? "It's gotten pretty twisted," I admitted. "It'll be interesting to see how it all plays out."

"And why do I get the feeling you've already decided how it's going to play out?" Adam Crowley asked pleasantly. I'd been so intent on trying to read Kyle's expression that I hadn't even noticed Adam walk up to the table. Kyle was on his feet before I could say anything, more out of defensive strategy than proper manners.

"You're interrupting our dinner," Kyle said.

"She's interrupting my life, so I think you're still on the upside of this deal," Adam responded.

Kyle's hand went to his hip, and for an absurd moment, I thought he was going to draw his gun, but he stuck his hand in his pocket—probably so I couldn't see his clenched fist—and looked at Adam. "Is this one of the jerks from last night?" Kyle asked me after a long beat.

"Kyle, this is Adam Crowley," I said, not wanting to get into whether or not he was a jerk because I was still undecided on the topic. While his crashing my dinner date didn't exactly enhance his current standing, I also found myself remembering the warmth of his mouth against my ear, which was highly embarrassing with Kyle right there in front of me. The real frustration was, I wanted to talk to Adam. But not here, not now.

Adam stuck out his hand. "And you are . . . ?"

"Kyle Edwards," Kyle said, giving Adam's hand a perfunctory shake. "I'd invite you to join us, but I don't want you to."

Adam yanked over a free chair from the table next to us, startling those people as much as he startled us, and sat down. "This won't take long."

"You got that right," Kyle said, still standing.

I could see our waiter and the hostess hurrying over, looking worried. I shook my head to reassure them, and they stopped anxiously several tables away. "How did you find me?"

"I called my brother, and he couldn't wait to tell me what fun he was having with you and your friends."

Kyle's eyes moved over to me long enough for me to register his displeasure, then snapped back to Adam. "Let me call you in the morning, Adam," I suggested. "We can talk then."

"Why delay the fun?" Adam asked.

Kyle sat down, leaning forward with his elbows on his knees, in part to look casual and in part to keep his hands within grabbing distance of Adam. "One good album doesn't make you king, Crowley."

Adam leaned in to him in a parody of friendliness. "Guess I better make another one, then. But before I run out to the studio, I just have one question. And then she doesn't have to talk to me ever again. Unless she wants to."

Kyle sat back, pinching his bottom lip, and I knew he wasn't considering Adam's question, he was debating how hard to hit him. "Okay," I said with a touch of warning for them both.

"One." Adam looked at me with a smirk and Kyle gave me a disapproving frown. But he let go of his lip. I shifted back to Adam. "But if you get one, I get one."

"That seems reasonable."

"Better than you deserve," Kyle muttered, going back to straightening his silverware.

"So, Adam? Your question?" I said, trying to move things along before Kyle lost his patience.

"Is my brother paying you?"

My first instinct was to laugh, but I knew Adam wouldn't appreciate that at all, and I wouldn't get to ask my question. "Paying me for what?"

"For whipping up this ridiculous stuff about the tapes. And Russell's and Dad's deaths being linked. You're dragging up a bunch of ancient history insanity, and it's upsetting people I care about."

"All I'm doing is researching an article about Olivia. This 'stuff' about the tapes comes from her, and it's between her and your mother. And Jordan was the one who said the deaths were linked, not me."

"Yet none of this started until you showed up."

"She didn't show up until Russell Elliott died," Kyle said, eyes on the knife that he was standing up on the table.

"Are you some fellow conspiracy theorist?"

"I'm a homicide detective. NYPD," Kyle said, looking up from the knife in time to see Adam struggle to control his reaction.

Adam looked back at me, confused and irritated. "And now you brought the police into this?"

I was going to let him off the hook and explain the dinner was purely social, but Kyle answered more quickly. "You don't think we should be involved?"

Adam's brow furrowed, pulling his black eyebrows down into diagonal slashes. He looked so much like his father. "You're the ones who told us Russell's death was accidental."

Kyle nodded thoughtfully while I knit my fingers together in my lap to make myself sit still. What was Kyle doing? Playing with Adam? Teaching me a lesson? "You comfortable with that?" he asked Adam.

"Shouldn't I be?"

"Not everyone is."

"Yeah? Well, whoever isn't is messed up. Or looking for attention. Probably both."

The interesting thing was, Kyle was just telling him things he actually already knew, but with the weight of Kyle's badge behind them, Adam was taking them much more to heart. What fascinated me most was that Kyle had not said he was actually investigating Russell's death, but Adam had made that leap. Was it Kyle's air of authority? Or Adam's guilty conscience, reminding him there was something worth investigating? Adam leaned back toward Kyle. "Did Olivia ask you to reopen the case?"

"Who else would want us to take another look?" Kyle tossed back quickly.

Adam took a deep breath. "I think most of us would welcome it, if you think there's genuine reason to suspect something," he said firmly, if not confidently.

"Anyone who wouldn't?"

Adam paused long enough that it was evident someone specific came to mind but he didn't want to share. Was this the extra information that'd had him smiling back at the apartment? He wasn't smiling now. "Whoever did it, of course," he said after a beat. "Assuming someone did do something."

"Who might have liked to do something?"

Adam turned back to me again, the look on his face more

beseeching than angry now. "This is really out of line. I want it stopped."

"You've done a fine job of that on your own," I said, worried now that Kyle was going to push him too far and we'd be in a nice group shot in tomorrow's gossip columns.

"Fine job of what?"

"Stopping this. Our meal. Not exactly showing the instincts of a future club owner."

Kyle looked at me sharply as Adam answered, "What are you talking about?"

"Aren't you and Ray Hernandez developing a club?"

Adam shifted, surprisingly uncomfortable. "Who've you been talking to?" Before I could answer, he pushed on. "You can't believe most of what Olivia says."

There was a belief the brothers had in common. "Funny, you seem close."

"Deep down, she hates me. But she's had to pretend otherwise so long, she forgets." He tried to put a mocking tone on it, but there was genuine hurt in his voice.

"Why would she hate you?"

"She resents the time and energy her father put into my family instead of putting it into his own."

"Sounds like a legitimate gripe," Kyle offered.

Adam smiled with effort. "Maybe it's as simple as the fact that my family's more fun."

"At least, maybe your mother was more fun," I said.

Kyle's eyebrows arched, but Adam's face stiffened. "I'm not going to dignify that."

"So you're also not going to tell me how long your mother's been sleeping with Gray Benedek?"

I might as well have stabbed him with my fork. He sat stock still for a long time, then stood, easing his chair out from the table. I thought I'd misjudged the reaction I'd get until I saw how white his knuckles were where he gripped the top of the chair. "That's more than one question. Good night."

Adam walked briskly from the dining area, head down slightly to avoid eye contact with the patrons. I started to rise and follow him, but Kyle caught my hand and shook his head. I glanced around to note the number of diners who were looking in our direction, wondering if anything tip-worthy had happened, as Kyle urged, "Let him go. That's as much as you're going to get out of him tonight."

"Why?" I protested, but I sat back down.

"You crossed the line."

"With him? How?"

"A man never likes to think about, much less talk about, his mother having sex." Kyle squinted, as though he were banishing a relevant thought from his own head. "It's just wrong."

I smoothed the napkin back in my lap. "How about thinking about your mother committing murder?"

Kyle's squint intensified. "Not as common an issue. You believe his mother did it?"

"If the election for murderer were held today, I think she'd win. Do you think he did it?"

"Why would I have an opinion?"

"Because you were questioning him."

Kyle pulled one of those lopsided-smile expressions men make instead of rolling their eyes. "I was asking him a few questions. There's a difference."

"I don't think he could tell. I'm not sure I could, either."

Kyle picked up his knife again. I wasn't sure if he was thinking about questioning Adam or about to start questioning me. "I don't know," he said after a moment. "Guess I'm just wired to ask questions."

"Yeah, so am I." I hated how defensive it sounded, one of those comments that you wind up hoping maybe someone else said and it just bounced into your conversation through a trick of acoustics so it can be laughed off and moved past.

But Kyle wasn't laughing. He was looking at me with such intensity that for once I wasn't thinking about the color of his eyes, I was just hoping he'd blink. "Yeah, I know," he said slowly and regretfully.

My stomach started to slither toward my toes. Were we going to have this conversation now? Here? Yes, we needed to have it, but I'd been hoping that somehow we'd get away with squeezing in a few fun and carefree dates and enjoy being back together before we had to confront the nitty-gritty of where things had gone wrong between us previously and how/if we were going to be able to avoid those land mines this time around.

But this was difficult territory. I was more than caught between a rock and a hard place, I was pinned between the man of my dreams and the job of my dreams. And while I have no problem apologizing for something when I genuinely feel I'm at fault, I couldn't apologize for being in a position that most women I knew would envy. Yet I felt as though Kyle were waiting for me to say I was sorry or that I'd been wrong or stubborn or prideful or any of those other lovely things women get called when they stand their ground. Not that I wanted to turn this into some sort of political manifesto, but—

"I'm sorry."

It took me a moment to get the lobbyist in my head to stop ranting and listen to what Kyle was saying. I was tempted to ask him to repeat it, just to be sure I'd heard it right, but I didn't want to appear to be enjoying it too much. "For what?" I asked.

The waiter came then, with that exquisite timing waiters have. I've long suspected that even the most elegant restaurants have an infrared surveillance system that runs back to the kitchen, so the waiters can gather around the monitors with glee and watch until, "Table six is about to propose! Get their soup out there now and spoil that moment!"

At least our waiter presented our salads with a special flair and a bright smile, but maybe that was because he was trying to figure out how important we were, given that both Crowley boys had shown up here because of us. I half expected him to take a demo CD out of his shirt pocket and ask us to get it to Adam or Jordan or both, but I was anxious to return to the conversation. I even refused the freshly ground pepper, though I was sure my salad would benefit.

"For what?" I reminded Kyle gently as the waiter finally moved away. I'm usually on the offering end of apologies, so I don't have much practice at eliciting them gracefully from others.

"For telling you to leave this alone, then nosing around in it myself."

I'd been expecting something slightly more profound that reflected on the state of our relationship, but this was still a very positive step. Our central problem was that he didn't approve of what I did and I didn't want to stop doing it. While I'd apologized for stepping on his toes or the toes of his colleagues, this was the first time he'd seriously acknowledged the irresistible pull of an unanswered question.

"Thank you," I said. It would have been gracious to stop there, but yeah, like I was capable of that. "How much nosing around did you do?"

"Just took another look at the file."

I felt a little thrill, vaguely victorious. Was he actually getting drawn in to a case he had sworn was not a case? Had I persuaded him, or was he caught by information I didn't have yet? I took a moment to poke at my salad so I didn't appear too eager to ask, "And . . . ?"

He frowned. "Some of the statements were a little odd. No one could pinpoint any indication that Elliott was suicidal, but no one seemed shocked by the possibility, either."

I leaned in, my enthusiasm getting the better of me. "But don't you think that's an instance of people accepting the reason that's presented in the moment, because there's no overt sign of foul play?"

His smile stiffened. "You talking about the police or the family?"

"The family." I took a deep breath, trying to pace myself. "I mean no disrespect to the officers involved. And I see how it looked like suicide to them and it was polite to call it an accident so everyone could save face. But the family—they buy into that explanation in their grief, then when their heads start to clear, they're doing the same thing we're doing, looking at who had access and motive and opportunity and—"

Kyle held up his hand, and I skidded to a stop. I wasn't sure what I'd said wrong, so I forced myself to stay quiet until he finally asked, "We?"

I could have kicked myself for poor pronoun selection. As delightful as the image was, "I know we're not going all Jerry Bruckheimer here and teaming up," I said with an overly bright smile. "I was just pointing out that we're both responding to the same things. Great minds and all that."

"You're good at what you do," he said, which struck me as a hopeful beginning.

"Thank you."

"And I'm good at what I do."

"Yes, you are."

"And they're two different things."

"Yes, they are."

"And they should stay two different things."

From discussion to negotiation in less than three seconds. I would've been impressed if it hadn't made me nervous. Where was he headed? "Yes, they should," I said this time, though I said it a little more warily.

"Cool," he said, tucking into his salad.

I stared at the top of his head for a moment before it dawned on me that, as far as he was concerned, that was the end of the discussion. Only I'm genetically incapable of letting things go that easily. The fact that he felt the need to point out to me that there was a difference between being a police detective and being a journalist either meant that he was writing for *Sesame Street* on the side or that he felt I had not been respecting boundaries.

"Cool?" I asked, a little sharply.

He looked up at me with a worried smile. "Okay, if we're going to argue, let's not do it here."

"I don't want to argue," I said, which was true. I wanted this to work. But not according to terms dictated to me. "I want to discuss. Reasonably. Maturely. Quietly."

The smile slid up his face into an irresistible grin. "Man, you've changed."

I had to laugh. "Now you're being a jerk."

"You only call me a jerk when I'm getting too close to the truth," he pointed out.

"Imagine what I'll call you when you get it completely right."

With startling quickness, his hand shot across the table to take mine. "I've missed you, and I want this to work, but you've got to understand where I'm coming from, what was making me crazy, and it's all about the jobs."

I didn't even realize how upset I was until my vision clouded. I opened my eyes really wide in the hopes that the tears wouldn't spill over and nodded. "Okay, then. You do your thing and I do mine and never the twain shall meet."

He released my hand so abruptly, I almost dunked my cuff in the boat of raspberry vinaigrette. "They will meet, I know that. Sometimes. But we don't have to force them to. And we can put some extra effort into carving out a work-free zone in our lives. Starting now."

As fabulous as this was, I was completely unprepared—emotionally or conversationally. Clearly, Kyle had put a lot of thought into this in the time we'd been apart; that alone was moving and exciting. But the fact that he was also willing to make elbow room for the chief sore spot of our first go-round, my journalistic investigations, was startling. Delightful, but unexpected.

Which meant I was totally unprepared for sitting here over a lovely dinner and talking about anything and everything but work. While we'd been apart, I'd thrown myself into my work more than ever, to keep myself busy. What else was there to talk about?

He seemed to have a similar problem, since he started the conversation by filling me in on his partner, Ben. I responded by bringing him up to speed on Tricia and Cassady. Then we progressed to the books we'd read and the movies we'd seen since we'd last seen each other. Slowly, we started to relax and move toward each other with a comfort that surprised and pleased me.

Two hours later, I drifted into my apartment, trying to sustain the feeling of comfort and relaxation and quell any sense of expectation. Still, my heart was racing as I turned to ask him if he wanted a drink. But he wasn't right behind me. He was still near the door, watching me with an odd expression on his face.

"Aren't you coming in?" I asked quietly.

He gestured for me to walk back to him as he asked, "Do you remember the first time we kissed?" I nodded as he continued, "Right here." He pulled me to him, kissing me as I concentrated really hard on not swooning.

To steady myself, I snaked my arms around him and tried to draw him into the room, but he resisted. Reluctantly, I stepped back. "What?"

He ran his thumb along my cheekbone, and I could feel the flush rising under his touch. "We're starting over. From this spot. And taking our time." And he kissed me one more time, gently but tantalizingly, and walked out. Leaving me there to marvel at his self-control. Which led me to examine my own lack of self-control. Which led me to consider what happens when people lose control or what they'll do to maintain control. Which somehow led me to wonder where, at that moment, Adam Crowley might be.

9

What is at the root of the American obsession with celebrity? We built a whole industry to create stars, and now we've built one to tear them down at every possible opportunity, critiquing their weight and their clothes, their lack of fidelity and their lack of underwear, their sexual orientation, the people they date, marry, and divorce (not necessarily in that order), the way they raise their children, the causes they embrace, even the pets they choose. We want them to be perfect and larger than life, yet we ache for the moments that they prove to be only human and we get to pounce and proclaim to the nation, "See, this one may be rich and beautiful and talented, but she has wretched taste in evening gowns and worse taste in men!"

And we don't limit it to actors. Rock stars. Designers. Athletes. Politicians. Rich kids with no clear contribution to society. We blur the lines and offer them all intense scrutiny, scathing criticism, and gleeful satisfaction when they tumble from the pedestals we put them on. Why?

Somewhere around two a.m., half dozing in front of Turner Classic Movies, which was showing the Mason-Garland *A Star Is Born,* I decided it was a vestige of our Puritan heritage: Those who elevate themselves have committed the sins of pride and vanity and must be brought down.

At four, waking with a start as Dana Wynter screamed at Kevin McCarthy in *Invasion of the Body Snatchers,* I decided it was an outgrowth of our innate distrust of people who seem so completely different from us.

At six, when my fitful dreaming had melded with *The Spy Who Came in from the Cold,* turning it into a story about trying to get Jordan to switch recording labels, I decided it was time to get up.

At six-thirty, while I was in the shower, Tricia left me a giggly voice mail announcing that she'd just gotten home from her night out with Jordan and she'd call me when she woke up, and I decided that we have a hardwired biological response to fame: The bird with the brightest plumage gets its pick of mates.

At ten, Gray Benedek told me it was all about drama. "People love a good story, and in Western culture, we're trained to expect a three-act structure, which generally means a rise and a fall and then a second chance if it's a happy ending. Or not, if it's a tragedy. Aristotle to Shakespeare to *Entertainment Tonight.* You with me?" he asked as he put his left elbow behind his head.

When I had called Gray, I'd hardly expected to find myself discussing dramaturgy with him an hour later. And when he had agreed to talk to me and suggested I come by his studio, I'd been thrilled at the prospect of getting to watch Gray Benedek at work producing an album as a happy by-product of the interview. However, the studio in his exquisite Central Park West home to which I was summoned was not his recording lair, but an extra room in his apartment dedicated to yoga.

Never mind that this "extra room" was nearly the size of

my entire apartment and had a view that people sit on waiting lists for decades to get. Never mind that one of the sex symbols of my adolescence was stretched out on the floor at my feet, sweaty and magnificent in a snug T-shirt and snugger gym shorts. It was all intoxicating in its own way, but what unnerved me most was his cheery invitation to join him.

I declined as politely as possible. I've tried yoga. More than once. The idea that you can work out and chill out at the same time is pretty intriguing, but I'm beginning to think that some people are congenitally unable to relax at the level required by yoga—and I'm one of them. I breathe, I twist, I submit, but I finish the session more worked up than worked out. Neither my body nor my mind will relax enough for me to get to that meditative place where serenity and good posture reside.

Gray Benedek had no such problem. He moved through a variety of poses as though doing choreography to a song I couldn't hear, not getting out of breath or losing his place, even while speaking to me. It was equally impressive and irritating, and I made a mental note to try another yoga class. Just one more.

I had come looking for some confirmation of his relationship with Claire Crowley and what he knew about the existence of the Hotel Tapes. So, of course, I had told him on the phone that I was writing an article about Olivia and would be very interested in talking to him since he'd been so close to her all her life.

Now, standing over him, I was having an extremely difficult time concentrating. Yes, Adam and Jordan were stars, but Gray Benedek was a megastar. An icon from my past. And even better-looking up close than my glimpse of him in the theater hallway had suggested he might be. I'd felt quite professional while his assistant, a very intense young man who looked more like an MBA candidate than a rock star's right hand, led me down the hardwood hallway lined with museum-quality abstracts.

But as soon as I shook Benedek's hand, I got a trifle star-struck and even stammered when he greeted me. To cover, I'd made a joke about his blowing all my theories about the social constructs of fame. But instead of laughing it off, he'd suggested his own interpretation, ending with the drama statement. Not at all what I'd expected.

"And it's in your hands," he continued now, "to decide whether this one's a comedy or a tragedy."

Not what I'd expected there, either. "I'm not sure I follow."

"You can portray Olivia as the broken little girl who can't overcome the shadow of her famous father, especially since she's surrounded by people with similar issues. Or you can portray her as a young woman who's making her own path, missteps and all, and going to succeed at it," he said crisply.

"Which one do you think she is?"

"Ah, there's the catch. I don't see her—or much in life, in fact—in those simplistic terms. But there's no way my complex point of view can be accommodated by the glossy web you're spinning, so why bother getting into it?"

When the Big Bad Wolf leapt out of bed and revealed himself to Little Red Riding Hood, was her first reaction disappointment? For a moment there, I'd thought I was going to get a memorable, intellectual discussion with Gray Benedek as he offered his unique worldview, shaped by an education as a classical pianist that had strayed into a life as rock royalty. Instead, I was getting sandbagged.

I couldn't decide whether Gray was venting his general dislike of the press or if he had some specific issue with me, but the false bonhomie with which we'd begun made his quick turn all the more irritating.

Careful to keep smiling, I said, "Mr. Benedek, if you're not interested in talking to me, you could have said so on the phone."

He stood and picked up a towel, wiping the back of his neck first. "But I'm very interested in talking to you. Especially if you call me Gray. This is a wonderful conversation."

"Because you get to demean what I do?"

He sniffed and wiped his nose with a corner of the towel. "Do you feel I'm being inappropriate? Perhaps you aren't aware of how your work looks from the receiving end."

"You know my work?" I asked skeptically.

"Claire had plenty to say about you, so I did a little Googling. The pictures from your publisher's Christmas party were very nice, by the way. You should wear your hair like that more often."

The room wasn't all that warm, but I was suddenly uncomfortable and opened my jacket. "What do you want to know?" I asked him, and felt great satisfaction when his eyebrows shot up.

"You're the one who asked for this interview."

"And I can see now that you wouldn't give someone like me the time of day unless you had a specific goal in mind. Either you want something, or Claire Crowley told you to get information out of me that she doesn't think I'll give her myself."

Gray buffed the back of his neck with the towel with enough vigor that I could tell I was nearing the truth. "How about that? Smarter than she looks."

I bit my tongue, but only briefly. "Oh, so I can't draw conclusions about Olivia based on research, but you can judge my intelligence by my looks?"

"Apparently not." He smiled lazily, and I resisted the temptation to teach him a new pose involving my knee and very specific parts of his body. Perhaps sensing my plan, he sat in a plain wooden chair, crossing his long, well-muscled legs. "I'm sorry, I didn't mean to offend you."

"Yes, you did," I said with great certainty.

He smiled with what I chose to interpret as appreciation. "I'd prefer to think of it as figuring out exactly who you are."

"I'm a reporter. It's that simple."

"Not according to Jordan."

"I can't be responsible for what he says."

"Or what Olivia says?"

"Or what Claire tells you. Which you should be accustomed to, since everyone around here tells me not to believe what anyone else says. Have the people in your circle always been so paranoid?"

"Must be all the coke in the eighties. Or everything else in the seventies," he said, chuckling.

The further we got into this, the more he was enjoying it for some reason. "Doesn't all that mistrust take a toll on relationships?"

"Please. Life takes a toll."

I sat across from him, perching on a matching chair, so I could look him directly in the eye. "How long have you been sleeping with Claire Crowley?"

His laugh soared to the ceiling like a beautifully sung note and bounced off the mirrored walls for a moment. In isolation, it was a very nice sound, but right now, especially since it was directed at me, it made my teeth itch. "She's been screwing me for about thirty years, but I've never had sex with her, if that's what you're asking."

"Why would Jordan say differently?"

Gray blinked incredulously. "I know you're new around here, but you must have already figured out that Jordan says what he thinks will get the biggest reaction, not necessarily what's true."

"Was Claire Crowley sleeping with Russell Elliott?"

Gray blinked again, more slowly, and considered his answer just a few seconds longer than he should have. "It is possible to be friends with a woman without sleeping with her, or haven't any of the boys in your world figured that out?"

I took that as a "yes" for Claire and Russell but thought it would be best not to linger on the point at the moment. "So you do her bidding just because you're such good friends."

"Claire's been part of my life since I was in college. She's family." Gray had no children and had never married, though he'd had several well-documented long-term relationships, mainly with large-eyed, soulful singer-songwriter types who were generally in their mid-twenties even after he'd left his twenties well behind. Unlike the other members of the band, Gray had stayed close to the center of the Crowley universe even after Micah died. So I could buy the "family" label. The question was, did he see her as a wife or a sister or something else?

As suddenly as if someone had flipped on the radio, I could hear "Icon," one of the few Subject to Change songs Gray had written and on which he sang lead: "The center of my solitude, the locus of my pain, / The reason I'm a madman, but whoever wants to be sane . . ." The song built to a riveting piano solo that made people freeze in place during parties when I was in high school and college—unless they were making out, in which case it fueled their passion. "Icon" was described as a "blistering anthem to the love/hate relationship the band has with fame," if I'd memorized the liner notes correctly; but looking Gray Benedek in the face now with the song echoing through my head, I wondered if he'd actually written it about someone he loved who didn't or wouldn't or couldn't love him back. Someone like Claire. And I wondered if Micah had known.

But I'd pushed on that point as much as I could for the moment, so I swallowed all the questions it raised and said, "People do even more for family than they'll do for friends."

"Depends on the family and on the friends, wouldn't you think?"

"You're right."

"I wanted to talk to you. Claire told me something interesting about you, and I wanted to find out for myself."

"I doubt she finds me either pretty or smart, so it must be something we haven't covered yet."

"She says you know where the Hotel Tapes are."

Now it was my laugh that rocketed forth, but to my chagrin, it sounded closer to the squawk of a seagull than the silver tone he'd produced. I cleared my throat and plowed forward. "And did she also tell you she denied that they exist? That she claimed she burned them?"

Gray's jaw set. "Maybe she didn't get them all."

"Your theory or hers?" He looked out the window, so I pressed on. "And assuming the tapes do exist, I don't know where they are. They were stolen."

"Allegedly."

"So you suspect me of withholding information, but told Claire you'd charm the tapes' true whereabouts out of me—for what? A share of the royalties?"

"I already have that," he said with the beginnings of a sneer. "There's a separate agreement covering anything released after Micah's death, we all share equally in the royalties."

"All?"

"Me, Rob, Jeff, David, Claire, Bonnie, Russell. Usually the bulk of royalties goes to the songwriter. That's why you tour, so the guys who don't write make some money. Micah wrote almost all our songs, so he was always legions richer than the rest of us."

"Was that an issue?"

"Only when we wanted to tour and he didn't. But he had this near miss OD when we were playing the Meadowlands with the Dead, and after that, Micah said if he went early, he didn't want it to end the party."

"But it did." In an industry where Elvis topped the charts as often after he died as before, it was interesting that there hadn't been any new Subject to Change releases after Micah died. Though "interesting" didn't match the expression on Gray Benedek's face.

"Because Claire felt there wasn't anything worth releasing."

"And she gets final word?"

"She and Russell. But he always deferred to her." He went back to toweling himself off, the speed and vigor picking up even more. "Same thing with licensing songs. Every major ad agency in the world wants to use our songs in commercials, and she said no, it cheapened the music. 'Ironman' sells trucks, Daltry and Townshend are basically TV theme writers, and Claire is worried about the purity of Micah's almighty artistic legacy. Of course, she can afford to be idealistic."

"Why don't you license 'Icon'? Isn't that yours?"

Pleasure that I knew the song was his raced across his face for a split second, then disappeared behind his anger. "That's not the one they ask for."

"You hardly seem to be scraping by," I said, pointing to the postcard-perfect vista of Central Park through the window.

"You don't have to be poor to be cheated," he snapped. "And she's not trying to maintain a presence in the marketplace. Who has the Hotel Tapes?"

He grabbed my arm, almost pulling me out of the chair,

and his world-renowned hand felt strong enough to yank my shoulder out of the socket if he decided it was necessary. My breath caught in my throat, but more than frightened, I was brokenhearted. All the friends I'd laughed with, all the boys I'd kissed while this same hand played awesome music in the background, all the lazy afternoons and hazy midnights I'd spent listening to this man's music . . . I'd been a fan for such a long time. I wanted to like him, and I wasn't sure I could. I wanted him to like me, and I knew he didn't. But most of all, I wanted to have a meaningful conversation with him about rock and roll, fame, Olivia, and who might have killed Russell. And he was treating me like the enemy.

"Olivia says Claire has the tapes," I said, searching his eyes because I was getting upset enough not to be distracted by how gorgeous they were. He glanced away, and I realized, "But you already know that."

"As we've established," he said, recognizing his mistake and pointedly looking at me again, "you can't believe everything Olivia says."

Pain flickered through his gaze, and I seized on it. "Even if you want to?"

"Why would I?"

"Because you suspect Claire of having the tapes, too."

Releasing my arm with sudden self-consciousness, Gray sat back in his chair. "Of course I don't."

I leaned toward him now, wanting to take advantage of the shift in momentum while I could. "Because that would mean Claire is keeping things from you. Which is never good in a relationship. If you can't be honest with each other, there's no point in being together. I know, I just went through it myself."

Gray put his bare foot on the edge of my chair, brushing lightly against my thigh. I wasn't sure if he was trying to intimidate me or was simply thinking about kicking my chair out from under me. Either way, I knew I'd be better off standing up, which I did. After a moment, he dropped his foot and stood with me.

"Russell used to talk about it in hypotheticals. 'Wouldn't it be great if we could release the Hotel Tapes?' That sort of thing. Maybe even pair it with a 'reunion tour,' with one of the boys in Micah's place. Claire always shot it down because she assumed the sound quality would be so bad, but Russell insisted that technology had gotten to the point that the tapes could be cleaned up. . . ." He made a frustrated rolling gesture with one hand, indicating that the conversations had rambled on beyond that, and I nodded. "But ultimately, it didn't matter because no one knew where the tapes were."

Gray took a deep breath, then continued, "Not too long ago, Russell started talking about the tapes again. 'If we had them and could clean them up, what would we want to do with them?' That sort of thing. His biggest worry was that it would look mercenary to release them." The pain flickered through his eyes again. "Russell was too pure-hearted for his own good."

"That's what I've heard," I said softly. "When did he start talking about the tour and everything again?"

"Right before he died," Gray said equally softly, shaking his head and giving me a warning look. He knew how it sounded, and he wasn't comfortable with the notion, had probably been fighting it since the moment Russell died.

The question was, how much did Gray know about the details of that moment? I'd come into this room hoping he could tell me a little more about the players in a general sense, but standing so close to him, I could feel the anxiety sheeting off him, no matter how many yoga poses he'd struck.

Keeping my voice low, I asked, "If the quality was good, why wouldn't Claire want the tapes released?"

"She thinks they'd dilute the audience for the boys' new albums. Why buy the second generation if you can get brand-new stuff from the master? Which is ridiculous, because releasing the tapes would actually be great publicity. The boys are talented enough to handle the comparisons."

"Boys?" I repeated, confused. Everyone was waiting for Jordan's new album, I knew that, but how did Adam fit into this?

Gray smiled bitterly. "I'm putting Adam back in the studio. Supposed to be all hush-hush so it doesn't look like the brothers are competing, but that's more of Claire's hysteria."

"Didn't Adam quit?"

"He stopped. There's a difference." He grabbed my arm again, just as urgently as before. "For some of us, it's not about wanting to play. It's about needing to play. You can't stop. You tell yourself you can walk away, embrace something new, but it's futile. It drags you back."

"Is the music dragging Adam back or are you and his mother?"

"You don't understand."

"Actually, I do. Millions of dollars are at stake, the balance of power is upended because Russell Elliot's dead, but we're all going to pretend it's about art. I understand completely. And I also understand how maddening this must all be because I bet when you heard what Russell had done with the tapes, they sounded amazing."

"Incredible." He nodded with his eyes closed, so completely lost in the memory for a moment that he didn't quite process what he'd just admitted to: that the tapes were real, and Russell had been preparing them for release. But as his eyes opened again, his hand went slack and I knew it had sunk in. "Incredible that you do understand after all, I mean."

"I know what you mean, Mr. Benedek." If Claire hadn't taken the tapes from Russell by force, there was a distinct possibility Gray had. It might not have been his intention, but it could have been the result. Years of art and commerce colliding could wear down a few moral distinctions, no doubt, and I could see Gray trying to persuade Russell to stand up to Claire with him. And pushing too far.

Whatever Gray saw on my face worried him. Pushing a false smile forward, he said, "We've gotten a bit off track. Isn't your article about Olivia?"

"As you said," I answered, matching his smile, "the article can go two different ways: look at the brave daughter carrying on her father's brilliant legacy, or look at the poor orphan surrounded by the people who killed her father."

What had Olivia told me her father said to her in that final phone call? Something about his work being used against him. Maybe he was referring to work he'd done cleaning up the tapes, which Gray was using as leverage to get him to go against Claire: The tapes sound so great, you've worked so hard, it's a shame not to let people hear them. I could see Gray pouring him a drink or two, maybe not even knowing Russell had taken the pills, just trying to get him malleable enough to give up the tapes. That explained why the tape deck was sitting out so casually in the middle of the room: Russell impetuously wanting to share his work in progress with Gray—and maybe with Claire, too—and pulling out the deck to have them listen right then and there. And setting the wheels in motion himself.

I continued, "The tragedy's compounded by the fact that if someone killed Russell to get the tapes, how can they do anything with them now without admitting they were involved in Russell's death?"

Gray snapped the towel between his hands. “The person who has the tapes isn’t necessarily the person who killed Russell.”

I smiled icily. “Prove it.”

His smile was much, much colder. “After you.”

10

"*Am I too old* to be a groupie?"

The young lady behind the counter blanched, thinking that Tricia was directing the comment to her and wisely not wanting to enter into a conversation that began in such a treacherous place. I shook my head hurriedly and pointed at myself, but the poor girl still fled to the cappuccino machine with eyes averted while I responded, "No, but I do think you're a bit mature to be this excited at the prospect."

Daylight had not diminished Tricia's giddiness over meeting Jordan Crowley. I couldn't really blame her: He was handsome, charming, and famous. And she hadn't been exposed to the venomous oddness of his inner circle yet, which was what was dulling his shine for me. Besides, Tricia had been single for a while now, and that increases your sensitivity to new and exciting potentials, the way not eating before a cocktail party makes that first drink hit you twice as hard. It was nice to see her buzzed. We were just going to have to make sure Jordan didn't wind up being one huge hangover.

"The issue isn't your age as much as it is the age of the boy," Cassady pointed out with a snarky smile.

Tricia narrowed her eyes in warning. "He is not a boy."

"If he's younger than you are, he's a boy," Cassady said. "It's an algebraic principle."

"You're just jealous because a *man* paid more attention to me than to you. For once," Tricia insisted.

Key among the immutable facts of life as a friend of Cassady Lynch is you're always going to be the second one people notice. Men in particular. Tricia and I have learned to accept that, but, as Tricia was revealing, it still chafes from time to time.

Studying the contents of the bakery case with feigned interest, Cassady looked as if she were going to be gracious and let it go, but then she returned the lob after all. "I don't need to shop. My cart is full."

"Really?" Tricia asked, eyebrows rising along with her voice. "How long since anyone scanned your basket?"

"Now, now, ladies, let's be careful," I said quickly. We were in line at the Dean & DeLuca by Rockefeller Center, a busy and very public place, not the most ideal location for this kind of discussion. We'd already frightened the barista and were well on our way to entertaining the other people in line, a prospect that didn't entice me in the least, given my recent media exposure.

Following my workout with Gray Benedek, what seemed appropriate was a good stiff drink or a hot-fudge sundae, but it felt self-pitying and irresponsible to give in to either impulse when it wasn't even noon yet. So I'd called Cassady and Tricia so they could talk me into eating vegetables or something equally saintly, but they'd agreed I should go for the most dessertlike coffee possible in the hopes that tapping into the twin wellsprings of caffeine and sugar at the same time would revive me. I would have preferred a quieter, less touristy venue, but this had worked out to be a central location for where they were each headed for lunch: Cassady was accompanying Olivia to see her lawyer and get some specifics on the intellectual properties aspect of Russell's estate, and Tricia was meeting up with Jordan again to discuss a party he wanted her to do for him so he could try out some new songs on a select group of friends and family. The two of them were mixing better with the Crowley clan than I was.

That left me to ponder my next move. As I'd left Gray's, I'd called Kyle, but gotten voice mail, which was probably just as well. I was less apt to get myself in trouble by rambling on about how much I missed him or ranting about how frustrated I'd been by my visit with Gray if I didn't talk to him until later in the day, when I might, I hoped, have my thoughts about Russell and the tapes analyzed more clearly.

I snapped back to the conversation as Cassady said, "I'm having dinner with Aaron tomorrow night, so I'm planning on checking out then." The barista froze in the act of handing Cassady her coffee, again looking slightly panicked until she realized Cassady wasn't talking to her. It had to be miserable to interact all day with people who were having conversations with other people, either in person or on their phones, while you're trying to serve them. I dumped my change into the tip jar.

"I'm glad to hear that," Tricia said as we moved outside. It was a gorgeous November morning, with enough sting in the breeze to put color in your cheeks, but not so cold that you dreaded the quickly approaching winter. Even here in a concrete canyon, the scent of fall leaves crushed underfoot added spice to the air, and I was sure I could smell roasted chestnuts just around the corner.

Pulling our jackets around us, we skittered across the street to huddle against the wall and watch the skaters below on the rink, sliding and twirling with varying levels of success. Tricia continued sincerely, "I was starting to worry that you two had hit a serious problem."

"So was I, but I finally got hold of him yesterday and made him explain," Cassady said while I imagined sweet, quiet Aaron being on the receiving end of that cross-examination. "Turns out Molly was right with her student meltdown theory. More or less."

"Meaning?" I asked, reassured that I had been on track with some theory at some point.

"Aaron's preparing a paper for a conference in Boston, and a few days ago, he discovered a problem with an experiment one of his grad students had done. When he asked her to replicate the results, she couldn't. Turns out she'd doctored the results, to bolster Aaron's theory."

"The things we do for love," Tricia said with a sigh.

"Excuse me?" Cassady's eyebrow arched unhappily.

"Oh, I don't mean that there's anything going on between them," Tricia continued quickly, "it's just that the student must think the world of Aaron to have gone to such lengths, all because she wanted to help him, see him succeed. I can remember a few profs along the way I would've bent a few rules for."

The things we do for love . . . Was that an element in Russell's death that I was missing? Money and fame were the only objects of love in evidence, but I could sense an underlying issue that I hadn't tapped into yet. Had Gray really loved Claire, maybe even back when Micah was alive, and thought he might be with her someday, only to have her get involved with Russell? I thought of the lyrics of "Icon" again: "Everything I've lived for will be the death of me, / Didn't know till I locked in just how much it means to be free . . ."

Listening to my inner iPod, I watched as a little girl on the rink, no more than six years old and picture perfect in her bright pink skating outfit with the white fur trim, flung herself into a grand spin, only to crash inelegantly onto her backside. I winced in sympathy. My footwork was all tangled up, too. I was letting myself get pulled into the emotional swirl surrounding Olivia and the Crowley clan, and that was hampering my ability to weigh the evidence empirically, the way Aaron had to.

While I'd gotten Gray to admit that the tapes were real and that he'd heard them recently, it was clear I wasn't going to get anything else out of him without something substantial to sweeten the bargain. Olivia had all her cards on the table. Jordan was reveling in the chaos. Claire was going to be more unapproachable than ever if Gray went back to her and admitted his slip. I needed to go see Adam.

The more I'd thought about him—and I'd spent way too much time doing that overnight—the more certain I'd become that he was hiding something. What I couldn't be certain of was how willing he'd be to part with the information. Or what I could offer to persuade him to do so. The really tricky part was that his mother was almost certainly part of what he was hiding, and he was so protective of her that one misstep could shut me out completely.

"I gotta go," I told Tricia and Cassady, shaking my coffee cup to see if it was worth taking with me in the cab.

"Not without telling us your new inspiration," Tricia said, grabbing the collar of my coat and pulling me close. "I can see it in your eyes. Along with a fleck of mascara," she added helpfully, lifting that away gently with the tip of her pinkie.

"I'm going to talk to Adam," I explained. "Olivia told me where he rehearses. I'm going to apologize for how badly things went last night and see how much that gets me."

Tricia frowned. "I didn't know you thought things went badly last night."

"They didn't," I said, "except for missing the fabulous party with Jordan, of course. But I thought a conciliatory approach might get more out of him than the 'So where exactly did I fling that gauntlet down, because we can pick up from there?' technique."

Cassady feigned dismay. "But you're so good at that one."

"New dogs, new tricks," I said as I kissed them good-bye.

Tricia looked genuinely concerned. "Do you really think he's holding out on you? Isn't he the good son?"

"Which means you're running around with the bad son," Cassady said.

"For a change," Tricia said with a little spike of triumph at the end. "Besides, if the good might become the bad, the bad might become the good."

"Hope may be the most devious enemy a single woman has," Cassady said. "Let us know how it goes with Adam." They waved as if sending me off to a jousting match as I hurried back to Fifth Avenue to grab a taxi.

My cabbie was Jamie, a fiery-eyed young man from Dublin who told me that while he'd be happy to take me wherever I needed to go, he had an audition for *Law & Order* later in the afternoon, so if I didn't mind, he was going to work on his audition piece while he drove. I agreed, looking forward to hearing a great theatrical monologue delivered in his rich, rolling brogue. Instead, for the next thirty blocks, I listened to him chant, "Look out, he's got a gun!" with a variety of emotions, accents, and syllabic stresses.

Between renditions, I tried to think what might be the more persuasive way to elicit information from Adam once I'd apologized. Did I continue to frame my questions just in terms of the article about Olivia, or did I tell him I'd come across some intriguing/disturbing/potentially explosive/all of the above information while researching the article and see what he thought about Gray having actually heard the tapes?

And ask where he thought his mother might fit into the scheme of things, aside from her sex life?

By the time he dropped me off, Jamie had decided to go with a "terse yet impassioned" reading with an accent that sounded like Madonna's British one. I told Jamie to break a leg at the audition, that I'd be watching for him, while I fished my wallet and some Advil out of my purse. It wasn't until he was pulling away that I took a good look at where I was. There was a name in faded gilt above the front doors of the weary brick building in front of me: MONTGOMERY PREP. For a moment, I thought perhaps the name and the half-hearted ivy on the walls predated the current occupants, until the front doors opened and dozens of pretty, perky young girls in elegantly tailored school uniforms spilled down the front stairs, skirts hemmed just below their derrieres and jackets fitted as though they had whalebone stays. Half pulled out cigarettes, and the others pulled out cell phones. Ah, high school lunch break.

An Upper East Side address had struck me as interesting for Adam's rehearsal space, but this was even odder. Could he be renting space from the school? Maybe someone on the faculty was in his play. Or Olivia had written down the address wrong.

"May we help you?" A knot of leggy, patrician, ponytailed blondes with more poise at sixteen than I'll have at fifty approached me, the ringleader out in front. "You look a little lost, ma'am."

I decided to ignore the "ma'am," especially since her smile told me it was deliberate. "I am," I admitted. "I think I might have the wrong address."

"Are you picking up your child? Maybe we know her," the ringleader asked with a false sweetness beyond her years.

I began to retort with equivalent saccharin that it was mathematically impossible for me to have a child at that school, and then I realized that, had I been careless in my freshman year of college, I might have a freshman here now. I could feel the crow's-feet etching themselves into my face as I did the math. "I'm actually looking for an adult. A musician. I was told he has a rehearsal—"

The ringleader tossed her ponytail in merriment, and her posse followed suit. "You want to see Mr. Crowley," she sing-songed as the other girls giggled.

"Yes, I do."

"You're not a stalker or anything, are you? We do try our best to protect him."

Like Dracula's wives, no doubt. "We know each other."

"That's what they all say."

"I'm a magazine writer."

"For whom do you write?"

"Oh, nice. AP English?"

"Honors. And editor of the school paper."

"Are you the only one in the group who speaks?" I asked her, failing to repress flashbacks to my own high school days, filled with challenging relationships with the power cliques.

Her nose turned up even farther. "Must be lame, or you'd tell us."

Happily, I was able to repress my desire to yank on her ponytail and see what would happen. *"Zeitgeist."*

That got a gratifying chorus of oohs and aahs from the posse and an, "Oh man, you're Molly Forrester!" from one of the girls in the back.

"You read my column?" I asked pleasantly, not too proudly.

She looked offended for a moment, as though I'd suggested she still read Dr. Seuss. "No, you were in yesterday's *Post* with Mr. Crowley. He told us all about you!"

Not the reaction I was hoping for, but I'd take it since it caused them to sweep me along before them like so many chattering ladies-in-waiting delivering the new dancing girl to the king.

Inside, the school's age had been covered up a bit more, though there was still that essential mustiness all old buildings have, where the dust just hunkers down along the bottoms of your nostrils and taints every breath you take. My young escorts, who must have developed a tolerance for it, laughed and peppered me with unanswerable questions about Adam and Jordan as we hurried through the hallways, drawing interested looks from other knots of students but, fortunately, not picking up any other hangers-on.

Adam was in the dark and echoing auditorium, seated at the grand piano in the pit and playing something warm but mournful. The scene was more Robert Walker in *Song of Love* than Lon Chaney in *Phantom of the Opera,* and I found I was glad to see him again. He looked quite dashing and extremely handsome sitting there and smiled warmly as he looked up and saw us, so I had to remind myself that I'd come to talk to him about murder.

"They come bearing gifts!" he said, laughing and meeting us halfway up the aisle, allowing the girls to coo around him for a moment before sending them on their way. "This is a surprise," he said as the double doors closed behind them.

"Likewise. Olivia told me you were in rehearsal for a musical—"

"And you assumed I was workshopping some angst-ridden Off Broadway rock opera." He walked back toward the pit, and I followed him, trying to regain my bearings.

"Something along those lines."

"Well, they don't come much more angst-ridden or further from Broadway than the ladies of Montgomery Prep."

"You teach here?" I asked as he sat back down at the piano and leaned into a wistful, bluesy chord progression.

"Sort of. I'm a 'visiting artist.' Which means I have a friend on the faculty who wanted to figure out a way to bring me in, despite my lack of academic credentials. Which is a polite way of saying I never finished school. And none of this needs to be in your article."

"Why not? It's nice, that you're taking the time to work with kids like this."

Adam lowered his voice to a conspiratorial whisper. "They're my guinea pigs. I really am workshopping a musical, I'm just trying it out here first. It's a musical version of *The Prime of Miss Jean Brodie*. With a jazz score. A girls' prep school is practically required."

As the chord progression worked its way into a song, his hands moved as though they were autonomous, effortlessly coaxing the notes forward while the rest of Adam was engaged in conversation with me. It was fascinating, until I found myself remembering that movie where the concert pianist's hands are replaced with a murderer's hands after an accident and the hands start killing people despite the pianist's best efforts to stop them. I took a step back.

He didn't react. "I like the kids and they like me, it is what it is."

"But what is it?" I asked.

"Adam Crowley's search for redemption." The song turned so sorrowful, it gave me chills.

This was not the way I'd expected this visit to unfold, but I knew enough to surrender to the current. "Why do you need redemption?" I asked, trying to keep my voice steady.

"I had an amazing chance, and I blew it. Wasted something most people would kill for."

His choice of words was not lost on me, and I swallowed before asking him, "What did you blow?"

"My succession to the throne. Russell lined it all up for me. All I had to do was step into the shoes and *pow*. Rock royalty, the lineage continues . . ." He thumped, the chords suddenly discordant, building to an unresolved chord.

"You were young."

"One of my excuses. I've got tons. Wanna hear them?"

"You didn't fail, Adam."

"I didn't measure up. What's the difference?"

"Do another album."

"Yeah, it's that easy. Talk to my brother."

"I actually wanted to talk about your mother. And Gray."

Adam snatched his hands back from the keys as though they'd suddenly gone molten. "Ah, Molly. And we were having such a nice time." He rose from the piano, avoiding my eyes, and climbed the steps from the pit up to the empty stage.

"Don't you like your mother?" I asked, staying put to give him a little space.

"I love her," he said with his back to me and his voice devoid of emotion. "All sons love their mothers, right?"

"Let me check with Norman Bates."

Chuckling, he turned around, flexing his fingers to keep them warmed up. "Why do you care about how I get along with my mother?"

Because I want to know what she'd be willing to do for you, I thought. "Olivia has a very difficult time with her, and Jordan doesn't do much better. If you and Claire get along beautifully, it paints her relationship with them differently than if she's a woman who doesn't get along with any of the children who grew up in her sphere of influence."

He held out a hand to me as though he were inviting me to dance. Willing to play along for the moment, I picked my way up the rickety steps and joined him on the stage, taking his hand. He spun me slightly so I was looking out at the house. "My mother thinks this is what it's all about. Being center stage. Looking down at the audience. My father didn't hang on to it long enough, I barely touched it, and yet she's the one who feels cheated. The dynasty must continue. But Jordan doesn't take it seriously enough to suit her, and Olivia was never interested in music, which offended her."

"Where does that leave you?" I asked.

"Teaching little girls to sing." He tugged on my hand gently, and I remembered enough cotillion lessons to spin back to him. Settling his other hand into the small of my back, he whispered, "Trying to escape."

"From her?"

"From all of it. Her. Gray. Everybody wants me back in the studio, aping my father."

"And that doesn't interest you."

He pulled me in even more tightly, almost uncomfortably so. "You like your dad?"

"I love my dad. He's an amazing man."

"Is he a reporter?"

"No."

"So you love him, but you didn't follow in his footsteps."

"One doesn't have anything to do with the other," I said, getting a little breathless from the rigidity of his grasp.

"Tell my mother that." He stopped so abruptly, I almost stumbled over his feet. Taking a step back, I was caught by the rage darkening his face. "She demands that I love him, she demands that I be like him, and I don't want to do either."

The force of his emotion was like a shock wave, and I took another small step back to absorb it. I'm blessed: I adore my parents. But I've had friends who weren't so fortunate, and I know the kind of constantly gnawing pain that engenders. I could only imagine how it would be magnified if the father you could not adore was idolized by people all over the world and only grew closer to perfection in their memories after a tragic death. And to have Claire invalidating his feelings and his ambitions at every turn had to be torture.

"Have you told her?" I asked.

"Of course I have," he said bitterly. "You know what she tells me? That I'm dishonoring him. Like he didn't dishonor her when he brought Bonnie and Jordan into our house. And she says I've lost my way. Like he didn't lose his way with the other women and the drugs and the staying out on the road when he didn't have to. She tells me I have to be just like him, but she hates him and so do I. So where does that leave us? Where does that leave me?"

He held his arms open to the empty auditorium as he tried to swallow back the tears I could hear threatening. "She keeps saying, 'All it takes is one great song, a hook, a riff, and you'll find it. You'll be back on top.' Easy for her to say when she's never tried it, never failed at it."

I went to him instinctively, not sure what I was going to say or do, but before I could touch him, he grabbed me, swirling me back into a grinding samba step, humming something low in his throat, as though that expressed his thoughts better than any words he could come up with.

But isn't that the magic of music? It elevates and encapsulates at the same time, preserving moments of high-flung emotion like delicate flowers trapped in amber, so we can take them out again and again, take a shortcut to the place deep inside where those feelings live, happy or sad, repressed or treasured. And isn't that the allure of the singer, that he or she can take you on that trip in ways more thrilling than you'd imagined? And the gift of the songwriter, to be able to catch the moment to begin with?

But you can't write a great song just because you feel great pain or experience deep love or because your mother says so. And if you are told to write a great song and want to write one and still can't . . . The frustration had to be maddening. I'd never tried to write a song, but I'd searched for the perfect phrase for a column or article and had it elude me, so I'd had a taste of what was driving him.

As I allowed myself to sympathize with him, I recognized the song he was humming. "I love Jobim," I said, hoping I sounded like a true music fan and not an eager-to-impress groupie. My mother had a crush on Jobim when I was growing up and had several recordings of his songs, by him and by other artists. My father would stand at the bottom of the stairs and sing "The Girl from Ipanema" when Mom came down, dressed up for a night out. As kids, we laughed madly, thinking it was silly, but looking back now, I see it as romantic, sexy even.

He loosened his grip on me enough to look me in the eye, a surprised smile lightening his gaze. "Lovely, talented, and she knows her jazz," he sang, improvising his own lyrics without missing a beat, then segueing into scat. The song was Jobim's "Desafinado," which translates as "Off Key," But Adam was more than on-key. Even just scatting, the quality of his voice as he sang the jazz tune was completely different from what I'd heard on his rock album. There was a richness, an intimacy that was seductive.

"You should do a jazz album," I whispered. "You sound great."

"Tell that to the folks with the checkbooks," he whispered back, trying to hang on to whatever comfort the song gave him. "They seem to think that making me give up something I dearly want is a noble cause." His mouth was against my ear, like at Jordan's concert, and his voice snaked down into my chest and up into my head. He laughed low in his throat. "So much sexier than anything my dad ever wrote, I ever wrote."

I pushed out of his arms, trying to match his flirty laugh. "You're making me dizzy." He took a step toward me and I took a step back. "Wait," I said, holding up my hand. But he took another step toward me and the intensity of his gaze made me drop back again. "Don't you think if you explained how you feel to Gray—"

"He'd tell me why it would never sell. Again."

"Record it yourself. You have the connections, the resources—"

"Not if Gray and my mother blackball me." He stepped forward, and I held out my hand to keep him at arm's length. He grabbed my hand and pulled me into him again. "Passion can only take me so far. Though it might be interesting to see how far . . ."

I pushed out of his arms and made myself concentrate. "What about the money you were going to invest with Ray Hernandez?"

The taste of lightness the song had brought him was evaporating, his look darkening again. "I was going to invest the advance from the album. Which Gray won't give me if it's not rock."

"Forget the club. Do the album yourself. Or find someone else. There must be someone who—"

"Believes in me? Only Russell. And look what happened to him."

"What did happen to him, Adam?"

He flinched as though I'd slapped him. "Molly, every time we start to get in deep, really connect with each other, you have to spoil the mood by bringing up something I'd really rather not think about."

"Why don't you want to think about it?"

He stepped toward me again and I stepped back, not realizing how close I was to the edge of the stage. My left heel actually dipped into the air, and for a moment, I thought I was going to plummet backward into the pit and destroy my spine and a lovely grand piano. But Adam grabbed my hand, pulled me tight against him. I grabbed on to him gratefully, unable in my panic to let go even as he slid his other hand behind my neck, pulling me still closer and kissing me with the authority that comes from no woman ever saying no, then murmuring, "Because I've been thinking about that."

11

"Have you lost your mind?"

It would have been bad enough to hear it from Eileen, who was probably on her desk, dialing Henry's phone number with her toes while dancing with glee. Or from Kyle, who was bound to be rethinking his decision to come back into my life right about now. Or from Tricia and Cassady, whose definitions of what they considered breaches of good taste, common decency, and basic sanity had been stretched and twisted by our escapades over the years yet still remained remarkably flexible. But no, I had to get the lecture on journalistic ethics and basic comportment from Peter Mulcahey, a man whose relationship with either bordered on estrangement.

And it wasn't that I didn't want to defend myself. I couldn't. The only thing more stupid than putting myself in a potentially compromising situation with a subject in a story I was working on was doing it in front of teenage girls armed with cell phones that took better pictures than I got with my camera. Pictures that had rocketed around Manhattan before I had been able to detach myself from Adam Crowley and get back to the office.

I'd barely caught my breath from Adam's kiss when laughter erupted in the house seats and we saw that the ringleader and her posse had returned. They looked like something out of a Verizon commercial, all with right arms extended, cell phones aimed at Adam and me, mouths open in perfect circles of fiendish delight. "Girls," Adam protested halfheartedly, suspecting it was a lost cause, "please delete those."

"Oh, of course, Mr. Crowley," the ringleader chirped. She pushed a key on her phone, and her eyes widened almost comically. "Oops. I think I hit 'send' by accident." Her posse mimicked her exactly, and I remembered why high school had been such a blissful time of my life.

Adam told them he'd meet them in the headmistress's office, and they sashayed out defiantly. He offered to walk me out, but I told him the less we were seen together, the better. "I'm writing a story about someone you're very close to . . . ," I began.

"And a crime you think I'm involved in," he finished.

"I don't suspect you. Should I?"

"Isn't that why you came?"

"No. Is that why you kissed me?"

"No. You couldn't tell it was sincere?"

"I have to go." Not only could I tell it was sincere, it made my head spin, and I still didn't have my equilibrium back. I tried to focus on an image of Kyle's face, but the only one I could come up with was frowning pretty deeply. Telling myself that the kiss shook me up only because he was famous and I'd never kissed anyone famous before wasn't helping much, either. "I have to go," I repeated, more for my benefit than his.

On the way back to the office, I concentrated on everything but the kiss. Gray claimed to want Adam to record again, but Adam said he wouldn't let him record what he wanted. Russell had been supportive of Adam's move to jazz, but now Russell was gone. So were the tapes. Had Gray killed Russell in a struggle over Adam's musical destiny? Had he then gone back and stolen the tapes to control them, too?

Or, as he'd suggested, did someone else—like Claire—have the tapes? Did she have them because Gray had told her to go get them?

One thing Claire had for certain was a burning desire to talk to me. By the time I got back to the office, I had three messages from her on my cell phone, two messages on my office phone, a note on my desk from Henry's assistant that Claire was trying to reach me, and an angry editor in the aisle delivering much the same information in person.

Eileen was swathed in a black cashmere cowl-neck sweater and houndstooth wool skirt. The weather hadn't gotten that cold yet, but she dressed by the calendar more than by the thermometer. I'm sure the intent was a soft and warm look, but as she stood there tapping her Pliner-encased toe, the image was more Boston terrier than cuddly boss. Perhaps it was the growling that sold it.

"Do you need a chaperone, Molly Forrester?" she asked peevishly as I hung up the phone. I hadn't even had a chance to sit down yet.

"Thank you, it would probably help," I said, dropping my purse into my desk drawer and myself into my chair. I thought we were talking about Claire, but then Eileen reached over my shoulder and tapped a crimson talon on the space bar on my computer, and the screen sprang to life with a picture of Adam kissing me filling most of it. CROWLEY ON THE PROWLEY, the headline at this particular gossip site read. I could only hope that there weren't many more sites—and if there were, that their headlines were better.

"How do you explain this?" Eileen asked, fuming.

"They rushed. I'm sure the pun would be more clever if they'd taken a little more time," I said.

"What does this have to do with your story on Olivia Elliott?"

"Nothing." She growled again, and I stood up so the vulnerable back of my neck would be out of reach of her fangs if she pounced. "Honestly, Eileen, this has nothing to do with the story."

She leaned in to read off the screen to me and everyone else in the bull pen, since all work had ceased the moment she'd begun questioning me. " 'What's keeping Adam Crowley from his music these days? This lovely' "—Eileen paused to snort in my general direction—" 'reporter from *Zeitgeist* who's investigating the link between the deaths of his father, Micah Crowley, and music manager Russell Elliott.' "

"That's Jordan," I snapped. "He probably set this whole thing up, another chance to advance his theory." I didn't put it past Jordan to have that gaggle of Valkyries spying on Adam to begin with. Then I'd been stupid enough to let Adam put us both in this uncomfortable position.

Eileen would have frowned if the Botox permitted; instead, her eyes danced a little with the strain. "Unless it's your theory, too, it's rather stupid of you to let him use you to promote it." Which struck me as one of the most insightful things she had ever said to me. Unfortunately, my surprise must have shown, because her lip curled again and she growled, "Clean this up." She gestured vaguely to the computer screen and stalked back to her office.

As she passed, my colleagues fell back into their seats like newly shorn grass in the wake of a lawn mower. With the exception of Irina, who stood up and walked over to me, her shoulders rounded in diffidence. "You don't have time for me," she stated.

"It would be a welcome respite from screwing up my life," I said genuinely, patting the guest chair beside my desk.

She sat down so tentatively, she seemed to hover half an inch above the seat of the chair. "Is it bad form for an advice columnist to suggest that some people were born to be alone?"

"What an intriguing idea," I said, considering all the ways in which being alone might improve my life at that given moment. But then I looked at Irina again, with her intense gaze and sad mouth, and continued, "But I do think you'll find that most people who write in are interested in connecting with people more, not less. And if you're a person who deeply values being alone, maybe the column wouldn't be the best next step on your career ladder."

Irina sighed, her shoulders rolling forward even farther. "It probably doesn't matter. You're going to get kicked off this article and you'll take back the column and it will have just been a writing exercise anyway."

If she had any idea how worried I was that she was right, it didn't register on her expressionless face. "On the other hand," I said with all the brightness I could muster, "someone of your perception could have a lot of fun with the column. Please submit something."

She rose without answering and drifted back to her desk. I grabbed my phone, hoping it would act as a talisman to protect me from more visitors.

Claire Crowley didn't sound as happy to hear from me as her multiple messages might have suggested. "You and I need to talk," she said. "I'm concerned you're not getting a balanced picture of how Olivia fits into our family structure, as it were."

Relieved that she wasn't rampaging about the picture of Adam and me, I agreed to meet her at her apartment at eight o'clock. After hanging up quickly, I pushed on to my next call.

"Got a second?" I asked Kyle when he answered.

"Three or four."

"That's enough, because it's just that something happened

this morning and it's not what it looks like and I want you to know that and it's the stupid gossip sites, though I'm impressed how quickly they post stuff—"

"Molly, did someone try to hurt you?"

It was entrancing and occasionally troubling, the way his mind worked. "No, someone kissed me." There was silence at the other end. "And someone else took a picture." The silence deepened. "And I wanted you to know it's not what it looks like."

"What does it look like?" he asked in his official detective voice.

"Like I'm kissing him back."

"But you didn't."

"No," I said emphatically, even though I could still feel the warm pressure of Adam's mouth against mine. Which shocked me. How could I be talking to Kyle and thinking about Adam? What was wrong with me?

"Okay, then."

"Are we? Okay?"

"I am, are you?"

"Yes."

"Then we should talk about it later, because Ben and I are on our way into court."

"Sorry!"

"No, no, it's good, we're good. Glad you called, appreciate the heads-up."

I dropped the receiver into the cradle, wondering how much to read into the fact that he'd hung up without any sort of endearment. Though "it's good, we're good" came close in his lexicon. I might have sat there and deconstructed those four words for the next hour, evaluating inflection, tone, volume, but Bonnie Carson had other plans.

"Molly?" she said, appearing beside me like a sprite materializing in the middle of *A Midsummer Night's Dream*. Skyler was behind her, smiling smugly.

"You have a visitor," Skyler said, in case I hadn't figured that out for myself. She held up a small bag from the pharmacy in the lobby. "You gave Eileen a headache, so I had to get her meds. Your visitor was at the front desk, and I offered to bring her up."

"That's so thoughtful, Skyler, thank you," I said, confident that she knew I didn't mean it.

Skyler slunk back to her desk as Bonnie held out her hand. "Bonnie Carson. Jordan Crowley's mother."

How interesting that she felt the need to introduce herself that way, as though I wouldn't remember her after only a few days. Though maybe it had just become habit. Or her identity. "Yes, I remember. How are you?" I said, standing and shaking her hand.

She laughed a little, but it wasn't a happy sound. "I'm perplexed, actually. And I hate to be such a *mom,*" she said, emphasizing the word to the point that it became two syllables. "But what's going on between you and my son?"

To the dismay of my colleagues, I suggested we move to the conference room at that point. My relationship with one Crowley scion becoming tabloid fodder was a sufficient contribution to the drain on American productivity for one day.

I ushered Bonnie into the hushed conference room, the scent of dry-erase markers hanging heavily in the air, and grabbed two bottles of water from the minifridge, more to have something to do with my hands than because I was thirsty. "I'm not sure I understand why you're concerned, Ms. Carson—"

"Bonnie."

I nodded in acknowledgment and continued, "There's

nothing going on. Not that there's anything going on with Adam, either. But there's certainly nothing going on with Jordan," I assured her.

"All this speculation about Micah and Russell—"

"He started it," I said, knowing I sounded like a three-year-old, but not eager to take the blame for anything but my own messes at the moment.

There was a pause, then a sniff. Bonnie was crying. I scanned the room for tissues, but she pulled a linen handkerchief out of her Ferragamo Gancio satchel and dabbed at her eyes with that, careful to slide the handkerchief under the eyelashes so she didn't smear the mascara. "That's what I was afraid of. I almost hoped it might be some sort of publicity stunt you'd talked him into, but . . ." She took a moment to compose herself, and I waited, playing with a corner of the label on the water bottle. "The pressure's getting to him more than I knew."

"Pressure from what?"

Shooting me a sharp look that implied my question was somewhere between stupid and offensive, Bonnie said, "To finish his new album. He's such a perfectionist, he deserves to take his time, but Gray's pushing him, Claire's pushing him . . ."

"You're not."

"I'm encouraging him. That's what mothers do." She crafted a brittle smile. "Good mothers, anyway."

"What do bad mothers do?" I asked, knowing I was throwing open the door to a knock on Claire.

"They let their children quit."

While I had an urge to defend Adam, I didn't want to have to explain to Bonnie how and what I knew about his next album, so I let it go. Knowing Bonnie's take on it was worthwhile, too. "Then maybe you should encourage Jordan to stop stirring up the tabloids and get back to work," I said politely.

"You'll include him in your article, won't you?" she asked with equal politeness.

"Absolutely. From what I've seen already, he's a big part of Olivia's life. I think the way Adam and Jordan treat her like a sister is very endearing."

"Russell adored Jordan," she said with a wistful smile. "He saw Micah in my son from the very beginning, encouraging his musical aspirations long before I ever dared imagine. . . ." The handkerchief slid back up under the eyelashes and I waited to see what other items were on Bonnie's agenda, other than making sure Jordan didn't slide out of the spotlight for even a moment. "I miss him very much."

"Micah or Russell?"

"Well, both of course, but I was speaking specifically about Russell."

"Has it been hard for you to live this way?"

Her back straightened, and the handkerchief disappeared into her fist. "What way?"

"In Claire's shadow."

To my utter amazement, Bonnie laughed, an amazingly resonant and hearty laugh for such a delicate woman. "Is that how it appears to you? You haven't been paying enough attention, Molly. Our worlds happen to intersect, but mine is every bit as bright and worthy as hers. More so, even. And my son is absolutely the true heir to Micah Crowley's musical legacy."

I half expected her to send me to the Tower of London to await my execution. "I apologize."

She laughed again. "There's no need, it's a common mistake. But don't repeat it in your article, because I'd have to refer the matter to my lawyers and there'd be all sorts of unpleasantness, and my family deals with enough of that." I was impressed by how she'd slid from reassuring me to threatening me without her voice changing one bit. She stood up to let me know we were done talking. "And don't mention the tapes in your article, either, because that will only get people agitated and, again, the lawyers would have to get involved."

"Why would you think I'd bring up the tapes?"

"Gray said you were over there this morning, asking about them."

"Did he tell you what he told me about them?" I wondered how much energy Gray expended balancing the two widows. It had to be a full-time job now that Russell was gone.

"That he doesn't know who has them."

"That's all?"

"What more could there be?"

"That Claire's very anxious to find them. And lock them back up, so they don't dampen sales when Adam and Jordan release their albums."

Bonnie's smile froze so hard, I was worried her lips would turn blue. "The tapes would actually encourage sales, I'm sure."

"That's what Gray thought."

"Gray's a smart man."

"Smart enough to figure out where the tapes are?"

She looked at me, but she was looking far past me. "Wouldn't that be nice." I stood so she could leave after all, but she still didn't move for a moment, chasing some idea in her head. "We'll find them," she said after a beat, and I tried to decide whether I was honor-bound to warn Claire and Gray that Bonnie was on the warpath and headed in their direction.

I did feel compelled to walk Bonnie to the elevator and thank her for coming by to warn me to stay away from her son, even though neither of us phrased it that way. It was that gesture that put me in the right place at the wrong time, so Peter Mulcahey could step off the elevator right before Bonnie got on it and ask me if I'd lost my mind.

"Hello, Peter," I said in response, pleased with my composure, especially because Peter, normally the one who was all too cool and controlled, looked to be unraveling a bit. I debated suggesting the conference room to him, too, but something in his demeanor made me more comfortable staying in the elevator lobby. With lots of witnesses. "Nice picture, isn't it."

"What picture?"

It's so hard to stay current in today's fast-paced world. "Okay, then what are you upset with me about?"

"What did you say to Adam Crowley to make him pull out of the deal with Ray Hernandez?"

"I don't think I did."

"Think again."

I tried to remember, but thinking about it just made my lips sting and my heart race. "Okay, I might've said something along the lines of 'forget it,' but trust me, I don't have that kind of influence over him."

"You sure? Ray Hernandez just chewed me out because Adam called him to say he had better dreams to spend his money on or some starry-eyed crap like that, so now Ray's furious with me because this whole deal between the two of them was below the radar and Ray blames me for letting you talk Adam out of it."

"First of all," I said, trying to calm us both down, "everyone's giving me way too much credit here. Second, Ray will cool off and you'll still get your article. You might even get a front seat to either Ray wooing Adam back or Ray landing a new investor, which is a process that should enthrall all the wannabe Trumps who read your magazine."

Peter looked at me with amazement. I thought he was

impressed with my deft spin on the situation until he said, "Are you pitching me? Are you trying to apologize to me by pitching the fix to this story?"

"It's better than an empty apology, isn't it?" I said with a smile that was intended to be winning.

In spite of himself, he smiled back. "Actually, it is. Go on."

"Most importantly, I didn't do this deliberately. I was talking to Adam about his music, not about Ray and the club. The club comment was collateral damage. And again, I apologize."

Peter's smile darkened down a bit. "Why are you still hanging around with him?"

I frowned, then immediately rubbed at the wrinkle I was creating so it wouldn't set, a habit I'd picked up from Tricia. "I'm researching a story. Olivia's circle is pretty tight. You can't deal with one of them without dealing with all of them."

"That why you were kissing him?"

"I thought you didn't see the picture."

"I didn't want to get sidetracked."

"But now that you've got a fix for your story, you can nose around in mine?"

"Why were you kissing him?"

"He was kissing me. I was trying to ask him about Olivia and her dad, and the conversation wandered a little."

"A little?"

"Yes, a little."

"You must be getting close to something. He's trying to distract you."

While I knew there was some truth there, it sounded harsher coming from Peter than I wanted to hear. "Or maybe he likes me."

"If he has an ounce of sense," Peter replied.

"Thank you."

"Or maybe he's involved in Russell Elliott's death and is

seducing you to get himself off—off your suspect list, that is. Damn straight the approach I'd use."

One of the human emotional reactions that intrigues me most is the anger provoked by someone saying something you know deep in your heart but are trying to deny. Something you are quite capable of denying until another person has the gall to be clearheaded enough to say the denied truth out loud. Some sort of chemical reaction occurs between the warring heart and brain, and the central nervous system overloads. Which was why, right then and there, in the elevator lobby of my own workplace, I wanted to strangle Peter Mulcahey. Whether I liked it or not, he was on to something. The question was whether Adam had some actual knowledge of or involvement in Russell's death or if he was just muscling into the spotlight so Jordan didn't have it all to himself.

But I'd known Peter long enough to know that I'd never live it down if I acknowledged his direct hit. "Thanks for believing in the power of my charms."

"What do you think he knows?" Peter asked, trying to demonstrate his own.

Even if I'd figured that out, I wasn't going to tell him. "Peter, this isn't snack time. I'm sorry I've complicated your story, but I'm not going to make it up to you by giving you part of mine."

"That's not why I'm asking. I'm concerned about you. You've gotten into a lot of trouble since we broke up."

I had to laugh. "I've started writing about murders since we broke up. Which of those variables do you think is more relevant?"

"All the more reason I want to protect you," Peter said, almost convincingly.

"I appreciate that, Peter, but it's not necessary."

"And keep you from ruining my story."

"Oh yeah, that too."

Peter smiled with such a rare moment of self-awareness that I couldn't resist. "Thanks," I said, kissing him lightly on the cheek.

He caught my hand as it rested on his shoulder and kept it there for a moment. Just long enough for Kyle to say, "Is this the picture you warned me about?"

Peter and I were both startled, having been oblivious to the elevator delivering another set of spectators. Most of them dispersed quickly, leaving Kyle standing there, looking us over as though we were in a lineup for a felony.

"No, there's actually a different picture. Different guy," I fumbled. Attempting to recover, I said, "I thought you were in court," then hated the fact that it sounded like a lame alibi.

"Continuance."

"Good to see you, Edwards," Peter said.

"I bet it is," Kyle said. "Y'know, Molly, when I said I wanted to start all over again, I didn't mean you had to go back to being with him every time I turned around."

"I could start dating her again, if you want a running start," Peter offered, enjoying the situation far too much.

"You're a stand-up guy," Kyle said, more amused than he should have been.

"Anything to help."

"If the two of you want to go out for a beer together, don't let me keep you," I said, failing to match their lighthearted tone.

"I should probably take a rain check, since I came here to talk to you about something specific."

"The picture."

"No. Your buddy Olivia. She's been arrested."

12

"I owe you," I told Cassady.

"Don't be ridiculous. I'll bill her for it. That's how it works with lawyers and clients. Well, clients who aren't your best friend. And even then, in certain circumstances."

"I meant 'owe you' in a more emotional sense."

"Oh, that goes without saying."

We paused halfway down the steps of the police station and looked back to see what progress Olivia and Kyle were making. Not much, since she insisted on stopping and planting her feet each time she had a point to declaim.

"I'm not the one who broke the law!" she protested, not for the first time since we'd arrived to arrange for her bail. The tales of my adventures and how Kyle was handling them were spreading through the police community, and a friend of Kyle's at the Twenty-fourth Precinct had called him when Olivia was brought in. She hadn't called anyone by the time we got there, thoroughly convinced that she hadn't done anything wrong.

Kyle rubbed his face wearily. "Actually, you are." He glanced down at me, and I had a deep urge to blow him a kiss in thanks for all he was doing.

He walked down another two steps and got Olivia to follow

one more before she stopped again. "He broke into my apartment!"

Two steps. "It's not breaking and entering when you use a properly issued key."

One step. "I should've taken it back from him after Dad died."

Two steps. "Separate issue, not relevant here."

One step. "Of course it's relevant. I didn't want him in the apartment and he knew it."

Kyle backed up two steps, took her arm, and marched her down to meet us. "But that doesn't give you the right to strike him with a blunt object."

" 'Clobbering him with a Grammy' will sound much better in the press," Cassady said.

"You'd be doing everyone a favor if you kept this out of the press," Kyle advised.

"Getting the charges dropped would be even better," Cassady said.

"Isn't that your department?" Olivia asked.

"Given your long-standing relationship with the victim, there's a certain amount to be said for a direct conversation. One that includes an apology," Cassady said.

"I never want to talk to Gray Benedek again," Olivia said.

"Good luck with the whole apology thing," Kyle said, delivering Olivia's forearm into my grasp and kissing me quickly. "I need to get back to my precinct. Talk to you later."

"I should get back to the office, too. Share a cab, Kyle?" Cassady and Kyle hurried down to the curb, leaving me with a truculent Olivia.

"It wasn't my fault," she repeated, but her voice quavered a little this time, and I was sure she was going to dissolve into tears on me.

"Hang on," I warned her. "Let's go somewhere a tad less public and sort this all out."

"I want to go to Serendipity and get a Frrrozen Hot Chocolate," she insisted. Stomping her foot didn't seem far behind.

"I don't have all afternoon to wait in line," I said.

She looked at me with something from her "Poor, Poor Pitiful You" collection. "Don't you know anyone?" she asked, taking her cell phone out of her bag.

Half an hour later, through the skillful plying of interlocking friends of friends I couldn't quite follow, we were secreted at a corner table. The old-time ice-cream parlor ambience, with its Tiffany lamps and other cheery frippery, soothed Olivia enough for her to manage a smile. It was the most relaxed I'd seen her yet, though fatigue and distance from anyone else she knew probably had as much to do with it as the candy-colored charm of our surroundings.

"You'd make a good therapist," she said. "You're very easy to talk to."

Working around a mammoth pile of whipped cream, I scraped a curl of frozen hot chocolate onto the tip of my spoon. "Then you won't mind my asking what you think Gray was doing in your dad's apartment this afternoon."

"He told me he wanted Dad's notes on Jordan's album."

"Was that before or after you hit him?"

"After. I didn't know it was Gray when I hit him. I told you, I thought someone had broken in. I came in, heard noises in Dad's study . . ." She mimed smacking Gray with her spoon, then stabbed the spoon into her cup. "He forgot I was staying there. I forgot he had a key."

"He has a key, so does Claire. Anyone else?"

"Adam. Bonnie and Jordan. We've always treated it like one big house, with separate wings."

"Where does Jordan live?"

"Upstairs, with Bonnie."

These people were beyond cozy. I thought of the psychology experiment we learned about in college where the overcrowded rats start to eat one another to create some space. "I see why you moved out."

She made a wry face. "And I was miserable. I missed them all so much. Even Jordan, who used to tell me when we were teenagers that he'd drilled a hole in his bedroom floor so he could see down into my room and watch me sleep."

"Were you guys ever together?"

"No," Olivia said sharply. "Disgusting. It would be like dating my brother. He just liked to tease me. Still does, in fact."

"What about Adam?"

"He's always been very sweet. We have a warmer relationship."

"How did Adam and your dad get along?"

"Great." Her eyes widened. "What are you suggesting?"

"I'm not suggesting anything. I'm interviewing you about the dynamics of your childhood, especially now that I've met a few more of the people since the first time we talked."

She flattened the whipped cream with the back of her spoon as though beating it into submission. "No, you're trying to figure out if Adam could've killed my father."

"Hadn't even occurred to me," I lied. "Why does it occur to you?"

"It doesn't, it wouldn't. And I can't believe you'd suspect him, after . . ." She trailed off uncertainly and took refuge in a big scoop of dessert.

"After what, Olivia?"

She stalled for a few moments, then said, "After what happened today."

So she did know. "Did he tell you or did you see the picture?"

"Jordan called me about the picture, so I called Adam to find out what really happened."

"Who's setting up whom?"

"No one. Adam really likes you, and a friend of Jordan's saw the picture pop up on a site and called him. That's all."

That wasn't even scratching the surface. Jordan was a little too in touch with the gossip community for my comfort, and Adam confiding feelings about me to Olivia didn't sit right, either. I felt manipulated, but I couldn't figure out where the puppet strings ended.

"Do you believe Gray about this afternoon?"

"No. He was looking for the tapes, I know he was."

"How do you know?"

"Because he called me at my office to ask me what I'd told you about them."

"Before or after he grilled me?"

"After."

So Gray hadn't believed either one of us when we'd said the tapes were gone, and he'd resorted to going to the Elliott apartment himself and digging around for them. Which meant that he didn't have them. But he'd been the one to take pains to make the distinction between killing Russell and taking the tapes. Did that mean he'd killed Russell?

I wasn't going to discuss that part with Olivia, but it did lead to another question. "But if he was in your dad's apartment after he talked to you, that means he thinks you're lying and you still have the tapes."

Her nose wrinkled in distaste. "It also means he thinks I'm dumb enough to keep them in the apartment."

"Are you?"

"Molly, I don't have the tapes. Remember?" she asked indignantly.

"Just checking."

A relieved smile spread across her face. "Oh, like *The Great Escape,* when the one guy has almost gotten away and he's getting on the bus and the German says, 'Have a nice trip,' and he says, 'Thank you,' automatically."

I smiled, too. "All my best technique comes from old movies. When necessary, I can do a little soft-shoe to get my point across."

She slapped her spoon on the table with sudden force. "It's just not right that you didn't get to meet him. You would have adored each other."

"Your dad?"

She nodded, trying not to cry. "He was a great listener, too. Micah said that all the time, that Dad heard people's souls. And he always said the right thing, and he had such a nice voice." She sniffed loudly, I offered her my napkin, but she used her own. "Would you like to hear?"

"His voice?"

"Yes."

"I didn't know he ever recorded anything."

Olivia looked at me as though I'd blurted out nonsense, then took her cell phone out of her bag. After punching a few keys, she handed it to me, eyes still bright with tears. "Listen."

I glanced at the screen, which read "Saved Message," then put the phone to my ear. A pleasantly rumbling voice, somewhat slurred, said, "Olivia, honey . . . I need your help. . . . It's all a lie, why didn't I see that? Everything I've built, destroyed. What's most precious, used against me. How did this . . . I can't . . . Please, I need you—"

I sat transfixed as Olivia slid the phone out of my hand and instructed it to save the message. She reached to put the phone back in her purse, but I shot out my hand. "Let me hear that again." Smiling sadly, she keyed it up again as I asked, "Is this the message you told me about? From the night he died?"

She nodded, nostrils flared to keep the tears at bay. "The last time I heard his voice, so I keep storing the message over and over. I'm not ready to let go yet."

I took the phone again and closed my eyes as I listened, concentrating as much as possible. The call was so clear, it had to be from a landline. The missing phone from the brass table. There was faint music in the background, but I couldn't identify it at all. Was it what he'd been running through the mixing board? Had he been playing the Hotel Tapes for someone?

There was also a rhythmic beat louder than the music, separate from it. Maybe Russell tapping his fingers on the brass table while he spoke, but he sounded a little too far gone to be keeping good time. A separate rhythm track?

But the sound I wanted to be most certain of came at the end of the message. The nails-on-the-chalkboard sound of the phone being pulled across the brass table. Someone pulling the phone away from Russell, leaving the scratches I'd seen in the brass and ending his last words to his daughter prematurely.

The killer came back into the room and, finding Russell still conscious and calling for help, pulled the phone out of reach and hung it up. Then took the phone away, worried about fingerprints or Russell trying to make another call, and took the tape off the deck and the rhythm track off whatever was playing it. And left Russell to die.

Olivia held out her hand for the phone. "Is there anyone your father would have played one of the Hotel Tapes for?" I asked, reluctantly returning it feeling much closer to an answer while I had it in my hand.

Olivia resaved the message while considering my question.

"I don't know. He didn't play them for me, that's for sure," she said with mounting bitterness. "I'm not a musician, after all. I can't appreciate certain things the way the rest of them can. I've been surrounded by music and musicians all my life, but that doesn't count. In the things that really matter, I don't measure up." She snapped the phone closed with such force that I expected it to shatter in her hand. Stuffing it back in her purse, she kept her face turned away from me, but I could hear her sniffing.

"You're the therapist here," I said gingerly, "but I have to say, I understand why you're angry. For your dad to be such a big part of your life, but he keeps you out of such a huge part of his . . . that's got to hurt."

She yanked the rubber band out of her hair and combed it out with her fingers, then drew it into a new ponytail so tight that it gave me a headache. "I loved my father."

"I know. But the people we love can still make us angry and vice versa. Believe me, I'm an expert in that field."

"So I'm angry. So what? Are you trying to accuse me of having something to do with my father's death?"

"No, I'm suggesting that your emotions might be clouding your thinking and keeping you from helping me figure things out. I know the tapes are a sore spot, but can you take a minute to think again—whom might he have played them for?"

Unhappy with her hair, and probably a lot more, she yanked the ponytail out yet again and redid it. After she'd pulled on it until the rubber band had to be embedded in the back of her head, she finally said, "Adam."

"He might have played the tapes for Adam?"

"He told me he was going to. Gray had been complaining to him about Adam losing focus, they needed to get him back in the groove. Dad thought hearing 'brand-new' tracks of Micah's would inspire him."

"Did he?"

Olivia poked her spoon around in her melting confection, intent on smashing the remaining frozen bits. "I'm not sure. I never asked."

"But . . . ?" She was holding on to something because she didn't want to give it up voluntarily, probably because it would feel like betraying someone.

"They were supposed to get together that day."

"The day your father died."

"Yes."

"And you never thought to mention that."

"Because it doesn't mean anything. I told you, Adam wouldn't hurt my father."

I could hear Peter Mulcahey laughing in the back of my head. "You can believe it of Claire, but not of Adam?"

"Claire's a bitch. Adam's wonderful. You don't know."

"Maybe you don't know. Maybe Adam's hidden things from you."

Olivia pushed her chair back from the table, poised for flight. "How can you talk about him that way? He's let you in, he never does that, and you're going to turn around and say these terrible things about him?"

I could hear the creaking gears as the drawbridge was being lifted and I dove across the moat, digging my fingers into the wood to hang on. "I'm sorry. I'm just trying to make sure we're not overlooking anything. Your father deserves that."

That mollified her for the moment and we sat in silence, no doubt thinking the same thing: Turn away from Adam and you were looking right at Claire. Which Olivia had been saying all along and I'd been resisting, not understanding why Claire didn't just take Russell to court if she wanted the tapes so badly. Of course, I also didn't understand why Scott

Petersen didn't just file for divorce, so I was willing to acknowledge that people make poor choices for terrible reasons.

Olivia had afternoon patients, so I told her she could go and I'd take care of the check. Picking up her coat and purse, she paused for a moment. "Thank you for caring this much. And for bailing me out."

"No problem, but I am curious. Why hadn't you called anyone?"

"Who do I have to call?" She smiled sadly and slipped out of the restaurant.

Working and living where I do, I come in contact with a lot of people I envy. When I'd first met Olivia, I'd envied her, growing up among brilliantly talented musicians, hanging out with other celebrities, traveling, partying, being a cool kid on a global scale. I never would've guessed that she saw herself as the outsider, not good enough for her father's inner circle, no family and no friends she could turn to when she was in trouble.

Almost four o'clock. It was late enough and I had survived sufficient public encounters that I felt justified in hiding/working at home the rest of the day. I even chose to walk and see what that which passes for fresh air in New York City might do toward clearing my head. It's strange how invigorating the cacophony of city noise can be, like a grand, symphonic backdrop to your thoughts, *Rhapsody in Blue* swelling around you while you try to make sense of your life and resolve all its crazy chords.

But even as I strove to lay out the pros and cons of Adam being involved in Russell's death, my thoughts kept straying back to Olivia and her friendless state. So, preferring to think of it as appreciation rather than schadenfreude, I called Tricia as I walked, one more rude Manhattanite having a private conversation as she marched down Lexington Avenue. "Thank you for being my friend."

"A little early in the afternoon to be buzzed and sentimental, isn't it?" she asked cheerfully. "Where are you? I'll come join you."

"I've had nothing but caffeine and chocolate today."

"Oh, one of those moods. PMS or your story?"

"Way to stomp all over a heartfelt expression of gratitude."

"Okay, I'm guessing, PMS *and* the story."

"I'm guessing I'm hanging up and calling Cassady."

"No, wait, you can't do that until I tell you the most amazing thing that happened today."

"Yet another embarrassing picture of me is bouncing around the Internet and you haven't given me a hard time about it yet?"

"Let me rephrase that: The most amazing thing that happened today that doesn't have anything to do with you. Except in a very peripheral way because you introduced us."

"What happened?"

"Jordan Crowley wrote me a song."

"Wow. Rock muse is a role that suits you," I said, impressed both by what had happened and by what I must have missed. "How much time have you two been spending together?"

"He wants to do this party tomorrow, so we've been joined at the hip all day. It's going to be great, and you're invited, by the way. Nine o'clock at Pillow."

"Where?"

"An after-hours club in TriBeCa. Jordan hangs out there a lot and says it's a great space. I'm running over for a quick tour."

"So the song is an homage to your event-planning skills?"

"No, it's about how he can't stop thinking about me."

I could feel her beaming over the phone, and as much as I wanted to warn her about the craziness I was encountering in this group, I wasn't about to rain on this parade. "Smart guy.

He should keep you around. Adam keeps talking about how Jordan can't finish his new album. You're the influence he needs."

"He and Adam don't like each other very much, do they."

"Why?"

"Jordan told me Adam's unstable. Even attacked Gray once."

I stopped, trying to reconcile this with my own experiences with Adam, until the not-so-gentle nudges of my fellow pedestrians reminded me that I was in a crosswalk and I hurried to the other side before zipping taxis could slice me in two. "Apparently, Gray provokes that reaction in a lot of people," I said, thinking of Olivia more than trying to justify Adam.

"According to Jordan, Bonnie won't be in a room alone with Adam, but Claire won't admit anything's wrong, so he's not getting the help he needs."

Risa had commented on his bad temper, too. Could it be bad enough to be deadly? Peter Mulcahey was laughing again. "Did Jordan accuse him of killing Russell?"

"Oh, no, no," Tricia said hastily. "He was probably just trying to make himself look better by comparison, but I thought I should mention it."

"Yeah, thanks." The storm cloud had passed right over her parade and dumped on mine. Tricia and I had both spent the day with rock stars and what did we have to show for it? She had a song. I had a murder suspect.

13

Dear Molly,

What makes bad boys so captivating? Why will good girls who know much, much better make stupid decisions based on the behavior of a bad boy? Do we really think we can save them, or do we actually want them to break us down? Or is it that we know that chances are, it's going to go badly no matter what and it's easier to walk away from a scoundrel than a saint?

Signed,
Quivering Quandary

"Hey, Molly, are things serious with you and Adam Crowley?"

For a moment, I thought it was Peter again and I considered making a pointed hand gesture to underscore my annoyance with his joke. Thankfully, I hesitated just long enough to see that the silhouette in front of my apartment building entrance was far rounder than Peter. And seemed to be wearing a bush jacket and carrying a camera.

In midflight, my gesture morphed into an awkward wave, saving me from the third installment in my Triptych of Humiliation. "Hello," I said as he stepped out from under the awning, giving me a clear look. "I remember you. You spoiled my breakfast yesterday."

He lifted the impressively complex camera to his eye. "Where's Adam?" he asked as the shutter *whoosh*ed.

Of course he was going to take my picture. I'd just walked over twenty blocks in a wind strong enough to make my hair, which normally won't do anything, twist itself into balloon animals. "I'd make a ridiculous face to try and ruin your picture, but that's the one you'd try hardest to sell, right?" I turned my back on him, but he circled around in front of me, snapping away.

"You're not answering my question."

I had too many questions of my own to answer anyone else's, which was the main reason that, while Adam had called my cell six times since I'd left the school, I hadn't returned a single one. Men always pick the wrong time to get talkative.

I covered my face with my hand. "Because you didn't ask the right one, which is: May I take your picture? How 'bout I ask you one: How did you find out where I live?"

"You must pay those assistants at *Zeitgeist* lousy."

I dropped my hand. "Who was it?"

He stopped snapping for a moment and frowned thoughtfully. It was a pleasant enough face when there wasn't a camera in front of it, apple-cheeked with a scruffy beard, warm brown eyes. A sort of Santa-needs-some-time-in-rehab charm. "Do you reveal your sources?"

"No."

"Neither do I."

"Not quite the same thing."

"No difference from where I sit."

"May I suggest where you should sit, then?"

"Come on now, I thought we were going to be friends."

"Are your photographs as creative as your thought processes?"

I said with a frown that he instantly photographed. "I don't even know your name."

"Kenny. Kenny Crandall." He wiped his hand on the thigh of his jeans before he offered it to me, which struck me as very thoughtful. As was the fact that he didn't crunch my hand when he shook it, though his hand was large enough to easily inflict injury.

"So be honest with me, Kenny Crandall. My own mother wouldn't find my comings and goings this interesting. You're after something specific."

"A shot of Adam Crowley leaving here in the early morning with a big smile on his face."

"You weren't planning on holding your breath, were you?"

"My editor said to sit on you until I got something, and no way I'm gonna tell him no."

"Come on, Kenny. Who's your editor and what did I ever do to him?"

"Jeremy Berkinholtz."

"Oh."

Pop went the balloon of righteous indignation. Yes, I knew Jeremy Berkinholtz. Worse, I knew exactly what I had done to him. We'd worked together at *Bottled Lightning,* a quirky magazine with the lofty aspiration of "examining the creative process," and I'd had much better luck getting ideas approved by the editor than he had, a fact that Jeremy attributed solely to the editor's desire to sleep with me. A theory he chose to espouse in front of the editor. So the editor chose to fire him.

To this day, according to the publishing grapevine, Jeremy blamed me for derailing his career and exiling him to tabloids like *Slice,* his current domain. His whining wouldn't have bothered me at all except that he turned out to be dead on about the editor's intentions, so I wound up quitting the job Jeremy had so coveted. He'd been a first-class jerk about the whole thing, but he'd also been on to the truth while I'd been in complete denial. Maybe it wasn't guilt I felt as much as embarrassment.

"How is Jeremy?" I asked.

"A pompous cretin, but he's the boss. So when's Adam coming over?" Kenny looked at his watch. "Do I have time to grab a burger?"

"Adam's not coming here. The picture this afternoon was a mistake, I'm not involved with him."

Kenny stroked his beard as he analyzed me. "You're actually telling me the truth."

"Yes."

"I tried to tell Jeremy that the dude was already hooked up, but he saw that shot of the two of you and just lost it, wanted to slap you and Adam all over the paper."

"Adam's hooked up?" I asked, then quickly clarified, "I'm asking for professional reasons, not personal. He hadn't mentioned that."

"Really?" Kenny asked with a tantalizing hint of how shocking I'd find the name once I'd heard it.

Given what Risa had said about Adam's romantic history, his current attachment was probably fashionable but disposable and had no bearing on my investigation. Except that he'd hidden it from me, along with his penchant for roughing people up, and the thing I need to know most is whatever people won't tell me. Kenny was going to enjoy this more than I was. "Go ahead. Tell me who it is," I said, letting pride fall before a story.

Kenny smiled so broadly that his cheeks nearly obscured his eyes. "What're you gonna give me?"

"Hey! What happened to our being friends?"

"Guess you were right, I didn't have enough imagination." I deserved that one, so I couldn't do anything but laugh.

Pleased, Kenny joined in for a moment, then said, "Seriously, what're you gonna give me?"

I held out my hand. "You're gonna give me your card, and I'm gonna get you a meeting with Connie Hamilton, our photography editor."

Kenny's shaggy brows drew down, casting a shadow across his jolly face. "That's not funny."

"Cross my heart and hope to stay on your good side. I know how difficult it is to get your break. I can't speak for Connie, but I can get you in to see her. Unless moving from your rag to our rag doesn't strike you as upward mobility."

Kenny fumbled a business card out of his wallet, eyes on me the whole time, as though I would make a face or otherwise betray my insincerity the moment he looked away. Not until the card had been stowed in my wallet did he seem to relax a bit and consider trusting me.

"So, who's he with?"

"Olivia Elliott."

I felt like laughing again, but at myself this time. I should have asked a few more questions before buying into the concept that Kenny had worthwhile information. "No, he's not," I protested, ready to renege on my promise to bring him in to Connie.

"Friend of mine's been watching the Crowley brothers for a while now, got this tip that Adam's been spending quality time with Olivia Elliott. Checked out."

"So they spend time together. That's not a surprise, they're practically brother and sister."

"You meet your brother at the SoHo Grand? On a regular basis?"

What is it they teach you in driver's ed about skidding on the ice—despite your instincts otherwise, don't slam on the brakes, steer into the skid and pump the brakes? "I'd meet my brother for drinks there. The SoHo Grand has several nice bars."

"So you'd think they'd stay downstairs and enjoy them now and then."

I was going to protest one more time, that the nicest bar at the SoHo Grand was on the second floor, but sometimes, no matter how hard you pump the brakes, you skid off the road and slam into a tree. Olivia and Adam? No. That would mean they'd both been lying to me. On multiple fronts. Which threatened the integrity of everything I'd constructed about Russell's death. Could I have been that foolish, that starstruck, that taken in? There had to be some explanation we were missing. Didn't there?

I tried to figure out what Kenny stood to gain by lying. Nothing. "You're being straight with me."

Kenny nodded. "Sorry."

"No need, because there was nothing going on. But it does give me food for thought on a couple of other levels." I shook his hand again. "Thank you, Kenny. I'll talk to Connie tomorrow and give you a call."

Kenny thanked me with a dubious smile and, after a moment's hesitation, drifted down the street. I knew he didn't believe I'd bring him in. I also knew there was a chance he was going to lurk around the corner for another couple of hours until he accepted that Adam wasn't going to show up, but that was his prerogative, and I couldn't spend time right now convincing him otherwise. I had work to do. More than I'd realized.

In my apartment, I got into research mode. I changed into my writing clothes—supremely broken-in Diesel jeans, a Washington Redskins sweatshirt, and bare feet—tore open a bag of cheddar-and-sour-cream Ruffles, poured two Starbucks DoubleShot Lights over ice, and put *Film at Eleven* in the CD player. With the groove dug, I slid in and began the teeth-grinding process of reexamining everything I thought I knew.

Suppose Kenny was right. I skipped right over what that said about Adam being manipulative and my being gullible and all the emotional issues that called up, and did my utmost to concentrate on the fact that it was now even less surprising that Olivia was upset at my suggestion that Adam was involved in Russell's death: I'd accused her boyfriend of knocking off her dad.

But if they were seeing each other, why hadn't either one admitted to it? Why hadn't anyone else in the family mentioned it? Or didn't any one of them know, either? Why would Adam and Olivia keep it secret?

Claire.

If Claire had so much control over Adam's professional life, it wasn't hard to believe that she watched his personal life rather carefully, too. Based on Claire's low opinion of Olivia, she would not be Claire's first choice as a partner for her little boy, so it made sense that they'd keep it to themselves. And since they all lived on top of one another on Riverside Drive, slipping away to a hotel did a lot to help maintain the secret.

But why not tell me? I wouldn't have exposed them. At least until press time. Why lie to me? So he could flirt with me and she could befriend me and they could keep tabs on what I was figuring out about Russell's death? They only needed to worry about that if they were concerned I was going to find out something that put them in a bad light. Then they'd be playing innocent so I'd think they were. What did they know? Worse, what had they done?

I answered the phone so automatically that it didn't really register it was in my hand and I was talking until Cassady said, "He's cheating on me."

"No, he's not, because we weren't together and I'm not

a hundred percent sure they're together, but it does look pretty bad," I said, feeling a queasiness exceeding the Ruffles-Starbucks combination.

"Hey, Molly? Let me try this again. *He's* cheating on *me*."

The fact that there were other people in the world came back to me a little belatedly. "Wait. Aaron?"

"Yes, Aaron. He's the only man I'm seeing right now because he's the one who's cheating, not me."

"I refuse to believe that."

"Based on?"

"The fact that there's got to be one good man in the world."

"Sure, but you're dating him, not me."

"Let's come back to that. What makes you think Aaron's cheating on you?"

"I called him. At home. And the grad student answered."

"She of the bogus results?"

"The same."

"So he's giving her a second chance. That proves he's a marvelous and compassionate human being, not that he's cheating on you."

"She was in his house."

"I thought his students hung out with him a lot. Weren't you the one that said it was charming that he was so accessible to them?"

"I think his definition of 'accessible' might differ a bit from mine. And she was laughing."

"She had a brush with academic annihilation and he snatched her back from the brink."

"Why are you defending him?"

"Isn't that why you called me? So I could talk you down?" There was a long pause. "Did you talk to Aaron?"

"Yes."

"What did he say?"

"That the whole research group was there and they thought they'd found a way to salvage the paper," she said, sounding as though I were forcing her to admit that she still believed in the Tooth Fairy.

"More cause for laughter!" I said, happy myself that someone's problems seemed fixable.

"So I'm a jealous shrew," she sniffed.

"No, you're a woman in love who's frustrated that she can't see her guy as often as she'd like."

"Why am I so angry?"

"Because you don't handle being vulnerable very well, not having had much practice. Hard not to be in the driver's seat, isn't it?"

"I'm going to ignore that question. By the way, speaking of driver's seats, Olivia's lawyer was a little reticent on specifics, since the estate hasn't been administered yet, but Russell's death doesn't seem to improve Claire's position at all."

"Really?"

"Olivia and I told him we were interested in doing a multimedia project that would feature the music of Subject to Change, and in light of Russell's death, we wanted to know who had to sign off."

"Besides Claire."

"In his original will, Micah left control of the music to Claire and Russell. Equally. But not too long before he died, Mr. Drug-Addled Rock Star got a little paranoid about who would control things further down the line. So he had the language amended so that upon Russell's death, all control over the music would be redistributed equally between Claire and 'the three children,' as the lawyer referred to them the entire meeting."

"Olivia, Jordan, and Adam?"

"Right. With Russell, she had veto power. Now, she's one against three."

"So Claire loses rather than gains."

"And she didn't know that, according to the lawyer, until after Russell's death. But if she did know, it takes away her motive, doesn't it?"

I actually shivered as I considered the implications but made one more try. "Unless she feels she can control the three of them. And couldn't control Russell."

"Hmmm . . . If we're motive surfing, I'd think it more likely that one of the three of them wanted more of a say in things."

She was right, of course, but that meant accepting the notion that Adam was involved in this, which I was still resisting for some intuitive reason I couldn't force out into the light. "Thanks for going with her."

"It was almost fun. I think I'd make an excellent producer. I don't have to apologize to the scholastic siren, do I?" she asked without even taking a breath between the two thoughts.

"Have you called her names, flamed her Facebook page, or sold her identity to foreign nationals?"

"Remind me never to cross you."

"You'll have dinner with Aaron tomorrow night and all will be well."

She sighed, but happily this time. "I knew I'd feel better after I talked to you. I should know better than to jump to conclusions."

We agreed to touch base later in the evening and hung up. Gnawing on the inside of my cheek, I wondered whether I was jumping to conclusions or seeing the light with Olivia and Adam. It was easy to reassure Cassady because I wanted things to be good for her and Aaron. Was I resisting believing Olivia and Adam were together because I didn't want to accept that I'd missed it or that Adam had played me for a sucker?

If Adam was involved in Russell's death, Olivia couldn't know—could she?

My contemplation of that horrifying thought was short-lived, because the doorman buzzed. But rather than Todd on the phone, it was Kyle. I could picture Todd cowering in the corner. "Tell me you haven't eaten."

I looked at the appallingly empty bag of chips. "I haven't."

"I'm coming up, and you better have red wine."

I had a bottle of Barboursville Sangiovese, and he had lasagna, garlic bread, and chopped salad from a café around the corner from the precinct run by a guy he'd gone to high school with. I uncorked the wine while he opened the containers, but I watched him out of the corner of my eye the whole time, wondering if he was waiting for me to kiss him or if I was supposed to wait for him to kiss me. This whole going back to the beginning business, while intensely romantic, was also confusing.

"Am I allowed to kiss you?" I asked lightly.

"Encouraged," he said, licking tomato sauce off the back of his hand.

I slid into his arms and kissed him slowly, savoring the taste of his mouth and the traces of tomato sauce. He smiled, holding me tight against him. "I've never kissed a celebrity before."

I dropped my head back in mock anguish and he kissed the hollow of my neck, so he couldn't have been too upset. "Did you see the picture?"

"Gotta check out the evidence," he murmured against my neck.

"It's not what it seems."

"Never is."

"There really is an explanation," I said.

"You mentioned."

"That mainly involves my being an idiot."

He scooped my face into his hands and kissed me hard on the mouth. "Stop."

"But I want to explain." I also wanted to talk through the "Adam as killer" scenario with someone who'd be brutally honest—and force me to be, too.

"After we eat. The lasagna's getting cold."

Not wanting to stack the deck or come between a man and his pasta, I demurred. We jostled in my little kitchen while we dished up the food, bumping into each other on purpose, just generally goofing around. Even if this wasn't exactly where we'd started the first time, it was a good place to start again.

The lasagna was amazing, though I didn't want to think about what it was going to do to my cholesterol count, but the best part of the meal was that we ate it sitting side by side on my couch, feet up on the coffee table and ankles entwined. The moment was beautiful in its simplicity and even more so in its rarity, and I hated to be the one to let reality intrude, but as Kyle started to top off my wineglass, I had to. "Hang on. I have to go out for a little while at seven-thirty and I can't be buzzed. Can you stay? I'll hurry back."

"Something for work?" he said, leaving my wineglass as it was and pouring more into his own. Guess that meant he was staying.

"Yes."

"Adam Crowley?"

"Related. Literally. His mother. A command performance, and she did the commanding."

"You in trouble for kissing her son?"

"I hope not."

"Tell her it was research."

"It was. I went to see him because things other people were saying about him weren't adding up, but then he got all passionate with me—"

"Passionate?" He tried to arch his eyebrows, but it wasn't an expression that came naturally to him, so he looked vaguely ridiculous.

"Everybody tells me something different about him, and I can't get a good read on him—" I stopped because Kyle inhaled as though he were about to say something of some gravity, but he stopped. "What?"

He paused a split second, then said, "You've got satellite, I'll keep myself amused."

"What is it?"

He shook his head and picked up his wineglass. "Might even read a book."

"You were going to say something and you stopped."

Swirling the wine in his glass, he held it up to the light. "I know it's supposed to cling to the sides, but I can never remember why."

"What were you going to say?"

"Has anyone ever told you you're tenacious?" he asked with a touch of sharpness.

"Why?"

"Because that's really just a nice way of calling someone stubborn."

"Is that something you'd like to do?"

He set down his glass firmly. "I was going to say something about your little friend, and I stopped myself because we agreed that we were going to stay out of each other's work. So you need to let it go now."

I couldn't let it go, but I couldn't ask him again, not after that pronouncement. Scraping at the last little bit of mozzarella sticking to my plate, I hoped the burning desire to ask him what he'd been going to say would pass, but it didn't. I was about to sacrifice all the ground we'd gained by insisting he tell me anyway when someone knocked on the door.

I made what I hoped was a charming face as I went to answer it. "Which neighbor smelled the lasagna and wants to join us?" At the door, I looked through the peephole at Adam Crowley.

Swamped by a wave of conflicting emotions, I threw open the door. Predominantly, I was irritated that he'd come, doubly irritated that Todd had let him up without calling. The fact that Todd was standing at the elevator with a huge, google-eyed grin didn't help at all.

"You know Adam Crowley! That's so cool!" Todd enthused as he disappeared back into the elevator.

"Sweet kid," Adam said, an odd tone to his voice. He leaned forward, apparently planning on kissing me, and lost his balance. It wasn't until he thrust out his arm awkwardly to brace himself against the wall and almost missed that it registered that he was drunk. Plowed, actually.

"How did you know where I live?"

"I have the world at my fingertips," he said, waggling the fingers of his free hand in my face. "Google." He leaned in to give me a wink and nearly toppled over.

I pushed him back up into a vaguely vertical position.

"What the hell are you doing here?"

"I need you," he said, having trouble staying steady even while holding on to the wall.

"No, you don't. You need to leave."

"You're the only—"

"Stop. Don't jerk me around, Adam."

"Don't be mad. . . ."

"You're a liar."

"No . . ."

Kyle's hand brushed lightly across my back as he stepped into the doorway with me. He looked Adam over quickly and frowned in disapproval.

"Call a cab, I'll take him back downstairs."

"No," Adam said thickly. "Need your . . . help . . ."

"Yeah, lean on me, brother, and leave the lady alone." Kyle reached out to take Adam's arm, and Adam pushed away, stumbling and flailing. The frown on Kyle's face shifted quickly, and he grabbed both of Adam's arms, peering into his eyes. "What are you on, Adam?"

"Nothing . . ." Adam tried to focus on Kyle's face, but he didn't seem to be having much success.

"Where have you been?" Kyle asked.

"Not sure . . ."

"Were you alone?"

"Maybe . . ."

"Were you given anything to eat or drink?"

"You think someone drugged him?" I asked.

Kyle didn't answer, but Adam's head tilted toward me oddly, and he might have nodded if he hadn't been busy collapsing to the floor.

14

Showering with a man is a pleasure I've experienced only a few times. Showering with two men is one I hadn't even dreamed of. But had I dreamed it, standing under ice-cold water fully dressed and hoping that one of the men didn't throw up on the other would not have figured as prominently in the scenario as they did in real life.

Kyle had swept Adam off the hallway floor and into the bathroom before I could even process that he'd collapsed. By the time I joined them, Adam was vomiting furiously into the toilet as Kyle hung on to the back of his jacket with one hand and cranked up the shower with the other. When Adam's stomach seemed to have emptied itself, Kyle hauled him into the shower, barely allowing me to strip off Adam's leather jacket, which had to have cost more than my rent. I tossed the jacket into my bedroom and doused the bathroom with Lysol spray. Then Adam lurched and fought him a bit, so even though there wasn't really room for all three of us, I stepped in to do what I could to help. It was easy to be noble knowing that everything I was wearing was machine washable.

"Good thing you got him in here before he started getting sick," I said, squinting against the water.

Kyle shrugged, oblivious to the water and the cold. "I induced vomiting."

Adam moaned. I started to ask Kyle how, then knew I didn't really want to know, so I clamped my mouth shut. Adam moaned more loudly, eyes struggling to open, flailing a little.

Kyle smiled. "I won't even make you tell me what you were going to ask that time."

"You're a better man than I am, Gunga Din. Or at least a wetter man."

"I'd applaud, but I might drop your buddy."

"No buddy of mine. He made a fool of me, to throw me off course," I said, angrier than I'd be willing to admit.

"You think he's involved?"

"Excellent chance."

Adam roused a bit more, trying to free himself from Kyle's grasp and getting nowhere. Kyle squinted at him. "Maybe I should drop him."

"Just do it hard."

"Not that he'd feel it. He's not just drunk, he's on something. Question is, what?"

"Oh no," I said, my own stomach lurching as an awful thought hit me. "Valium and Jack?"

Kyle recognized the song and remembered the stories about Micah and Russell, but I hadn't told him about the concert. I filled him in while we hauled Adam back out of the shower and I pulled every towel I had off the shelves. "A combo like that, anyway."

Adam was awake enough to sit on the toilet while Kyle stripped off wet shoes and shirt. "You seen him naked?"

"Of course not," I said indignantly.

"Keep it that way. Step out and let me do this. Grab that old blue-and-white bathrobe of yours, I'll throw him in that."

"What about you?"

"My old—" He stopped, smiling ruefully. "I don't have any clothes here anymore, do I?"

We'd been so close to living together that he'd had a nearly complete wardrobe here, but it had all left with him. All but one piece. "Actually, there was a pair of sweats that I never got back to you."

"Good planning."

By the time Kyle guided Adam out of the bathroom, I'd changed clothes, too, putting on my favorite Ralph Lauren linen pantsuit, my lucky armor for tough interviews. But as I tried to fluff my damp hair into some sort of shape, I almost changed back into my jeans. What was I thinking? I couldn't go meet with Claire Crowley while her drug-laden son crashed in my apartment with my boyfriend.

"Why not?" that boyfriend asked. "She doesn't have to know he's here. In fact, it'd be interesting to find out where she thinks he is, if she gives any indication that he might be in trouble."

Propped up in my leather armchair, a flannel throw tucked around him, Adam looked oddly vulnerable. As he struggled back to coherency, it was impossible to see the charming and seductive fellow who had danced me around earlier in the day. The image of the tortured artist, the bad boy with a song to sing, was gone completely. All I saw was a damp, shivering mess. But now that he'd shifted over to the suspect list, I couldn't feel sorry for him. "Do you think he did this to himself? Another Crowley OD?"

Kyle, on the other hand, looked even better than he had when he'd arrived, although his wet hair was a little crazy and he was wearing gunmetal sweats and an old flannel shirt of mine that he hadn't gotten around to buttoning yet. Another reason I didn't want to leave. But Kyle was practically shoving me out the door. "My gut says no, but I'll sober him up while you're gone, try to find out."

"What if he killed Russell?"

"I've been around murder suspects before and survived. And if he confesses while you're gone, I'll write everything down, I promise."

"You're sure he doesn't need a doctor?"

"I'll call at the first sign of trouble. I know the number."

"Mine or the paramedics?"

"Molly, do you trust me?" Kyle grabbed the door and swung it half-closed so I couldn't go back into the apartment and check on Adam again.

"Of course I do."

"Then go do your job. I'll take care of him." He said it with firmness bordering on irritation, so I backed away from the door.

I didn't know how to thank him for his help without making it sound as though I thought he was working with or for or through me or whatever. I opened my mouth to see if something lovely and inspired would come out, and he pointed to the elevator. "Go."

Todd scrambled up to me as I came out of the elevator, babbling something about never having seen a rock star up close and was he going to be staying long. I cut him off. "Do not tell anyone he's here. Anyone. If word gets out, I'll know it was you, Todd, and it won't be pretty." Todd stood at attention and mimed locking his lips and throwing away the key. I felt so safe.

The true feeling of danger didn't wrap its icy hands around my digestive tract until Claire Crowley was facing me, sitting on the other side of a dining room table that could double as a bowling lane, given its sheen and length. A fully loaded cocktail tray, deposited on the table by a Filipino steward who had come and gone in silence, sat at her elbow, featuring cut crystal decanters with a rainbow of contents. I wondered which one had the Jack and which had the Valium but decided to hold that question until a more opportune time.

Claire was dressed to intimidate in a plunging Roberto Cavalli silk halter and towering Steve Madden red leather slingbacks. Perhaps she had an event to go to after she finished scratching out my eyes and was confident that she'd do a skilled enough job that she didn't need to worry about getting blood on her outfit.

"You've been avoiding me," she began, her voice measured but her unhappiness coming through loud and clear.

"Not intentionally," I said, deciding to start with breezy, then see how the conversation devolved from there. "But several of your inner circle have kept me quite busy, so I'm sorry if I've appeared neglectful."

Claire folded her lips into a thin arc that was a distant relative of a smile. "I want you to leave my son alone." She tapped on the tabletop with a crimson nail for emphasis.

Kyle was right. I was going to get yelled at for kissing Adam. "That implies you think I've been bothering Adam," I said, going for a slightly hurt tone.

"Pursuing, bothering, whatever you'd like to call it."

"It must be difficult to be the mother of a very handsome, very talented man. My mother wanted to put up an electric fence and my brother was only varsity basketball, with none of Adam's money and only half his charm. So I understand that you're compelled to eye every woman who draws breath within a mile of him with suspicion, but I've been chasing a story, not your son."

"How do you explain that picture this afternoon?"

"A joke." In so many ways. "Ask him. Or his real girlfriend."

"He isn't seeing anyone."

Discretion is hard for me, but I gave it another try and didn't say anything about the alleged trysts with Olivia at the SoHo Grand. "What a shame." Maybe she didn't know. Was it possible that despite her location at the center of the Crowley solar system, with all its bright stars and wobbly satellites, there were holes in her knowledge? What else might she not know about? If Adam did have something to do with Russell's death, could she genuinely be unaware?

Claire glared at me briefly, impatient with my thoughtful silence, then slid a plain manila envelope across the table to me. It was flat and not obviously ticking, but I was still reluctant to pick it up. "Go ahead," she urged. "It's for you."

"You shouldn't have," I said, my hands still in my lap.

"Open it. It's your article."

"You couldn't have." Incredulous, I opened the envelope and let the contents, photographs and documents that looked like press releases, slide out.

"We didn't actually write it for you—"

"Thanks for that—"

"—but Gray and I did assemble everything you'll need to write a lovely and well-balanced piece about Olivia."

"Without talking to anyone else."

"Exactly."

"And by 'well-balanced,' you mean a piece that presents your point of view as the only correct one."

"I think you'll see that's best for everyone. Care for a drink?"

Taking a drink from her seemed to rank right up there with taking an apple from a humpbacked witch in the woods, so I declined. Sliding the items back into the envelope, I tried to imagine the thought process that had led up to the filling of the envelope in the first place. Who would think that I would take it with a smile and say thank you? A woman who was awfully used to getting her own way and traveling in pretty tight circles. Still. "I have to ask you, Mrs. Crowley, what makes you think that I'll take this information and go away?"

"If you refuse, I can either tell your editor and publisher to kill this story . . . or I can write you a check."

"My choices are blackmail or bribery? I'm shocked, Mrs. Crowley. Shocked."

"You're offended. I get that. I can make the check out to the charity of your choice, if you prefer. If you haven't embraced a particular cause, I can give you some suggestions."

Willing not only to bribe me, but to structure the bribe so it was politically correct. Here was a full frontal shot of the control freak who'd been lurking under the surface all along. It was rather amazing to see her reveal herself so blatantly. I pushed the envelope back to her. "No, thank you."

"You're being foolish. There's no story here."

"Then why are you trying so hard to keep me away from something that doesn't exist?"

"Because you're stirring up a lot of ridiculous talk and unnecessary attention that Adam and the others don't need. They've been subjected to it enough in their lives. Forgive a mother for wanting to protect them whenever possible."

"Even if they don't deserve protecting?"

Her hands slapped the tabletop with such force that my own palms burned. "This is what I'm talking about. Speculation. Gossip. And the wrong kind of attention. My son didn't do anything wrong. None of us did anything wrong."

"But Russell Elliott's dead."

"His choice."

"Like Micah before him."

"Do not go there."

I started to ask her where she thought I was going, then I

saw it on her face. "You mean, to where the two men who had having you in common both killed themselves?"

She was hurt, and I didn't feel bad about that at all. She had no trouble impugning my character, so as unused to it as she seemed to be, she could take a little impugning right back. "Is that what you're worried about? People are going to start talking about that? Aren't you just glad they're still talking about you at all?"

Claire stood, nails whisking along the sides of her skirt, looking for something to claw and being restrained from reaching across the table for my face. "How unprofessional."

"Says the woman who just tried to buy me off."

"I offered you something for your trouble."

"Exactly. If there really were no story here, you'd ignore me. You might as well hang Christmas lights on the fact that you're hiding something."

She came around the table so quickly, I didn't have time to back up or get away. Anger had drained most of the color from her face, and her hand was ice cold as it squeezed down on mine, grinding the knuckles of my index finger and pinkie together.

"All I ever tried to do is protect my family," she said with a grim huskiness. "My husband had a child with another woman, but I kept us together, kept us happy. He died, but I kept us together, kept us happy. Now my best friend is dead, too, and I will not let it destroy us."

"It's not me you want to crush, you want to destroy the story. And it's too late. Everybody's talking about the Hotel Tapes, about who's got them. You can get me tossed, but the story's going to keep bumping along until someone gets an answer they like."

"Those damn tapes," she snarled, pushing away from me

and retreating to her side of the table again. "I'd burn them again, just give me the chance."

"Why?" I asked, saving the discussion of whether she'd truly burned them for a later moment.

She dropped one ice cube into a crystal tumbler and stared at it, as though waiting for it to request what should be poured over it. "Imagine being married to Pablo Picasso and discovering an entire warehouse filled with sketches and paintings he'd done while he was apart from you. One day, you get the chance to go through the warehouse and you discover that the art in there is beautiful. Breathtaking. More wonderful than any of the work he's ever shown you. But in that entire warehouse, you find just one sketch of you. Only one."

Distracted by the four fingers of vodka she poured over the ice cube, I was a beat behind her. "You burned the Hotel Tapes because there was only one song about you?"

She smiled at me sadly. "I loved Micah Crowley from the moment I saw him, hunched over his guitar, sitting on the brick wall outside the college bookstore. He had nothing and I didn't care. I believed in him, sacrificed for him, forgave him. And he wrote me one single song. The selfish bastard."

According to Lennon and McCartney, "In the end, the love you take is equal to the love you make." Does that imply the existence of other mathematical theorems useful in computing the tipping point of a relationship? To quantify when the love that's gained is negated by the hurt that's inflicted, when the promises that are made are overwhelmed by the lies that are told? We all keep tallies, even if we never intend or expect to even the score. Whatever accounting method she'd used, Claire had crunched the numbers and found Micah wanting.

"Which song?"

She shook her head. "He never even recorded it. Except on those damn tapes. So it's gone forever."

"Why did you stay with him?"

She wasn't prepared for the question, and I wasn't prepared for the spasm of vulnerability that crossed her face. "I have a son."

Rock-and-roll royalty at its proudest. The dynasty must continue, my son must rule. Even at the expense of other people's lives. "A high cost for a son who doesn't care about rock and roll very much," I said quietly.

I'd meant to offer some perspective, but I could tell by the rage in her eyes that I'd gone too far. "He's finding his way back, seeking inspiration," she said in very careful syllables. "His next album will be brilliant."

"The jazz album."

For a moment, I thought she was going to vaporize and, just maybe, take me with her. Then she gathered herself with such force that the air pressure in the room shifted. "He must have put on quite a show for you."

I had my feet too firmly planted and couldn't dodge that zinger. "Meaning?"

"This esoteric jazz bullshit. It's misdirection, to diminish expectations before his second album." She said it with great authority, but I wasn't convinced. He might have been feigning a lot of things, including his innocence and his interest in me, but his passion for jazz had been clear. "Rock is in his blood," Claire continued.

"Like a virus?"

"Like his DNA. He writes and sings just like his father. And all it'll take is one great song to get back on top."

"So he mentioned."

"He'll write it, he'll feel that fire, it will all come flooding back."

"Are we talking about recording music or resurrecting your husband?"

She smiled, a dark and oily smile, pleased that she was seeing some great truth I was missing. "Both," she said.

Unease gnawed at the base of my neck, teasing the hairs upright. Could this be why I'd been resisting Adam as a suspect? "Did Russell feel the same way?"

"Russell loved Adam and wanted what was best for him. Would have done anything for him."

"Except give him the Hotel Tapes."

Claire's face twisted, her eyes corkscrewing shut as though she were battling an instantaneous migraine. "They're gone!"

"Russell wanted Adam to find his own way. You wanted your husband back, even if it meant force-feeding your son his music."

"Good night."

"Did you drug Russell so you could search his apartment, or did you plan to kill him all along so Adam would have no support?" I hadn't intended to accuse her, but the pieces were all sliding together so neatly, it practically said itself.

"Get out." Claire walked out of the room without a look back. The steward appeared to make sure I went straight to the front door, did not pass other doorways, did not collect more hypotheses. But I did sweep the manila envelope off the table for curiosity's sake.

When Olivia had first suggested Claire was responsible for Russell's death, I'd been framing it in terms of money and control of the estate. But Claire wanted to control the family. Specifically, her son. Get the fulfillment from him she hadn't gotten from her husband. Once she got him back into the limelight where she wanted him, Adam had better make sure to write her an awful lot of songs.

How could I prove it was Claire? As Kyle had said all along, there wasn't much evidence to work with. But if she'd gotten help from someone, like Gray Benedek, there might be a way to play them off against each other and force the weaker hand. Especially if it looked as though Adam were in trouble.

I hoped Adam would be able to explain more about what had happened to him by the time I got back to the apartment, but he was so deeply immersed in a game of cribbage that he was reluctant to talk to me.

Rather than sheltering a tense and quiet vigil, my living room had become the setting of a happy little house party. In my absence, Tricia and Cassady had arrived, hoping to surprise me, and declared themselves responsible for Kyle and Adam until I returned. Popcorn had been popped, shoes had been kicked off, cocktails had been mixed—for everyone but Adam—and the mood was much more convivial than when I'd departed. More on the order of the cool kids keeping an eye on the new exchange student than a group of interested parties keeping an eye on a wounded soul.

Adam nursed a chai latte so large, I suspected Cassady had made it in one of my cereal bowls. His face was haggard, but it had returned to a color with some hint of life in it. Kyle told me that Adam was getting progressively more lucid but was still pretty hazy on where he'd been and whom he'd been with before he'd arrived on my doorstep. Tricia had kept him talking by asking him questions about growing up in a famous family, though Kyle pointed out that most of the stories put Jordan in the "punk kid brother" role, which Tricia found less than amusing. Cassady had been more interested in topics like the most embarrassing thing anyone had ever asked him to autograph.

I told him I'd gone to see his mother, and his expression curdled. "Why would you do that?"

"I was summoned."

"It was about me, wasn't it," he said flatly, setting down the latte with unsteady hands.

"She accused me of bothering you," I said, earning sidelong glances from the other three people in the room.

"I'm sorry," Adam said, managing a small smile.

"That's okay. I accused her of killing Russell Elliott."

I'm not sure who gasped loudest. I think it was a tie between Tricia and Adam, while Cassady and Kyle went for the more reticent dropping of the jaw.

"Why did you do that?" Kyle asked tightly.

"Because it all added up."

He pinched his lip and I knew he was already calculating if this put me in harm's way, how it impacted Adam, whether to send Tricia and Cassady home. He looked over at Adam, prepared to say something diplomatic or to apologize for me, but the look on Adam's face stopped him. It was the tight smile of a patient who'd been trying to convince himself the test results were going to be fine but knew deep down that they were anything but. "Adam?" Kyle asked with concern. Apparently, they'd gotten comfortable with each other in my absence. Maybe it was something about wearing my clothes.

"It makes so much sense," Adam said.

"Way to honor thy mother and father," Cassady said darkly.

Adam shook his head, over and over, until Tricia slid onto the couch next to him and braced his head against her shoulder. "Russell must have told her 'no' one time too many."

"I'm not sure she meant to do it, Adam," I said, explaining my theory.

"And you told her that's what you were thinking?" Kyle asked. He sighed heavily when I nodded. That was a discussion we'd be having later.

"The piece that doesn't fit is you," I told Adam. "What happened to you tonight? Your mother's not going to hurt you."

"An accomplice who's double-crossing her?" Tricia suggested.

"Or someone who's on to her and trying to get back at her," Kyle said.

"Or someone with their own agenda and good timing," Cassady voted.

"No. No way. None of that," Adam said with some force.

"Why not?" I asked.

"Because the last person I remember being with is Olivia."

15

"Do I look like enough of a slut?"

"Not all my fans are sluts," Adam protested.

"Just the popular ones?" Tricia undid another button on her blouse, which was already perilously close to sliding off her torso.

"I don't want to spoil your fun," Kyle said from his place on the couch beside Adam, "but there's a lot to be said for the low-key approach."

"Where's the challenge in that?" Cassady asked, tying her blouse so it exposed her enviably flat tummy.

When Adam had told us that his last memory was being with Olivia, I asked him if they'd been at the SoHo Grand, a question that had thrown everyone, including him. I didn't bother explaining about Kenny because Tricia gasped, "You and Olivia? Isn't that some form of incest?"

Adam grimaced. "We're not sleeping together. She's my therapist."

"And you meet her at a hotel?" Kyle asked, not buying it.

Trying to summon enough energy to be agitated, Adam explained, "I don't mind people taking pictures of me going into a hotel."

"But you do mind them taking pictures of you going to the therapist," Tricia said.

"How quaint," Cassady said. "Rather have your fans think of you as a dog than a whack-job."

Adam looked at me in response. "How does it feel to have your life randomly taken out of context and judged?"

I was sympathetic, but I couldn't let us get sidetracked. "Was anyone else there with you this evening?" I asked, pressing ahead.

Adam frowned, trying to focus. "Someone stopped by the table, but . . ."

"Did Olivia leave you alone with that person?" Kyle asked.

Adam's frown deepened, but he came up blank. I grabbed the phone and dialed Olivia. Voice mail. I left a terse message that I needed to talk to her immediately and hung up.

Kyle shook his head dismissively while I announced that I was going to go to the hotel and see what I could find out, but Tricia and Cassady warmed to it quickly. Adam didn't look very happy, but then again, he might have just been nauseated again.

Tricia and Cassady returned to rummaging through my closet in an effort to dress up like trashy rock groupies, even though I assured them there was nothing like that in my possession. But they quickly proved that trashy clothes, like dirty jokes, are all in the presentation. Roll a waistband, unbutton a shirt, or adopt a sneer, and the preppiest of outfits can become cheap and provocative. I took it as a sign of success that Kyle looked appalled when we emerged from the bedroom.

"This is such a bad idea on so many levels," he muttered to me as I pushed my skirt down as low on my hips as it would go.

"The outfit or the idea?" I asked, startled by how cold my stomach was. I inched the skirt back up.

"Yes."

"We're just going to find out if anyone saw who was with Adam tonight, help him piece together how he got this way," I said.

"He probably got this way because someone wants to kill him," Kyle said, his voice hoarse. "That's not the kind of attention you need to attract."

"No one's going to hurt me, I don't have the tapes," I said firmly, to convince us both.

"They don't know that. And you don't have any backup, either."

Those two thoughts diverged in my whirling brain, and I went with the latter one. I wasn't sure if he was offering, but I wasn't going to ask. I couldn't put him in that position, emotionally or professionally, if I wanted to keep him in his current position romantically. "I'm going to ask a couple of questions and then come right back."

"When's the last time anything you did was that simple?" He plucked at his shirt, and I could tell he was thinking about changing his clothes and coming with us.

"Someone needs to stay here with Adam," I said, "and the three of us chatting up people in a hotel bar will be more inconspicuous than you going."

He squinted at my outfit. " 'Inconspicuous' doesn't apply."

"Thank you," I said, coaxing both a kiss and a smile out of him.

Actually, we didn't stand out as much as we might have. Our definition of glamour fell smack in the middle of the spectrum represented at the SoHo Grand Bar & Lounge. It's a marvelously warm space, full of rich fabrics, deep-seated chairs, and glowing light. The SoHo Grand Hotel calls it the neighborhood's "living room," and while it achieves that goal architecturally, my living room has never been host to such an eclectic and dazzling array of fashions and personalities. In our shiniest, shimmeriest best, we blended right in.

Or as much as we can ever blend in when Cassady's with us. She was showing extra cleavage and thigh this evening, and the men in the room came close to bearing her on their shoulders to a seat at the bar. Tricia and I did our best to keep up, but I had to walk more slowly than usual because I couldn't get over the sensation that my skirt was about to fall down.

The cocktail waitress arrived before we'd even put our purses on the bar, her tray bearing three tangerine martinis from a donor who wished to remain anonymous, at least for the moment. Again, a benefit of going somewhere with Cassady, especially when she's dressed for the hunt. Cassady looked at me like a little kid who knows better than to ask for dessert because she hasn't finished her vegetables. "We should say 'no,' right?"

"If you don't take them, I'm going to get such grief from the guys who sent them over," the waitress said, her smile never wavering. She was lovely, with Mediterranean features, glowing olive skin, and amazing upper-body strength, because the tray didn't so much as tremble as she held it out, waiting for our decision.

"We can't have that," Tricia said, snatching the drinks off the tray and placing them on the bar.

"Thank you." The waitress smiled wearily. "You just saved my evening."

"Wanna do us a favor in return?"

Her brow wrinkled in anticipation. "I really can't tell you—"

"No, something else. We hear Adam Crowley, the singer, comes in here a lot."

Her expression shifted to a sympathetic smile, and she looked us over. I held my breath, hoping our groupie-esque costumes would pass muster with her. "Yeah, he does, but you missed him." She turned away from us, but Tricia slid a twenty onto her tray and she paused for a moment. "He usually comes in Mondays and Thursdays. Come back Monday."

"I'm sorry, I didn't get your name," I said amiably.

She smiled warily. "I know." She held my gaze comfortably while I waited. After a full thirty seconds, her smile warmed. "Vicky."

I was pretty sure that wasn't her real name, but we'd make do. "Was he alone, Vicky?" I asked.

She pursed her lips. "Adam's a really cool guy."

"Yes, we know," Tricia said enthusiastically.

"What I mean is," Vicky clarified, "I don't talk to the tabloids. Especially about cool guys."

Vicky: one; outfits: zero. Still, I wasn't going to let her shake us loose that easily. "We're not from a tab," I said. "It's just . . ." I looked around as though I were worried someone was going to overhear and dropped my voice confidentially. "A friend of ours said she hooked up with him tonight and we don't believe her."

Vicky appeared offended on Adam's behalf. "Yeah, don't. She's lying. He came in, had drinks with a couple of friends, and then left."

"How do you know our friend wasn't one of his friends?" Cassady asked.

"Because I recognized them both. One was Olivia Elliott, they're super tight and they come in here a lot."

I couldn't help it. "I heard they were more than friends," I said with a significant waggle of my eyebrows.

Vicky sighed. "I don't think she'd mind, but it's not happening. Trust me, working a job like this, you get a pretty good sense for those sorts of things."

Cassady's eyebrows waggled now, more at me than at Vicky. "So you think Olivia likes him?"

"That's not any of my business," Vicky said, shifting her weight back onto her heels in preparation for leaving us.

"Okay, so who was the other person?" I asked quickly.

"Not your friend, unless your friend's a guy," she said shortly.

Ready to literally buy another moment of her time, I slapped a twenty on her tray. Her weight shifted back and forth a moment as she decided. "Older guy. Great cheekbones. He knew them well. I think he used to be a big deal."

Gray Benedek. Tricia, Cassady, and I exchanged looks, confirming that we were thinking the same thing. But why, after pressing charges against Olivia earlier in the day, was Gray having drinks with her and Adam in the evening? No one in this group had given any indication of being able to get over a grudge in under ten years.

"Was it a pleasant conversation?" I asked.

"More fun than this. Why?"

Cassady slid a twenty onto her tray now, with more grace yet more insistence. "Because if Adam stormed out after a fight, he's less likely to have hooked up with our friend in the lobby than if he went strolling out of here in a good mood."

"The guy pretty much carried him out," Vicky said. "I was out front catching a cig and watched him pour Adam into a cab."

Cassady snagged her twenty off Vicky's tray before Vicky could stop her. "Liar."

Vicky, Tricia, and I all looked at her with the same confusion. Vicky snatched back the twenty. "Am not."

Cassady pointed to the charm around Vicky's neck, a pearl enamel ribbon. "That's a lung cancer ribbon. You seem too smart to smoke, especially if you've lost someone to lung cancer."

Vicky touched the charm reflexively, then stuffed the

twenty deep into her tip glass. "Okay. I followed Adam and the guy out because I was worried."

"About Adam being drunk?" I asked.

"No, Olivia left them alone for a while, and the two guys got into a pretty nasty argument. They kept their voices down and everything, but you could tell it was bad."

"Where did Olivia go when she got up? Did you notice?"

"Out in the lobby. She got a phone call, and I guess she wanted a little quiet."

"Or a little privacy," Tricia suggested. It was true: Depending on who had called her, it might have been something she wanted to keep from Adam and/or Gray. And why not? These people kept everything from one another except their anger.

"Oh, man," Vicky said suddenly, "now I get it."

"Get what?" Cassady asked.

Vicky pointed at me. "You're the new girlfriend. From the Web site. And you're checking up on him. Points for the extra effort and all, but you could've just asked. You wouldn't be the first woman to come ask what her man'd been up to in here."

I wasn't sure how to react, but I was determined not to laugh, even though Tricia and Cassady weren't being very successful in hiding their smiles behind their martini glasses. "I'm not—" I began, but Cassady kicked the very pointed toe of her Michael Kors snakeskin pumps into the hollow behind my anklebone; I felt it all the way up to my molars.

"It's gotta be rough," Vicky said sympathetically, patting me on the knee as if we were old pals.

"Are you insinuating my friend is difficult to date?" Cassady asked.

"No, it's just that both Olivia and the guy were trying to get Adam to open up, confess his feelings."

"About her?" Cassady and Tricia asked in perfect harmony.

"Makes sense." Vicky shrugged. "Olivia kept saying, 'It's okay, you can tell me,' and with the guy, it was all about 'I need to know' and all that male bonding crap. He even came up to the bar and asked Crissy to make some special drink because he needed 'to loosen Adam's tongue.' "

"Did you bring the drink to them?"

Vicky hesitated, and Cassady got a twenty on her tray so quickly that it startled me. "I should've, house rules and all, but he took it."

Which meant Gray had had the opportunity to add something to it to really loosen Adam's tongue. Maybe not to kill him, but certainly to force the truth out of him. The question was, what was Gray asking about, and what answer did Adam give?

"I understand why you're concerned. But I think they were encouraging him to be more honest with you, not to dump you or anything. I'm sure you'll be fine."

Tricia slipped another twenty onto her tray. "Thank you. And give the gentlemen who sent the drinks over this." She placed a card beside the twenty. "My, this is an expensive place to drink," she said as Vicky sashayed back to work.

"You did not send them your business card," I said.

"It's a card for a plastic surgeon. I'm doing his son's bar mitzvah. Nice little ego check." Tricia grinned as she sipped her drink.

"Much as I'd like to stay and see who checks his hairline, we're leaving," I said, grabbing my purse and my resolve. "Toss 'em if you want 'em." Tricia and Cassady, both too well raised to let a fine drink go to waste, grabbed their glasses and did just that. I joined them, just to be sociable.

Martinis weren't designed to be tossed, so we were feeling rather pleased with ourselves when we arrived at Olivia's building and told the doorman that he needed to convince Olivia to see us immediately or the consequences would be grim and public. After a brief phone call upstairs, the doorman allowed us to go up in the elevator, but Olivia was waiting outside the door of her father's apartment and did not hurry to invite us in.

"I'm sorry I haven't had a chance to return your phone call," she said preemptively as we got off the elevator.

"That's okay. I'm not here to see you," I said, walking over to Claire's door and banging on it.

Tricia and Cassady were as surprised as Olivia, but they stood their ground while she dashed down the hallway to pull me away from the door. "But you had the doorman call me."

"Because I knew there was no chance Claire would let me come up. But I need to talk to her or Gray Benedek, and I can't get either one of them on the phone. Unless you can tell me where Gray went after he left the SoHo Grand."

Olivia's face sagged. We were right. I raised my hand to knock again, and Olivia grabbed it. "What did Adam tell you?"

"Why do you assume I've talked to Adam? Did something happen I should know about?"

Olivia shot a worried look at the door. "Shut up."

"Does that sound like a confession to you, Cassady?" Tricia asked.

"It's certainly not a denial, Tricia," Cassady answered.

"She's not amused, guys," I said. "Let's run it by Claire and see what she thinks."

"Claire's not home," Jordan said from Olivia's doorway. He leaned against the doorjamb, dressed in a white broadcloth shirt and skintight black jeans, his arms and ankles crossed as if he were posing for an album cover.

"Hey, Jordan," Tricia said brightly.

"Hey, angel, this is a pleasant surprise," Jordan said, almost convincing me and completely convincing Tricia. He strode over to her and threw his arm around her shoulders, kissing her on the cheek. Me, he looked at less warmly. "What's up?"

"Do you know where Claire is?" Tricia asked helpfully, smiling up at Jordan like a smitten teenager.

"No, but I passed her in the lobby. She and Gray were going out as I was coming in about half an hour ago," Jordan answered, watching me carefully and absently tapping his fingers on Tricia's arm. "I didn't stop to talk to them, they were in a hurry."

Tricia, Cassady, and I all knew better than to look at one another in reaction to that, but the fact that all three of us looked at the floor at the same time probably made Jordan and Olivia just as suspicious. But I knew my friends were on the same wavelength with me. Gray drugs Adam, gets the information he needs, pours him into a cab, and sends him home. But Adam doesn't go home, he goes to my place. And Claire freaks out because her son is missing and demands that Gray help her find him. And Gray, not wanting to tell her what he's done, plays along and joins the hunt, maybe even worried that he went too far and Adam is unconscious or worse somewhere in Manhattan.

"Why're you looking for Claire this late?" Jordan continued.

I corrected course a bit. "I'm actually looking for Adam," I said.

"What'd he do now?"

"Why does everyone assume Adam has done or said something?" Cassady asked.

"Because he usually has," Jordan said.

"I just need to talk to him," I said. "And I'd really like it to be tonight."

"You haven't fallen for him, have you? I thought you were smart," Jordan said with a sour grin.

"Almost as smart as Tricia," I said, eyeing his arm still around her shoulders. Jordan's smile didn't waver, but Tricia's did.

"I misplaced him," Olivia said crisply. "I was hoping you knew where he was."

"Misplaced him? What happened?"

"I met him for drinks at the SoHo Grand, which you obviously already know somehow."

"Gossip."

Olivia gave such a tight little shake of her head, it was more like a shudder. "Gray joined us. He'd been looking for Adam, and Claire told him where we were."

That supported the "happy hour therapy" scenario; if Adam and Olivia were sleeping together, Adam would never admit to his mother where he was meeting Olivia. "What did Gray want? To see how you enjoyed your arrest?"

"To apologize to both of us."

"No way," Jordan interjected, then explained to me, "He doesn't know how."

Olivia continued impatiently, "He's not pressing charges, he was just upset."

"And staying on your good side in case you turn up with the tapes since he couldn't find them in your apartment."

Jordan shook his head, and I felt some of Olivia's impatience myself. "This isn't about the tapes," he said.

"Really?" I said pleasantly, though I was not at all happy with his spitting on my central thesis.

"Gray and Claire are just tearing each other down. Bad breakups lead to stupid behavior."

"Like Gray breaking into Olivia's apartment?" I didn't see where that fit with Jordan's theory.

Jordan shrugged grandly. "I don't get that, either. Ask him."

"I'd love to," I said, trying to conceal my frustration, "but he isn't around, is he?"

"You're not being very helpful," Tricia said chummily to her new friend, sensing the rising temperature of her old friend.

"I don't have to be, do I? Adam will come home sooner or later, hung over and trailing paternity suits behind him," Jordan said with a sunny smile that had probably been getting him out of trouble since the cradle.

Cassady snapped us back on track. "Why did Gray want to apologize to Adam?"

Olivia hesitated a moment, then said, "Gray was sorry about arguing with Adam over his album, and he wanted to make a clean start."

"How'd that go?" I asked.

"I don't know. I got a phone call, so I excused myself."

"Who called you?"

"I did," Jordan volunteered. "Funny thing, I was looking for Adam, too."

I had a sudden insane image of all the children hunting for the Golden Ticket to Willy Wonka's Chocolate Factory, but instead of devouring candy bars to get it, they were devouring one another. Why was everyone so worried about where Adam was? Did they all think he had the tapes? Or did they think his mother had the tapes and he knew where they were and could be persuaded to divulge?

That made sense at least for Gray, who might have decided Adam's new obsession with jazz was beneficial; if he was turning his back on rock and roll, he wouldn't care about the tapes as much and would help Gray get hold of them. And Gray had been so casual about slipping Adam something and not paying attention to whether Adam survived or not—could that mean Gray's callous pursuit of royalties had already claimed one victim and he didn't care about making it two? Had Gray killed Russell, too, and then just not been able to find the box with the tapes before Olivia showed up?

I didn't realize how long I'd been lost in thought until I heard Cassady ask Jordan, "Why were you looking for Adam?"

"I wanted to talk to him about singing with me tomorrow night at the terrific party Tricia's planning."

"Because it went so well last time?" I asked.

"To make up for last time."

"Why does everyone suddenly want to patch things up with Adam?" Tricia asked.

Jordan shrugged, pulling her closer to him. "Who knows what Gray's deal is, I just felt bad. He's my brother, after all."

"So did you talk to him?" I asked.

"I wouldn't let him," Olivia said quickly. I caught the look she zapped to Jordan, that slightly wide-eyed "play along, please" look that hovers between confidence and desperation. She was either spinning this hard or making it up as she went. "Adam was so upset, I didn't think it was the time for them to talk."

"How drunk was Adam?"

Olivia elongated her neck, offended. "He wasn't. He's very careful about his drinking, which is understandable given what happened to his father."

"I thought his father was murdered," I said, as much to Jordan as to Olivia. "Just like your father. Which means he shouldn't just be careful about drinking, he should be careful about who buys his drinks."

Olivia's neck drew back down, and she flushed a deep, unexpected shade of red. "Are you accusing me?"

"No, should I be?"

While Olivia sputtered, Jordan said, "She's accusing Gray, Ollie. Cool it."

Olivia gasped again, and she flushed even deeper, which I wouldn't have thought possible. "Oh no, what if Gray hurt Adam and that's why we can't find him?"

I agreed with her on the first half, but her grave concern about the second half distressed me. Before my guilt, which lives very close to the surface, could get the better of me, Cassady said, "Adam and Gray were seen leaving the hotel separately. I'm sure Adam's fine, wherever he is." It's like MasterCard says, "Friends who know when to lie for you: priceless."

"And when he turns up, would you ask him to give me a call?" I said, guiding Cassady and Tricia back to the elevator. A plan was beginning to take shape in my tangerine-flavored brain, and I didn't want us to overstay our welcome.

Tricia and Jordan bade each other a flirtatious good-bye until Cassady pulled Tricia in one direction and Olivia pulled Jordan in the other. As the elevator doors closed, Tricia sighed happily and I felt like an absolute creep.

"You really like him?" I asked.

"He's handsome and he's fun, and that's all I'm considering right now," Tricia said.

"And he wrote her a song," Cassady reminded me.

"You're working really hard on his party, too, aren't you?" I asked.

Tricia looked at me uneasily. "Yes, but why do you sound so unhappy about that?"

It was my turn to sigh. "Because I'm going to ruin it."

16

The most dangerous part of my job isn't the occasional fanatic who takes a swing or a shot at me. It's spending so much time with people who are willing to lie, steal, or worse in order to get what they want that I start accepting that as the normal course of events. So it's really good for me to stop and remember how nice it feels to do something good for another person. And to consider what lengths people will go to for me once I've done something sweet for them.

In the doorway of Connie's office, evolving paparazzi Kenny radiated a whole new vibe, eager and earnest. Who knew? He smiled at me over Connie's shoulder as she thanked him for bringing in his portfolio on such short notice and promised to give him a call for something in the next issue. I told Connie I'd be right back and escorted Kenny to the elevator.

"How much does she owe you?" Kenny asked, gun-shy and trying to get to the punch line before I did.

"About twenty-three large," I said in my best moll voice. Kenny flinched, then I explained, "We take bunco very seriously around here." He snorted and made a face. "She doesn't owe me anything, Kenny. It's one of those greater good situations—break for you, benefits the magazine, helps out Connie, so why not?"

"Would've expected you to be more cynical at your age."
Kenny shrugged.

I felt kindly toward him nevertheless. Plus, "There's something else."

"I knew it," Kenny said with the satisfaction of a man seeing his worldview vindicated.

"You really ought to come by Pillow tonight."

"The club in TriBeCa?"

"Jordan Crowley's having a listening party for some friends."

"What, you haven't gotten your picture taken in twenty-four hours?"

"I was thinking you might want to get a few shots of what happens when people hear a very special announcement about Micah Crowley's Hotel Tapes."

Kenny lit up as though I'd handed him a winning lottery ticket. "Who's making the announcement?"

I winked. "An announcement will be made," I said, hoping I didn't sound too much like I was dictating the press release.

"Who else knows?"

"In the press?"

"Yes."

"Just you."

Grabbing me in a bear hug that reset my spinal column more efficiently than a chiropractor, Kenny said, "You won't be sorry."

He had no idea on how many levels I hoped he was right.

The night before, I hadn't been able to get Kyle saying "They don't know that" out of my head. After we'd talked to Jordan and Olivia, the fact that no one knew I didn't have the tapes because no one knew who did have the tapes blossomed into a plan. Which was why I'd told Tricia I needed to ruin her party.

At first blush, she hadn't been pleased, which was to be

expected. Not only had she been working around the clock, she'd been enjoying hanging with Jordan; she didn't want either of those efforts to go to waste, and neither did I.

"Ruin how?" had been her first question.

"Unleash a little pandemonium," I said.

"That helps most parties," Cassady said. Her dazzling eyes flicked back and forth between Tricia and me, weighing us as much as watching us. The elevator doors opened, and Cassady swept us out in front of her.

Halfway across the lobby, I stopped and asked the doorman if I could leave a message with him for Mrs. Crowley. When he said I could, I took out a business card and wrote on the back of it.

"You don't have cards for your new job yet, do you?" Tricia asked.

"I think I have to prove I can hold on to the job for more than a week before Henry will authorize the expense," I said. I wrote, "LIAR," on the back of the card, handed it to the doorman, and followed my friends out to the street.

In the taxi back to my apartment, I explained my plan. Since everyone in this group was lying to me—and to one another—about everything, I was going to play the game by their rules and tell a whopper of my own. I was going to announce that I had the Hotel Tapes. While the ensuing chaos might ruin Tricia's party, it would also force whoever really did have them to take some action.

"Like shoot you!" Cassady exclaimed, horrified.

"They don't seem like a gun-toting crowd," I said with optimistic justification.

"I can't believe you're doing this to Tricia," she tried again.

"That's why I'm apologizing in advance."

"I don't know that an apology's necessary," Tricia said, her voice strangely tight. She was looking out the window, so I couldn't see her face, and for a moment I panicked, thinking I had made her cry. But Cassady poked her, probably thinking the same thing, and Tricia turned to give us both a dazzling smile. "Can you imagine the publicity?"

"Oh, God help us all," Cassady said, sighing.

"I've got such an old-money, blue-blood clientele—not that I don't love them, but this will introduce me to a whole new community, one that throws parties constantly," Tricia said with growing enthusiasm.

"And you'll take credit for her suicidal stunt, like it was part of your planned entertainment for the evening?" Cassady asked with growing incredulity.

"Hey, you're the one who usually encourages envelope pushing," I said.

"If one of these maniacs doesn't kill you, Kyle will," Cassady said with a tone that implied I'd tripped over the elephant in the room several times without noticing. "In a metaphoric, emotional sense, of course, but nevertheless. I don't think he'll appreciate your using yourself as bait in this type of situation."

One of the most valuable things about true friends is the perspective they offer you about life. One of the most annoying things about true friends is they offer that perspective when you're least receptive to it. I considered my "I can play this game" strategy to be bold and clever, worthy of a Thin Man movie or at least of an episode of *Law & Order* that would give some very deserving cabdriver his big break. Self-as-bait had not occurred to me, and I disliked the image of a worm impaled on a hook that sprang to mind now. But surely there was a way to explain my plan so it would win over Cassady. And Kyle.

"No."

Kyle looked at me as though I'd just asked permission to try a swan dive off the George Washington Bridge. Cassady and Tricia got a glance as he determined if they were in on this, then the smoldering glare swung back to me. He pointed to Adam, who was sound asleep on my couch, a position I envied deeply. It was after midnight, and I had reached the point in the evening where my feet felt permanently fixed in the shape of my Stuart Weitzmans and my thoughts felt squeezed through cheesecloth. I was sure it was a good idea, maybe I just wasn't expressing it properly. "Haven't you ever told a suspect that you had a piece of evidence that you didn't really have, just to see his reaction?"

"I'm unplugging your television."

"You're avoiding my question."

Tricia grabbed Cassady by the hand and yanked her out of the line of fire. "We're going to the bathroom. Call us when it's okay to come out."

"You don't have—"

"Have fun, ladies," Kyle said grimly. He looked down at the floor, waiting to hear the bathroom door close, while I cast a flustered look at the sympathetic but worried faces of my departing friends.

The door snicked closed, and I lowered myself toward a chair, anticipating a lengthy lecture about professionalism and boundaries and a bunch of other things I couldn't argue with. But before my knees had bent more than seven degrees, Kyle grabbed my arms and pulled me back up. For a fleeting, hopeful moment, I thought he was going to kiss me, but instead he looked at me with a ferocious intensity that made my throat go dry. "I have to be there."

"Where?" I asked quietly.

"At your damn party. To watch your back."

"But you just said—"

"That I didn't think it was a good idea. And it's not. But

it's your call, not mine. I told you I want to make this work. You're not making it easy, but I'm trying."

When he did kiss me, he had to keep holding me by the arms so I didn't collapse from the heat. Losing myself in the moment, I tried to slide my hands up under his shirt, but his hands shot down to my wrists and stopped me.

"One unconscious male on the couch and two giggling females in the bathroom," he said by way of explanation.

"Send them home. He'll sleep through anything, don't you think?" I whispered, not wanting the heat to dissipate.

"Taking our time," he reminded me firmly.

"You're showing off."

"Yeah, right."

"Because you have more self-control than I do."

"Maybe I just want you all to myself when the time is absolutely right," he said, running his fingers to the base of my throat. If he'd asked me to go rob a bank right then and there, I would have asked him what denomination bills he wanted.

Instead, after a brief conversation with Tricia and Cassady about our after-dawn plans, we sent them home and curled into the club chair together, dozing off as Rita Hayworth and Glenn Ford clawed their way through *Gilda*.

When I woke up, I was in the chair alone and Adam and Kyle were in the kitchen, clenching their jaws and brewing coffee. I hurried in as fast as the crick in my back would allow.

Adam greeted me first, smiling sadly. "I'm sorry."

"What are you apologizing for?" I glanced over at Kyle, but he was slicing a cantaloupe with great vigor and didn't look at me.

"I'm not sure. But I don't remember big chunks of last night, which usually means I need to apologize for something."

"I told him your theory about Gray Benedek drugging him," Kyle said, still slicing.

"I can't believe that bastard thought I was holding out on him," Adam said, "why he didn't believe me when I said I didn't know where the tapes are. This is my mother's fault."

The pause in the rhythmic beat of knife to cutting board told me that this surprised Kyle as much as it surprised me. "You think your mother told him to do it?"

"No, but if my mother would let him license a couple of songs, he wouldn't be so desperate." Adam let out his breath in a silent whistle. "So what do I do now?"

"You're willing to work with me?" I asked.

Kyle turned and looked at Adam, waiting for an answer, and I kicked myself for having missed the conversation—or lecture or bargaining—that preceded it. Adam looked as though he were going to try to negotiate one more point, but his lips had barely parted when Kyle gave him the look of disbelief you give a child who's been practicing his cursive writing on the living room wall.

"Yes," was Adam's reply.

Deciding I'd have to hear that story later, I explained the agenda for the day. For Adam's part, that involved lying low, once he'd called his mother and let her know that he was all right. No point in having her flipping over his unknown whereabouts. Not because I cared about how she felt at this point, but I didn't want to give her an opportunity to put a crimp in our plans.

Adam wasn't thrilled until he learned that a baby-sitter with fabulous legs was part of the deal. Since Tricia needed to spend the day with Jordan getting the party ready, Cassady had volunteered to work from my apartment and keep an eye on Adam while Kyle and I went in. And my day started with planting a seed with Kenny.

Once I had sent Kenny on his way and thanked Connie one more time, I circled back into the bull pen, stopping at

Skyler's desk. "Do you have something for me," I said, "besides envy and disdain?"

With a cool smile, Skyler handed me a file folder. Thicker than I'd expected, the folder contained the audition letters from those staffers aspiring to take my place. "You don't understand how much I admire you," she said.

"Because once an atom splits into all those little teeny bits and quarks and whatever, I can't keep track of things that small."

"You're confusing the notion that I don't like you with the fact that you don't like me."

The hurt she injected into that statement was the most genuine emotion I'd ever heard from her. Either she was circling the truth or she was taking acting lessons. "I could've sworn it was the other way around."

Her eyelids dropped into the hooded expression of a cat about to pounce. "The letters are coded, and Adrienne in Henry's office has the key."

"Which one is your favorite?" I asked.

Skyler rolled her lips, either thinking or checking her lipstick. "The letters should speak for themselves."

"Very nice," I said, having been braced for a self-serving answer that either pointed out her letter or slammed someone else's.

"Eileen wants your vote by the end of the day."

"And Claire Crowley wants your head," Henry said as he walked up to us. He didn't look like a man carrying a death warrant, with his hands in his pockets and a smile on his lips.

I checked my watch. "She's lethal early today."

Eileen's office door flew open, and she stepped into the doorway, gripping the doorjamb with her talons. It was like watching a mole clamber to the top of its burrow because it sensed danger. Or fresh meat. "What have you done this time, Molly Forrester?" If Eileen knew my middle name, she probably would have used that, too, in that special way your elders invoked your full name so you knew exactly how much trouble you were in as a kid.

"I turned down a bribe and rejected a prewritten article," I said, deciding to keep the part about holding her son hostage to myself as long as possible.

Henry nodded. Happily, what I was saying seemed to make sense in the context of what Claire had told him. "She didn't mention that part. But she did say you accused her of murder."

The bull pen wasn't fully awake yet, everyone still on their first cup of coffee of the morning, but that got them sitting up straight and paying attention, even though I wished heartily that they weren't. Eileen exclaimed my name with the same shrill tone you'd reprimand a puppy who'd wet in the house. Called on the carpet and now accused of ruining it.

I pressed on. "That might have come up in the course of the discussion. The same discussion in which she was trying to bribe me," I said, ready to defend myself however possible.

"You've got to be careful about those sorts of things," Henry said.

"I've told her that over and over," Eileen said, cutting in line for a top spot on my firing squad.

"We have to be able to document everything," Henry continued without acknowledging Eileen.

"In case she sues us," Eileen added helpfully.

"And if Molly sues her," Henry said.

"I kept the bogus article material she gave me," I said, letting my stomach settle back from being lodged in my throat.

"Good," Henry said.

"Henry. Are you encouraging her to continue, even though she's offended a prestigious cultural figure with a vast following?" Eileen asked.

"She didn't spit on the pope, Eileen. You're giving Claire Crowley too much credit, and Molly not enough," Henry responded. "I find that when people call and protest so vehemently about an article they haven't read yet, it's because the truth is being uncovered and they'd like it to stay buried."

Eileen's mouth worked soundlessly, like a goldfish lifted out of its bowl. "But you told me Claire was going to sue us."

"She threatened. I'm comfortable that she won't. We'll find a way to smooth her feathers."

Henry headed back to his office, but I called after him, "Would you like an opportunity to do it in person? She'll be at Jordan Crowley's private party at Pillow tonight and I can get you in."

I could've sworn I heard a collective sigh in four-part harmony as the bull pen pondered the joys of attending a private party at Pillow. From Henry's smile, I gathered the idea appealed to him as well. He walked back toward me. "Excellent strategy. Give Adrienne the information and I'll be there."

"I could get a car and pick you up," Eileen offered.

"Are you sure you're invited?" Henry asked.

He looked at me, Eileen didn't. I wasn't sure if she thought she was forcing my hand or if she just assumed, and for a split second, I thought about making her squirm. But then I decided that would just be mean. Entertaining, but mean. "She's invited," I said.

"I'll get there on my own, thank you," Henry told Eileen. "Go read, I'm anxious to compare notes with you," he told me, and gestured for me to walk past him to the conference room, shielding me from any effort Eileen might exert to drag me into her office. It was delightful to think he was deliberately running interference for me.

I closed the conference room door behind me, kicked off my shoes, and sat at the mammoth table with my feet up in a second chair, as if I were settling in at the campus library for a long night of studying. It was odd to be in a room alone and trying to turn my mind to things other than Micah's twisted family tree and its bizarre fruit. The chance to catch my breath made me want to call Kyle and see how he was doing, how we were doing, but I also knew I'd already made some extraordinary demands on his time and he'd been gracious above and beyond the call about accommodating them. I needed to give him some space and some peace at work, and I needed to read some letters.

An odd sense of anticipation crept under my rib cage as I held the folder, a mix of excitement and dread about the quality of what might be inside with equal chances of the letters being far better or far worse than I might imagine. Taking a deep breath, I hoped to be pleasantly surprised.

The first reply I read to the sample letter about whether it was possible to have a relationship when you feel as though you're struggling for control shifted the barometer from anticipation to dread. "If you want to be in control, you're not committed to the relationship." Okay, I thought, this is about interdependence versus independence, fair enough. But then it continued, "You need to find someone you're willing to surrender to, someone who makes you want to give up control." Not in this century, not in this magazine. That one went in the "no" pile.

Reading further, I found several that fell into the empowerment camp: "You deserve to be in control," that sort of thing. And a few that went for the deeper issue, raising the possibility that the angst was really about something else in life and the writer was taking it out on the boyfriend. They all got extra points for insight, as uncomfortable as the insight made me, and I put them in the "yes" pile.

Then there was the letter that started: "Of course control is an illusion. Everything in life is illusion. Life itself might be. So why not do what you want? Pedal to the metal!" I'd been trying not to imagine which staffer had written which letter, but that one just seemed to scream Seth in Art Direction, the one with Buster Keaton's face tattooed on the back of his neck, the eyes peeking out just above the collar line, which made walking down the hall behind him a surreal experience.

Halfway through the folder, it was well past lunch and my rear end was asleep from my bad posture in the chair, but I had several strong candidates, a couple of possibles, and a large pile of not quites. Then I came to:

Dear Balancing Act,

Men and women should both respect control, but they have to respect each other first. Just because you want to take the trip on your terms doesn't mean it has to be a solo flight. If you really have momentum in your life, find a man who's going to hop on board and ride shotgun as you build up speed, not one who's going to flag you down. Or a man who inspires you to slam on the brakes and have a picnic at the side of the road. Get there when you want to, how you want to, with whom you want to.

It touched me. It amused me. But most of all, it rang a bell.

Debating between calling Cassady, who was baby-sitting, and Tricia, who was party building, I grabbed the phone. Cassady won, because I knew she'd be more interruptible. "How's he behaving?" I asked.

"He's sleeping again," she assured me. "It's all been very Freudian. Poor boy really needs to work things out with his mother, whether she's harboring Gray or not. Oh, and Adam's taking us all to a jazz concert at the end of the month. Unless you wind up implicating him, too."

That explained the John Pizzarelli album playing in the background. "Hey, it's not like I get to choose who's involved here," I said. "But before we get into that, listen to this."

I read her the answer; a thoughtful pause followed. "The last line needs work."

"I agree."

"Molly, I thought you were leaving that job."

"I am."

"So why are you writing another column?"

Now the bell didn't just ring, it pealed. "Yes! That's why it sounds familiar, I wrote it!"

Cassady chuckled, but it had a worried tinge to it. "Have you been sipping out of Adam's cocktail glass?"

"No, no," I said as I tried to rise from my chair, slumbering hindquarters and all. "This letter was submitted by someone who wants my job. But I wrote it."

"Plagiarism *and* shortsightedness. A winning combination," Cassady said. "Hire that person right away."

I told her I'd check back with her in a bit and raced stiff-hipped back to my computer, ignoring the anxious faces that attempted to peer without being seen to peer, wondering what letter had provoked such a strong response that I would galumph through the office barefoot.

Cracking open my archive folder and searching my past columns for two- and three-word combinations, I was able to pull up five different letters I'd written, each of which was represented in the patchwork letter that lay crumpled beside my keyboard. The metaphors had been adjusted, but they were all there. Except the last sentence.

I looked up from my computer, and everyone in the bull

pen looked down, suddenly busy, like high school students who believe if they do not make eye contact, they will not be called on to answer the pop quiz question. Everyone except Skyler. Tensed, as though prepared to either call Security or dig Mace out of her purse if I moved too suddenly, she stared at me from her desk.

Could it be Skyler? All I had to do was get the key from Adrienne, assuming no one had tampered with the key, but she was all the way over on the other side of the building. Skyler was right in front of me and starting to sweat.

I picked up the crumpled letter and advanced on her, waiting for her to blink or bolt or, worse, buzz Eileen. As I walked up to her, I tried to imagine how anyone could believe they'd be able to pass off someone else's work as their own, even if they claimed to model themselves after that person, to be offering an homage to that person—

To be that person's son.

My freezing in midstep alarmed Skyler, but the idea struck me with physical force, and I couldn't move for a moment. It was like bracing myself at the breaker line when we were kids at the beach, the breathless exhilaration of staying on your feet as the waves crashed into you even while the water slapping into your face stung your eyes and throat and lungs.

Gray Benedek might kill for a new hit song, but anything he did with the Hotel Tapes, he'd have to share with Claire and the rest of the heirs.

But if Claire had the tapes, she could not only lay claim to the songs, she could reclaim her dynasty. In fact, the best way for Claire to guarantee Adam could become his father was to give him his father's songs and let him sing them as his own. And to kill the only person who knew they weren't.

17

The only thing worse than a plan that doesn't work is one that works too well. You revamp your diet to focus on organics, and either you discover you're allergic or you find that once you've shopped for groceries, you can't pay your rent. You flirt with someone to get his attention, and either he walks right by you or you discover he's not as much fun as you thought he'd be but you can't shake him. You construct a press leak, and either no one listens or you wind up getting indicted. Or the entire fourth estate camps out on your doorstep before you've had a chance to get presentable.

But I wasn't speculating on the potential press mishaps in my future when I slammed the letter down on Skyler's desk. Invigorated by my new insight into Claire's motive for killing Russell, I was psyched to smite a few ethical dragons before I left to get ready for Jordan's party. "You're kidding, right?"

"Rarely," she said, sounding nervous for the first time in our acquaintance.

"What were you thinking?"

"I wanted to try something new."

"By using something old?"

"I know there are copyright issues—"

"You better believe it."

"But I thought if you liked the concept, we could figure out the royalty issues with the songwriters and see if it was doable."

Her lower lip trembled while my mind slid to a stop. "You wrote the answer with the song quotes. The advice Cole Porter and Norah Jones might give."

"Yes," she said tentatively.

"Excellent answer."

She brightened slightly. "I thought you were upset."

"I am. But apparently, not with you. I need to talk to Adrienne."

Trouble was, I didn't make it to Adrienne. I made it all the way to the other side of Skyler's desk before Carlos stood up at his, phone in his hand, and said, "Molly, call for you."

Of all the people I considered on the way back to my desk, I did not consider Peter Mulcahey. "I'm the last person in the world you should be holding out on."

"I beg to differ several times over," I said. "What do you want, Peter?"

"What's the announcement about the Hotel Tapes?"

"I don't know what you're talking about."

"I've slept with you enough times to know when you're lying, Molly," he said with a certainty that annoyed me.

"So you knew it wasn't true when I told you how terrific you were?" I snarked.

"Don't bait me while I'm baiting you," he said. "I'm trying to get a story here."

"Peter, assuming I even know anything about whatever story it is you're chasing, why would I give the story to you instead of telling it myself?"

"Because you're too close to it. Give me an exclusive."

"To publish in your magazine."

"So your guys fire you. I'll get you a sweet deal over here."

"Thanks for checking in, Peter."

"At least invite me to the damn party."

The twisted notion of fixing up Peter and Eileen occurred to me, but I'd have to ask Aaron about the global implications of introducing an unstoppable pressure to an emotional black hole. "Yeah, see you there," I said, and hung up.

The word was out. And it had already gotten from the tabloids to the mainstream press. Or at least to Peter.

It had also reached the music community, because I'd barely cleared the line when it rang again. This time it was Risa, who announced she wanted to acquire the Hotel Tapes for her label. "I'll pay you ten percent over what anyone else has offered."

"Who told you I was selling the tapes?"

"You're the last person I discussed them with. I heard there was some big announcement coming, and I just assumed you were involved."

I had hoped the rumor that someone had found the tapes would be sufficient to force the hand of the person who really did have them: If I said I had them, Claire would be compelled to come forward and prove me wrong. Said rumor exploding into an auction for the tapes in the blink of an eye took my breath away. I just hoped the explosion didn't take me with it before Claire had been flushed out.

I told Risa that I didn't have anything to do with selling the tapes, but I'd certainly call her first if I heard they were for sale. After pushing a little more, she thanked me, I hung up, and Gray Benedek grabbed my shoulder.

"What the hell are you doing?"

Such is the power of stardom that a tall, muscular man with fury in his eyes and vitriol in his voice was standing over me, clearly meaning me harm, and my colleagues sat in their places, gazing at him with awe and adoration. I even heard giggling as

Gray leaned down into my face, and I hoped that was in honor of his fame and not in anticipation of my demise.

"Where's Adam?" he demanded.

"I've been looking for you to ask you the same question," I said with what I felt was commendable calm. "You were the last person seen with him in public."

Gray straightened up slowly, a cobra recoiling after a strike. "Don't try to make me look bad here, little girl. You're the sucker, falling for the charming act. You think Adam is the wounded party? He's the one who's got the tapes and is telling everyone he'll sell them to the highest bidder."

"Since when?" I asked, wincing at the anxious crack in my own voice. He had to have this wrong, didn't he?

"Who the hell knows? But I've got press up to my armpits wanting reactions and pictures and producers wanting a piece of the project, and what I want is Adam Crowley so I can teach the ungrateful piece of spineless scum about loyalty and respect, just one more thing his father never bothered to do for him."

Out of the corner of my eye, I could see that my colleagues' awe and adoration were ebbing into the discomfort and fear zone. Not that anyone was coming to my aid, but at least they weren't batting their eyes at Gray anymore.

"Why would you think this was Adam's doing?" I asked.

"He doesn't have his own songs," Gray said with distaste. "The best he can do is ride on someone else's riff."

The sour torque in my stomach acknowledged his point and the fact that I'd ascribed a similar motive to Claire yet kept Adam free of any culpability. The attractive option at this point was to attend medical school, probably in another country. The responsible option was to check on Adam and give him a chance to answer these charges. But I had to get away from Gray to be able to do that. Knowing how well he handled confrontation, I tried a different approach. "I'm really sorry that you're being bothered. Let me look into this, press my contacts. I'll see what I can find out for you, Mr. Benedek."

Gray actually smiled, and a soft group sigh filled the room behind me. "Good. Good."

"In fact, I'll walk out with you, get right on this," I said, scooping up my accoutrements and stuffing them in my bag. Even the offending letter went along; it would have to wait its turn in the long line of events wanting to mess with my life.

As I walked out with Gray, Skyler stood at her desk. "Wait! What about the letters?"

"Grab them out of the conference room and sit on them if you have to. I'll call you!" I called back. My giving her a mission seemed to please her, perhaps because she thought it meant we were friends now. Yeah, fine.

Gray and I seemed to be friends now, too, and we parted with professional politeness in front of the building. I wasn't sure how he'd feel about me at the end of the evening, which I was still hoping would culminate in the exposure of Claire, but my promise to track down Adam mollified him for the moment. I was willing to take that and run with it all the way back to my apartment, where both Cassady and Adam were happy to see me.

"Changing of the guard," Cassady proclaimed, scooping up her work. "I have to go find a fabulous dress to wear to dinner with Aaron. I don't suppose . . ." She wrinkled her nose at Adam, then shook her head. "Never mind."

Adam leapt to his feet, tossing down my well-worn copy of *One Hundred Years of Solitude*. "Let's go. Put me in drag if you have to, to get me through the press downstairs, but I need to go outside."

"He does need something to wear tonight," Cassady said.

"A condemned man deserves to go in style," Adam said.

"You're not a condemned man. Unless you're holding out on me and you've been working the phones," I warned, Gray's slams on Adam's character reverberating in my head.

Adam gestured at Cassady. "She confiscated my cell and listened at the door while I was in the bathroom."

"I was being thorough," Cassady explained. "You told me to keep him incommunicado and I did."

"We're on the same side," Adam said.

I hoped so, or the chopping block was going to have my name on it right next to his. Relenting, I said, "There's no press downstairs yet, but incognito is still the order of the day."

Which was why, one hour later, Cassady and I escorted Adam into Saks, his sunglasses on despite the overcast weather, his telltale curls crammed into a bright yellow baseball cap from a 5K for diabetes research that I limped through, his chin tucked down into the zipper of a ragged burnt orange zippered sweatshirt that had survived a Green Mountains camping trip with a little more flair than I had. Adam managed to be remarkably low-key as we entered the men's department, though I'd barely begun to sift through the stacks of shirts when he arrived at the customer service desk with a Marc Jacobs ensemble, black sateen trousers and a white sweater, plus a package of Calvin Klein knit boxers and black socks. Either the cashier didn't notice the name on his credit card or didn't care, because she didn't blink an overly mascaraed eyelash as she completed the transaction.

Adam strolled back to where Cassady and I waited and smiled. "Done."

Cassady looked him over with something that approached distaste. "Men just don't understand how to shop." She sighed and led us to the evening wear department.

While Cassady slid between racks, evaluating, dismissing, and moving on, Adam and I loitered near a table of merino sweaters that compelled you to stroke them. "I appreciate this very much," he said as I slid my hand between two sweaters.

"The shopping?"

"Your helping Ollie like this. Figuring out what happened."

"Don't thank me until it's over," I said, touched by his loyalty to Olivia but trying to imagine what his reaction would be when the blame came down on Claire. Especially since she seemed to have done it all for him.

"I'd like to do a lot more when it's over," he said with a smile I couldn't quite read.

"Like record a jazz album?" I asked, uncomfortable with the slick tone in his voice.

"Like take you out."

A little perturbed that he was playing with me again, I laughed it off. "You don't have to do this anymore."

"Ask you out?"

"Flirt with me to keep me from suspecting you."

"Is that what you thought I was doing?" His smile disappeared. "That's crap. I was trying to open up to you, share something special with you, and you thought it was an act? So you taking care of me, helping me out, that's been an act in return?"

"No, I genuinely want to help you," I protested.

"And I genuinely like you," he snapped back, not seeming to care for me all that much at the moment. "Which is why I want to take you out."

I deemed a new approach necessary. "That wouldn't go over well with Kyle."

"My other baby-sitter?"

"Yes."

For some reason, that pulled him up. "Sorry. I thought you were old friends."

Which pulled me up. "Old friends?"

"Or cousins or something."

Adam was not exactly a neutral observer, but he seemed genuinely surprised. How could the undeniable attraction Kyle and I felt for each other not be plainly obvious, even to him? Kyle and I were meant to be together. Fated. Destined. Force of nature and all that. Weren't we?

Though I told myself—repeatedly—Adam was giving me a hard time, I had difficulty dismissing his statement. Sufficient difficulty that when Kyle arrived at my apartment several hours later, looking more handsome than ever in a tailored black jacket I hadn't seen before and a deep blue shirt that made his eyes radiate, I grabbed him and kissed him as passionately as I could without getting into exhibitionist territory.

"So," Kyle said when I let him come up for air, "we're not going to Jordan's party?"

I allowed myself a glance at Adam, who sat on the couch in his new Marc Jacobs ensemble topped with a Simon Cowell scowl. "Interesting," Adam said.

"What?" Kyle asked.

"Nothing," I said quickly, shooting Adam the narrow-eyed frown that translates universally as, "Shut up. Now."

In the taxi on the way to the club, I wound up between the two men, holding myself in my own space so tightly that I could have cracked walnuts between my knees. I was experiencing serious eleventh-hour anxiety about my strategy, and I didn't need Adam playing with my mind, heart, or any combination thereof, either by declaring his own feelings or by questioning Kyle's. Was he doing it just to do it? Or because he really meant it? Or because he sensed I was closing in on his mother?

The question was, would the pressure of the press, paparazzi and legit, swarming all over the front door of Pillow work its magic on Claire the way it already had on Gray? If I got up onstage in front of the party tonight and announced that I had the Hotel Tapes, would Claire be provoked enough by the ensuing hysteria to grab the spotlight back for herself and insist that she had them—and, by doing so, admit that she had killed Russell Elliott?

I kept my eyes down as we walked the gauntlet of photographers to the front door of the club; I didn't want to be accused later of playing to the crowds. Adam smiled and waved at everyone, and Kyle focused on the front door. This evening was the polar opposite of his idea of a good time, and my heart pounded with appreciation for all the things he was doing for me against his better judgment.

But just short of the doors, I realized that the power of the press was that much more powerful when it was in your face. Asking Kyle and Adam to wait just a second, I backpedaled down the red carpet. "What are you doing?" Kyle asked, puzzled.

When I stopped in front of the knot of photographers straining against their velvet ropes, it was Adam who yelled, a little tightly, "What the hell are you doing?"

"Kenny?" I called, squinting into the nebula of flashes.

Kenny popped to the front of the crowd like a bubble surfacing in a glass of soda. "Hey, Molly, gimme a smile."

"Don't take my picture, just come inside," I said, tossing my head in the direction of the front door.

I'm not sure who liked the idea less, Kenny's fellow photographers or Adam, but Kenny needed no persuading; he ducked under the rope with surprising agility as his compatriots screamed questions about the announcement, about Adam and Jordan, and one exceptionally catty question about who did my hair. Refraining from replying, I walked up the carpet with Kenny, pausing beside Adam and Kyle. Brow knotted, Kyle asked, "What's going on?"

"Not out here," Adam hissed, casting a troubled look at Kenny. "But you better know what you're doing, Molly."

"She's using me and I'm fine with it," Kenny said with a cheeriness in direct opposition to his sour demeanor. He hoisted his camera. "I'm proud to record the announcement."

"What announcement?" Adam asked.

"Not out here," Kyle said, herding us past the doorman and into the club.

Pillow is an odd but intriguing space, dominated by the all-brass bar on one wall and the stage opposite it. The room is not that big, yet it's decorated with huge, billowing, jewel-toned fabric drapes and cushioned panels on the walls, an outer ring of booths with heavily padded banquettes, and then clusters of "pillow pits" elsewhere in the room, where fashionable New Yorkers in outfits that easily crossed into four figures basically sat on the floor, pretending to be pashas or praetorians. At least when they got too drunk, they didn't have far to fall.

Onstage, Bonnie conferred with the stage manager and the light-board operator, her small hands swooping through the air as she described some effect. She was dressed simply, more low-key than I'd ever seen her, yet she caught your eye immediately. She was luminous—with pride or excitement, I couldn't tell.

As I scanned the room, looking for Olivia, Peter, Henry, Eileen, Risa, or any of the other people for whom I felt responsible, Tricia rushed up to us, dressed in a stunning silver Robert Rodriguez baby-doll and acting like a giddy newlywed throwing her first party rather than a seasoned professional who did this sort of thing twice a week. "Isn't this a fabulous space? It's going to be a memorable night!" She winked at me a little too extravagantly, but Adam didn't notice. Kyle did, but his forehead was already furrowed as he examined the decor, so the furrows just deepened slightly.

The presence of Kenny and his cameras in our group threw her for only a moment. "I trust you," she said happily, patting me on the arm. "I also know where you live."

"So do I," Kenny said happily.

"No random snapping," I warned him.

"Got it. Announcement only."

"What's this announcement?" Adam asked again.

I didn't have to figure out how to answer because Claire swooped down on us at that moment, smothering Adam with kisses. Wearing a black Max Mara suit that accentuated her long, slender frame, she looked equal parts businesswoman and assassin. Or maybe that was less her fashion choice and more my subconscious talking.

"I've been so worried about you!" she said, not being all that discreet about checking if Kenny was immortalizing her maternal concern on film. It wasn't until she'd given Kenny the once-over that she registered I was standing next to Adam.

"Is this where you've been?" she asked him, her tone equating being in my company with wallowing in subterranean caverns rife with incurable viruses.

"Mrs. Crowley, I just had fresh champagne delivered to your table," Tricia said with the firm-handed cheeriness of a rehab counselor.

Claire didn't budge. "Things have been a little out of control, Mother," Adam said, his voice heartbreakingly weary.

"So you run off to hide with a woman who's crazy enough to believe she has your father's tapes?" Claire snapped. "Most of these people are here because she's making some fraudulent announcement, not to listen to your half-brother's new songs."

Kenny looked at me in surprise before Adam did. Adam turned to me slowly, as though reluctant to take his eyes off his mother, though I couldn't be sure if that was motivated by distrust, habit, or both.

"You've been talking to Gray Benedek," I said, and Claire flinched enough for me to know I was right.

"That's the announcement? You have the tapes?" Adam asked with chilly incredulity. "How did you get them?"

"One thing at a time," I said, hating the fact that I was causing him pain, but sensing Claire wasn't quite at the point of confessing yet.

"They aren't yours," Adam said angrily, his hand shooting out to grab my arm.

Before either he or I could react, Kyle was standing between us, catching Adam's wrist in his hand. "Bad idea," Kyle said quietly, but I wasn't as sure as I wanted to be that he was talking to Adam and not to me.

"You better be careful, Ms. Forrester, or I will wreck your world," Claire said, her voice alarmingly even.

"I'm sorry," I said, leaning forward as though I were having trouble hearing her over the sounds of the party. "You're going to rock my world?"

Kyle pulled me back in one direction, and Tricia shepherded Claire off in the other. Adam hesitated a moment, then followed his mother. I spotted Gray installed in the booth just to the left of the stage, receiving guests as though it were his party and not Jordan's. Claire shook off Tricia, took Adam's arm, and went to join Gray.

Kenny looked at me analytically. "Are you crazy?" he asked with no judgment.

"Yes, she is," Kyle said, not quite so judgment-free.

"It's a bogus announcement?" A wicked grin spread across Kenny's face, and he checked his camera for readiness. "This is gonna be great."

Groping for a defense, I was saved by the arrival of Cassady, who ran up to us breathless, Aaron doing his best to keep up with her in the crowd. "Did we miss anything?"

Kyle shook his head. "We're just getting started. Hey, Aaron."

The men shook hands, and Kyle introduced Kenny to both of them as Tricia ran up from the other side of the room. She greeted Cassady and Aaron briefly, saying, "I think we need to get Molly off the floor. I saved a booth for us, you should come sit."

"I'm not sure I can," Cassady said with a weird little trill in her voice.

"Your dress isn't that tight," I said.

"I'm just too excited."

"Why?" Tricia asked, yanking on her arm. "What happened?"

Cassady quivered a little and rolled her eyes at herself. "You're not going to believe this. I'm not sure I do." And she raised her left hand to show us a magnificent marquise-cut diamond in a raised setting with emerald-cut baguettes on all four sides.

Murder and thievery are all well and good, but if you can't stop a moment and squeal over your best friend's brand-new engagement ring, then what's your life come to?

18

Perhaps there's some law in physics that can explain life's continual need to flip itself upside down when you least expect it. It's an excellent characteristic in a roller coaster but makes crafting a balanced life nearly impossible. The friend you thought would be the last to get engaged goes first, the man you find perfect finds you flawed, the person you thought was totally incapable of committing murder turns out to be the most cold-blooded creature you've ever met. Maybe Aaron can explain it to me someday, since he's apparently going to be around for the duration.

Tricia and I nearly conked heads as we both dove in to hug Cassady. Laughing, we let go of her long enough to fall upon Aaron, then moved right back to Cassady.

"Isn't this the most ridiculous thing you've ever seen?" Cassady said, tears sparkling at the corners of her eyes.

"It's splendid," I said, choked up myself.

"Were you shocked?" Tricia asked, sniffing grandly.

"Stunned," Cassady answered.

"And here you thought he was up to no good," I said, turning her hand so the diamond caught the glittering club lights.

"Do you know why he's been standing me up? Because he

was too nervous and he needed to rehearse a few more times," Cassady said with an "isn't that sweet?" tone.

"So his student didn't have a problem?" I asked.

"Oh, she did, but he said he's not normally one to let work interfere to that extent. He was using it as a handy excuse," she said with proud relief, knowing now that it was all for the best. I felt a hot flash of guilt; how much of my insistence on the importance of my work was a defense mechanism, hedging my bets in case Kyle and I couldn't get the bugs worked out?

"Oh, this is so amazing," Tricia said, quivering with sympathetic happiness. "You wait right here, I have the most incredible idea."

She raced away, giving me the opportunity to hug Cassady all by myself. "I'm so happy for you."

"Who'da thunk it?" She laughed.

Over her shoulder, I could see Aaron explaining his method of proposal to Kyle and Kenny, who both smiled appreciatively. Kyle looked up long enough to catch my eye and wink. He didn't seem to be experiencing any of the pangs of guilt or, I admit, jealousy that I was feeling, but my head was too jumbled for me to decide whether that was a good sign. Besides, as thrilled as I was for Cassady and Aaron, I needed to stay focused on why we were there, beyond Jordan's singing.

Checking on the ringside booth, I could see Gray, Claire, and Adam sitting together, the men watching the stage expectantly, Gray spewing about something and Adam nodding absently. Claire stared daggers at me across the crowded room. Enchanted evening, my foot.

Onstage, Bonnie and the technicians appeared to have reached the end of their consultation, and I caught a glimpse of Jordan and Tricia whispering cozily in the wings with Olivia as a welcome third wheel. Olivia's hands flew to her mouth, and Jordan smiled dazzlingly at something Tricia said, then they both nodded. Tricia threw her arms around Jordan's neck, and they kissed with noticeable heat. How caught up in my own story—stories—had I been not to have noticed how involved my two best friends were with these two men?

Then Jordan walked onto the stage, skintight black leather pants, white linen shirt only partially buttoned. Bonnie clasped her hands together, radiating maternal pride, then threw open her arms to embrace him. Jordan scooped her into his arms and spun her around once before depositing her carefully back on her feet. The people who were watching the stage applauded, causing everyone else to turn toward the stage.

Jordan kissed Bonnie on the cheek, and now the whole room erupted with applause. I spotted Risa in the crowd, smiling and clapping in approval. Bonnie slipped into the wings as the band came out and Jordan strode up to his microphone, holding out his arms in welcome. "Good evening! Welcome to our little party for a few close friends." He grinned, gesturing to the full house. "We'll be starting in just a few minutes, so grab a drink, grab a date, and settle in. We're gonna be here all night."

This was a more gregarious Jordan than I'd seen before, and I wondered if that was a reflection on how things were going with his songs or with Tricia or something else. I glanced over at Adam, who was watching Jordan with razor-sharp intensity. Maybe Jordan was just enjoying have a leg up on Adam.

Bonnie and Olivia appeared at the booth to the right of the stage, smiling and waving to people as they took their seats. It was like warring dynasties clustered at the feet of the crown prince.

Tricia ran back to us, out of breath but carrying bottles of Veuve Clicquot in each hand. "Jordan has something special for you," she said to Cassady. "Come sit down and enjoy." She pointed to the booth next to Claire and Gray and led the way.

"I'm gonna start things off," Jordan said to a renewed wave of cheering, "with a song I've never performed in public before. In fact, only a couple of people have heard it at all until tonight. And I'm playing it for two very special people here tonight—Cassady and Aaron. Congratulations on your engagement!"

Tricia looked back over her shoulder and winked at Cassady and Aaron, who both blushed. A club filled with people who had no idea who Cassady and Aaron were cheered voraciously for them anyway. Jordan fired off an amazing riff that exploded into a sustained chord from the entire band, then they pulled it way back down into bluesy vamping as Jordan leaned into the microphone, eyes half-closed, voice husky with emotion. "Carve out a space where only we exist," he sang. "Lead me to a place that I would have missed."

Tricia parked the champagne bottles on our table and gestured to the stage proudly. "I asked him to play it for you," she shouted over the music.

"It's beautiful!" Cassady shouted back.

"It's the one he wrote for me. That's my song."

"Oh, sweetie, thank you!" Cassady teared up, clutching Tricia's hand with one hand and Aaron's with the other.

"Raises the bar on our engagement present to her, doesn't it?" Kyle whispered in my ear, trying to guide me into the booth.

At least it was a great song. Because it would have been doubly tragic if the chaos that ensued had been inspired by some disposable pop tune that you couldn't even remember three minutes after you listened to it. I was turning to answer Kyle when Claire Crowley came hurtling out of her booth beside us.

"Stop him!" she demanded of the room in general, despite the fact that the music was so loud, no one more than an arm's length away could hear her.

"Mother," Adam warned as he clambered out of the booth behind her. Gray stayed at the table, his head in his hands. It truly was a beautiful song, and I didn't understand why the three of them were so upset.

Frustrated by the general lack of response to her demand, Claire turned to us. "Stop him!" she insisted again.

"Mrs. Crowley," Tricia said in her best hostess voice, "don't you like it? It's my song." She placed a placating hand on Claire's arm, and Claire smacked it away.

"You awful little wannabe," she spat, "that's not your song. Who told you that?"

"Jordan wrote it for Tricia," I said, confused by Claire's lack of control and trying to figure out exactly where Kenny was standing and whether we should quickly modify our agreement about no preannouncement pictures.

Now it was my turn to feel the wrath of Claire. Her nostrils flared so wide that her top lip flattened out. "I knew you weren't as clever as you pretend. That's *my* song."

There's a ride at Disneyland that my devious little niece lured me onto last summer, where you're supposedly in the elevator of a haunted hotel and you rocket up just long enough to get a magnificent peek at the park and the city, spread out as a million sparkling lights below you, before the car drops so fast that your body rises up, straining against the seat belt for a moment, then slams back down in pursuit of your stomach, which has plummeted all the way to your ankles.

"The song Micah wrote for you?" I asked.

"Yes!"

A whole different answer to the puzzle of the Hotel Tapes, of Russell's murder, flashed before me even as my stomach and theories went into deadfall. I'd been so fixed on Claire as puppet master, jerking Olivia, Adam, and everyone else around for her own purposes, that I hadn't seriously considered the other branch of the family tree. I hadn't seriously considered that Jordan had been sitting on the tapes all along until he was ready to pass off the songs as his own.

"Jordan wrote it for me," Tricia repeated, wounded.

"It can't be," I said to Claire, not defending Jordan as much as trying to hold my theory together. "I mean, if you had the tapes and gave them to Adam to record, then you'd keep quiet."

"What?" Adam exclaimed in outrage. "That's what you thought?"

People in our vicinity were starting to take notice of the agitated body language and the fact that we were blatantly ignoring Jordan's impassioned performance, even though they couldn't hear what we were discussing. Most just turned in our direction, but a couple of men stood up, reacting to that male instinct for violence brewing. This could get very ugly, and not in the productive way I'd planned.

I didn't have time to explain properly to Adam, so I plowed ahead, hoping I'd be permitted to do all my apologizing at once, when this was all settled. "But how can he expect to sing Micah's songs and not have you expose him?"

"Jordan's not a genius," Claire sneered.

"And you can't prove the songs aren't his," Kyle pointed out.

Claire blanched, her mouth moving soundlessly for a moment. Behind her, Gray still sat with his head in his hands, having already figured this part out. "But the tapes . . ." Having never seen Claire at a loss, I found it disconcerting.

"You don't have copies. And Micah didn't write any of those songs down," I finished for her.

"Who the hell cares?" Adam said, storming away.

"Adam," Kyle said, on that testosterone wavelength.

"Leave him alone," Claire demanded.

"That's a really bad idea," I said, spotting where Adam was headed.

As the song reached its climax, Jordan was working the guitar with feverish dexterity, the notes swirling together, building to a melodic and emotional peak that had people on their feet, swaying and grooving as if it were an old favorite, even though they'd never heard the song before. But just before the final, tumultuous chord, Adam leapt onstage and punched Jordan in the jaw with admirable accuracy. Jordan tumbled back into his bass player, and Adam jumped on them, fists still flying. Feedback and guests screamed in unison, the drummer and the keyboard player dove into the scrum, Kyle ran for the stage, and I followed, only to have Cassady and Tricia yank me back. Aaron raced unimpeded after Kyle, while Kenny strained next to me, like a puppy wanting off the leash.

"Go for it, Kenny," I said. "The papers may not want them, but the courts will need them."

As Kenny and his camera raced to the fracas, Claire turned back to me. "This is all your fault."

Tricia and Cassady gasped for me, so I concentrated on replying, "Life must be such great fun when you never have to take responsibility for anything."

"Speaking of responsibility, your party's getting a little out of control," Cassady told Tricia, pointing out that even in the darkest corners of the club, people were now comprehending that something unusual was happening onstage. There was no panic, no clamor, just a breathless lull in the conversation as club security rushed forward and people waited for the next development. Which was Jordan jumping down from the stage the moment Kyle and Aaron pulled Adam off him. Unfortunately, the rest of the band grabbed Kyle and Aaron, not understanding that these two strangers were trying to help. Which allowed Adam to jump down beside Jordan, where the two of them began, of all things, a pillow fight.

After yanking a large pillow out from under a model with no posterior padding of her own, Jordan swung it full force at Adam. Adam staggered, almost fell, then caught a pillow tossed to him by Risa, surprisingly, who applauded merrily as Adam threw his whole weight into smacking Jordan. Jordan swung back, connecting soundly with Adam's chest and face, while Risa and several of her friends snatched up pillows and waded into the fray.

Tricia dashed off in search of more security. Completely misreading what was going on between Jordan and Adam, the guests flung themselves into the new party sport with glee and abandon. With dizzying rapidity, the dramatically dressed and coiffed guests dissolved into a screaming mass of five-year-olds. Designer shoes flew through the air as women kicked them off to improve their stances, tailored jackets hit the floor as men sought to free up their swings, and the wait staff scrambled for cover. Kenny popped up and down all over the room, it seemed, like a gopher with a flash in his hand. The Mad Hatter Tea Party air of it all was further elevated by Gray, who had made his way to the baby grand onstage and begun playing crazy, mad blues progressions that whipped themselves into a frenzied melody. "Blues for Chaos" seemed a fitting title.

Eager as I was to shoulder my way to the center of the storm and help separate Jordan and Adam, I was reluctant to leave Claire. But then I saw Olivia hurtling toward the locus where my boys and the bouncers were grappling with her boys despite the pummeling they were receiving from giggling guests, and I knew I had to lend whatever aid I could.

"Don't let her go anywhere," I told Cassady.

"May I have your permission to sit on her?" Cassady asked.

"Since we're running short of pillows, absolutely," I said.

"You can't treat me like a criminal," Claire protested.

"Sure we can," Cassady said. "Just watch."

"You still think I had something to do with this?" Claire asked me indignantly.

Fissures were appearing in my theory with alarming rapidity, but I couldn't shake the feeling that Claire was involved somehow. "Maybe you killed Russell because he gave Jordan the songs and now you're going to win public sympathy by discrediting him."

"Oh, I will discredit him, believe me," Claire said with the pent-up rage of two and a half decades. "But I didn't kill Russell."

"Watch her," I told Cassady again, and threaded my way through the obstacle course of swirling cushions and flailing knees and elbows to where Kyle and Aaron were giving the security guys their shot at wrestling Jordan and Adam apart while Olivia hovered fretfully.

Tricia had reached the stage and convinced Gray to stop playing long enough for her to announce, "Ladies and gentlemen, we'd like to wind down the pillow fights now and return to the music. So if you could all settle back in, our special surprise guest, Gray Benedek, will finish his set and then we'll get Jordan back up here."

Happily, the crowd was amenable, dropping their pillows and plopping back down on them to applaud enthusiastically as Gray started back up. The drummer and bass player grabbed their instruments and joined the jam. Attention was soon focused back on the stage by everyone except the small knot of people formed around Jordan and Adam. Kenny wandered back but had the grace to keep his camera down for the moment.

"No way in hell he's getting back up on that stage," Adam fumed. Kyle stood behind Jordan, pinning his arms back, while Adam leaned as far into Jordan's face as possible, given that Aaron was similarly restraining him. Security guards stood by, ready to help but respecting Kyle's shake of the head.

"Why not? What the hell's wrong with you, dude?" Jordan asked angrily.

"You stole my mom's song, you dirtbag."

"Your mom's a liar, man."

"Jordan, please," I said, digging deeply for my most diplomatic tone. "Everyone needs to put their cards on the table before anyone else gets hurt. Where'd you get the song?"

"It's my song."

"Jordan . . . ," Tricia said with an anguished catch in her voice.

Jordan looked at her for a long moment, then looked at the rest of the group, his eyes falling on me last. "All right. Someone else wrote it."

"Duh!" Adam exclaimed. "Dad wrote it. For *my* mother."

"No way!" Jordan exclaimed in return. "He didn't write it."

"It was on the Hotel Tapes!"

"No!" Jordan was so upset, he was trembling.

"My mother heard it, Jordan!"

Craning his neck, Jordan looked around the club as much as his pinioned position would allow. "No. Where is she?"

"Claire?" I asked.

"No, *my* mom."

Adam grimaced in disgust. "You infant."

"You don't get it, Adam. She wrote the song. She gave it

to me. Because I was having such a hard time writing songs for the new album. She said it was a gift and I had to keep it a secret."

Adam snorted in derision. Sensing the fight draining from him, Kyle let Jordan go. Jordan pivoted sadly in the midst of our group, scanning the club. "Mom?" he called halfheartedly.

Just as I'd thought: a mother willing to kill to get what she regarded as her son's birthright, to give him a leg up on claiming his artistic legacy.

Right theory, wrong mother.

19

"*I gotta get back* out on the road!"

Glowing with sweat, excitement, and champagne, Gray Benedek flung himself offstage as though a horde of screaming fans were waiting for him rather than the hysterical cluster of the Crowley inner circle. "That felt amazingly good. Anybody gonna tell me how great I sounded? Or at least thank me for keeping the show going?"

I moved to pull him aside and explain, but Claire cut me off, steaming up to him with her chin lifted in regal indignation. "Why don't you get back out there and make sure anyone gives a damn before you make too much of an ass of yourself? Maybe they all think it's just part of the joke tonight."

"Joke?" Gray recoiled from the artistic censure. "My music isn't any joke."

Kyle and Tricia hustled down the hallway, trailed by several security guards. "She's not in the club." They'd done a thorough sweep while Cassady, Aaron, and I herded Jordan and the rest of our cozy entourage backstage.

"Who's not?" Gray asked.

"Are you high?" Claire asked, stomping her foot so hard that she wobbled as her heel threatened to snap under the pressure. "Bonnie stole the tapes and gave Jordan the songs. Didn't you hear him singing out there? Couldn't you tell it was Micah's song?"

Gray gave Jordan a look brimming with nostalgic sadness. "I thought he'd finally tapped in."

Jordan sank into a chair, head hanging low between his shoulders, more weight than I could imagine pressing down. "So far from it," he murmured.

"You don't remember that song?" Claire asked Gray insistently.

"I'm lucky I remember that year," Gray said frankly.

"Where would your mother go, Jordan?" I asked.

"I'm not sure," Jordan said flatly, still trying to absorb the magnitude of what his mother had apparently done. For him.

"Flight risk," Kyle said, pinching his bottom lip.

"Can't you send the police after her?" Olivia asked shrilly. "An APB or something?"

"This doesn't really qualify," Kyle said.

"We can throw down another kind of net," I said quickly, sketching it out in my mind as I went. I hated to have to ask, but it was the best way. "Jordan, where's your cell?"

With a deep breath, Jordan sat up enough to look at me. The flat gaze told me that it wasn't as much a matter of his trusting me as his not having the energy to fight me anymore. He pointed to the dressing room. "In my jacket pocket."

"Your mom's number is in it, obviously?" He nodded. "Perfect. Olivia, grab it, please. Jordan, you need to get back out onstage. Play more. I don't care who wrote the songs. Sing some Who songs. Just get out there. Gray, Adam, go with him."

"No way," Adam said, eyeing Jordan warily.

"Adam. Jordan. I really need you to look at the big picture here. This isn't about all the years of jealousy and bickering and backstabbing and God knows what else your mothers put you through because you were the pawns in their self-righteous turf war."

"Just a minute!" Claire objected.

I was not about to stop, even for Claire. "This is about doing the right thing for the men who loved you and who always tried to do right by you. One of whom died for you. So can you reach down deep inside and try to find some love for each other as brothers and some love for Russell and your dad?"

Bracing myself for a cutting retort, I watched as Adam unexpectedly moved to stand beside Jordan, hand on his shoulder. After a moment, Jordan stood, patting Adam briefly on the back. However twisted their relationship, however deeply rooted their anger, they were still brothers at heart after all.

Now it was Gray who frowned and shook his head, pointing at Adam. "We both play keyboard."

Adam sighed heavily, already propelling Jordan toward the stage. "Get a grip, Gray. You take the piano, I'll take the Hammond."

Claire barred Adam's way. "What do you think you're doing?"

"Listening to Molly."

Claire didn't like that at all. "You don't know what she's planning. Why are you going along with this?"

"Because she's right about Dad and Russell. And she's the first person I've met in a long time who judged me on my own merits, low as they may be. And I trust her." Claire faltered, and while she groped for a comeback, Adam marched Jordan out onto the stage without a look back at me. Gray followed, dazed but itching to play.

Collecting herself quickly, Claire demanded, "Now what?" over the noise of the crowd welcoming the boys back to the stage.

"You're going to make a statement to the press," I told Claire.

"I am not. This is a private, family matter."

"Nothing about your family has ever been private. By your choice."

Olivia dashed up with Jordan's BlackBerry in her hand. "Molly, Jordan didn't know, I swear it. . . ."

"I believe you. Now pretend to be Jordan. Text Bonnie and ask her where she went, that Claire's about to make some big announcement about releasing the Hotel Tapes as a boxed set and she should get back here right away."

Olivia's thumbs flew over the keyboard with impressive dexterity and speed. Claire thrust an imperious hand into the air. "Don't you dare, Olivia." Olivia, to her great credit, kept texting. "I don't care what you say, I won't be a part of this."

"Okay, fine. Olivia, change it to 'Adam's making some big announcement' and we'll let him be the hero," I suggested. Olivia's head never came up, just bobbed in assent.

"What hero?"

"The one that lures Bonnie back here and exposes her."

The band started playing again, a song off Jordan's first album called "Dust of Dreams," and the crowd whooped. Claire's lips pursed, as though she were already tasting the sweetness of dethroning Bonnie after over twenty years of having to pretend she was happy to share the crown. "Change it back to me, Olivia."

"I never changed it to Adam. Forgive me, but certain relationship dynamics around here are predictable. But for my father's sake, don't screw this up, Claire," Olivia said, tasting a little sweetness herself. She hit the "send" button in punctuation, then turned back to me. "So what happens next?"

Cassady and Aaron went with Kenny to invite members of the press inside for the announcement.

Tricia and Olivia went to talk to Risa and Peter and give each of them Bonnie's number so they could text her and ask her why she wasn't part of the deal to produce the Hotel Tapes boxed set.

Kyle and I took Claire into the dressing room to collect herself and practice her announcement.

"Do you have some brilliant plan B in the event this doesn't work?" Claire asked tartly, fixing her makeup. Surprisingly, her hand trembled slightly as she relined her lips.

"Blame it all on me," I said, knowing full well that I'd be fired anyway if this train left the tracks.

Jordan's BlackBerry buzzed insistently in my hand. The message from Bonnie read: "BRB, keep Lying Bitch quiet."

Claire tensed, hearing the buzz. "Is that Bonnie? What's she saying?"

" 'Be right back . . . ,' " I started, then decided to let her read the rest for herself. Turning the BlackBerry so she could see the message, I asked, "Is that what she calls you to your face?"

Claire glanced at the text, then swatted my hand away and went back to primping. Kyle studied the toes of his shoes intently for a moment. "How exactly do you see this playing out?" he asked me.

"The paparazzi's already lathered up in anticipation of an announcement."

"What were you going to tell them?" Claire asked.

"That I had uncovered the tapes. So you'd be forced to come forward and denounce me, saying you had them." Catching her hate-filled look in the mirror, I shook my head. "Please. You can't be shocked. After you bribed me and your boyfriend drugged your son."

Claire's eyebrows shot up in genuine dismay. "He's not my boyfriend."

I was going to express my opinion of the fact that she chose to take offense at that part of my statement, but Kyle interceded. "So the press is foaming at the mouth . . ."

Taking a deep breath, I said, "So Claire goes out there, tells everyone she's found the tapes and is going to release them, Bonnie makes a scene because she has the tapes, Tricia gets her security guys to sit on Bonnie, your friends in the local precinct come scoop her up and discover it's all part of a much bigger story."

It sounded so simple.

And it got off to such a good start.

Posted outside, Cassady called me the moment Bonnie vaulted out of her cab. Aaron unleashed the paparazzi who had remained outside, the ones who'd been told—by Cassady and Aaron—that there'd been a huge fight inside and Bonnie had stormed out, but the rumor was she was returning to settle the score with Claire. The crowd of photographers delayed Bonnie's entrance into the club long enough for Tricia to give Jordan and Adam the signal to wrap up the song and for Jordan to address the crowd.

"There's been some pretty heavy stuff going down with me and Adam and our families lately," he told the rapt audience with scruffy, self-effacing charm. "Things got a little toxic earlier, and we're sorry about that. But we're sure rockin' now, aren't we?" He grinned as the guests cheered. "And we're gonna rock some more, but right now, I've got a really special announcement for you all from a true queen of the rock world, Claire Crowley."

Backstage, Claire didn't move. I couldn't tell if she was being stubborn or freezing up, but I put my hand on her back to nudge her along. "You can do this, Claire," I whispered, more warning than encouragement.

"Of course I can," she said, and strode out, arms open to

the applause, head tilted back, channeling Micah in some twisted fashion.

I started to slide around front to watch her, but Kyle grabbed my arm. "Stay back here. Better vantage point," he said quietly, his eyes scanning the crowd. "You'll want to track Bonnie from the minute she comes in."

"Good evening," Claire said, her voice dropping down into the smoky, sexy register. "Aren't these boys magnificent?" The crowd clapped in approval. "I'm so proud of both of them. They share such a special relationship and a unique musical heritage." She held out her hands, and Jordan and Adam came to flank her.

"Bingo," Kyle whispered, pointing out where Bonnie had entered the club and paused at the edge of the crowd.

"I hate to interrupt their show, but we all decided this was an ideal time to make a very important announcement. There have been rumors for so many years about recordings that their father, Micah Crowley, made while he was on the road."

"Wish I had binoculars," I whispered to Kyle, but even without them, I could see Bonnie's face twisting with anger.

"Tonight, it is my honor and privilege to announce for the first time in public that those tapes do exist," Claire said with an emotional vibrato building in her voice. The audience gasped in pleasure. "And with the help of Jordan, Adam, and Gray Benedek, I will be releasing them as a boxed set of CDs—"

"Why is everything about you?!" Bonnie screamed from her spot at the back of the club.

"Here we go," Kyle whispered.

I crossed my fingers, willing Bonnie to play her part the way I'd seen it in my head. The fact that she was the person in this group with whom I'd spent the least amount of time and

I knew the least flitted across my mind and quickened my pulse for a moment, but I was sure it would all come together.

The photographers in the club swung to take pictures as the crowd parted, even as its shocked whispers bubbled up into excited murmurs, to allow Bonnie to march up to the stage.

Claire stepped away from the microphone to address Bonnie with the illusion of privacy. "Bonnie—"

"'Bonnie' what?" Bonnie yelled, advancing. "'Bonnie, let me have the spotlight'? 'Bonnie, stay out of the way'? 'Bonnie, you whore, your son's a bastard'? What, Claire, oh-so-understanding rock star wife? So forgiving, so accepting. Lets everyone think it's all fine. Queen Claire, rock royalty. Keeper of the flame. Keeper of nothing but lies. What do you want to say? What lie are you going to tell them now?"

People had been on their feet, dancing, but now sat down in hushed attention, though I could see cell phones popping open everywhere. I wondered where Risa, Peter, Henry, and Eileen were and what they were making of all this.

Claire cast a concerned look toward me as Bonnie swept around the side of the stage and came up the stairs, and I nodded encouragingly. Jordan stepped forward to meet his mother, but Adam and Gray pulled him back. Bonnie didn't notice, she was so focused on Claire.

"I'm not lying," Claire said, returning to the microphone.

"Of course you are," Bonnie said, "because I have the tapes."

I wanted to throw up my arms in exultation but didn't want to distract Claire. Still, Kyle squeezed my arm, on the same wavelength.

"Now you're lying," Claire said, her face flushed and the audience forgotten.

Bonnie hadn't forgotten the audience. She turned to them, played to them. So here's the insidious cultural legacy of reality television: No secret is too sordid, too shameful, not to share it when there's an audience to entertain. Bonnie all but fluttered her eyelashes to emphasize her wronged position. "She was going to cut me out, just like she's tried to cut me out of things my entire life. But who inspired Micah to his greatest work? Who gave Micah his talented son?"

"She's disrupting the concert," Kyle whispered. "Tell Tricia to get security on the stage. Now."

As I fumbled for my phone, Jordan approached Bonnie. "Mom," he said, "don't do this."

He reached out for her, but she stepped back, defiantly pulling a simple cassette tape out of the ruffled Yves Saint Laurent bag on her shoulder and raising it above her head. The audience oohed as though she were holding up a great religious relic, which I guess to her mind she was. "I'm glad you're all here tonight," she told the guests, "because Micah loved an audience."

"Like you know what Micah loved," Claire scoffed.

"He loved me. He felt sorry for you," Bonnie said, turning to give the guests a special smile, acknowledging that she knew they were on her side. Chuckles fluttered through the audience, the tension level dropping as people sat back in anticipation of the next fight on the night's card. "I loved him most of all, so I should be the one to bring his music back. I deserve it."

"No, you deserve this," Olivia said, stepping up onstage and pointing a pistol at Bonnie.

The tension level rocketed back up through the roof. People screamed and ducked under pillows, flashes exploded, and Adam dragged Claire out of the line of fire. Jordan froze, his gaze fixed on the gun, and Gray pulled him out of the way. Knowing security would come of their own accord now, I raced onto the stage, half a step behind Kyle. When he stopped ten feet from Olivia, I assumed that he had an excellent, field-tested reason for doing so and stopped next to him.

"Olivia, put the gun down," I said as firmly as my quaking voice would allow.

"Everyone really needs to stop telling me what to do. You included, Molly," Olivia said with wholly inappropriate calm.

"I want to help you protect the tapes, that's all," I said.

All three women looked at me as if I were the one acting crazy. "What?" Olivia asked.

"Everyone's here because of the tapes, right?" I wasn't looking for an audience reaction, but I got one: a smattering of applause and some whoops of agreement. I flashed a strained smile at the crowd to be polite, but Kyle gestured brusquely for me to keep focused on Olivia. "So it would be a huge shame if you took a shot at Bonnie and missed and hit the tapes."

Bonnie huffed in offense, but otherwise she didn't move, her arm still above her head and her eyes locked on Olivia's gun.

"Why don't I take the tapes?" Claire offered.

"Don't move, Claire," Olivia warned. "You're hardly a neutral party here."

"How about I take the tapes?" I offered, taking a tentative step forward.

Bonnie pinned the bag to her side with her elbow. "I am not giving up these tapes."

"Over your dead body, huh, Bonnie?" Olivia said. "The same way my father felt, but that didn't stop you."

"I didn't kill your father!"

"Don't you lie to me!" Olivia took a step closer, steadying the pistol at nose level on Bonnie.

"It was an accident!" Bonnie blurted.

With everyone gasping at the same time, the air pressure in the club had to have dropped several points. I could swear my ears popped.

Bonnie pressed on, eyes still focused on the gun. "Russell wasn't supposed to know anything about our plan, and then Jordan had to play him his new demo tape, beg for his approval."

"Stop it, Mom," Jordan said, his voice dark and heavy.

"But Russell thought he recognized the song and wanted to compare it with the Hotel Tapes and realized a few were missing. He was so angry, he went a little crazy. Jordan called me, I came right over and tried to calm him down. I just mixed him something to make him settle down and give me some time to think. I didn't realize how much he'd already had. Olivia, I'm so sorry."

There wasn't a sound; not a single flash went off. People throughout the club froze in the face of naked emotion and the magnitude of the confession. Only Claire was smiling, her blatant joy at her rival's collapse disconcerting.

So Bonnie had taken a couple of Russell's tapes, hoping he wouldn't notice. Then once he was dead, she'd gone back and taken all the tapes so no one else would be able to play them and expose Jordan as an actual copy of his dad.

"Give me back my tapes," Olivia said, yanking the bag off Bonnie's shoulder with her gun-free hand.

Bonnie caught the purse strap. "No, don't take the tapes. It's not like I did it deliberately."

Claire threw herself at Bonnie as Bonnie yanked back on the purse strap, throwing off Olivia's center of gravity. For a moment, I thought she might bobble the gun, but she tried to use the purse strap to pull herself back upright against Bonnie's weight. The strap flew off Bonnie's shoulder and the purse crashed to the floor, disgorging its load of nearly a dozen tapes. Bonnie landed right beside them, Claire on top of her, screaming and kicking and biting. Olivia toppled over, the gun skittering away from her.

Patrons attempted to storm the stage, whether to help or to see better, I wasn't sure, but then others pulled them away or perhaps pushed them away in their own flight toward the doors. The party disintegrated into a multilevel meltdown.

Onstage, Kyle grabbed the gun and pulled Olivia away from the other two by her ankle. Jordan, Adam, and Gray dove to the floor like football players covering a fumble, not to separate the women, but to gather up the tapes, especially before guests could get to them. It was left to me to jump into the catfight and peel Bonnie and Claire off each other.

Men fight nasty, but women fight mean. In the brief time in which I writhed on the stage floor with the two of them, I dodged far more elbows, knees, and incisors than made mathematical sense. It was like falling into a pit of hyenas, and when security finally arrived and pulled the three of us apart, I was winded, bruised, and grateful.

Kyle handed Olivia over to them, too; she wasn't going to be able to get away with brandishing the gun in a crowded club, even though no one had gotten hurt.

Kyle helped me up off the floor while the guys finished collecting the tapes and themselves. Cassady and Aaron hurried up to make sure we were all right while Tricia took the microphone to announce that although the concert was over, the police were going to need a few statements, so people should feel free to stay awhile. A moment of silence followed her announcement, then, unbelievably, everyone applauded. In the blink of an eye, people were chatting, laughing, texting, and making calls, spreading the news all over town before we could even get out the door.

"You're all going to need to talk to the police," Kyle told the guys.

Gray indicated their fistfuls of tapes. "Can't we secure these somewhere first?"

"They could be considered evidence. We'll have to discuss it with the responding officers," Kyle said.

"Evidence? They'll be tied up for years," Gray moaned.

"We should just burn them," Jordan said grimly. He laid his hand on Adam's shoulder, and Adam nodded forlornly.

"Not until the police are done with them," I said.

Kyle gestured for the guys to go down the stage stairs first, then turned back to take my hand. "Let's go."

"No, I'm respecting your boundaries. It's in your hands from here on in," I said.

"There's a difference between respecting boundaries and passing off a problem," he said wryly. "I appreciate the thought, but we're both going to talk to them."

"I never intended to get you this involved," I said by way of apology.

"Good."

"But I appreciate your help."

"Yeah, but it has its limits."

"Such as?" I asked as I took his hand.

"Don't expect me to buy the boxed set."

20

"*What made you think* you could get away with it?"

It was a question worth asking a number of the people in my life at the moment, with Bonnie in custody in connection with Russell's death, Claire raising a ruckus, and Olivia, Jordan, and Adam trying to stay out of the crossfire and the public eye. Of course, it was also the first thing Ben, Kyle's partner, asked me when he joined the confab at the precinct house as Kyle and the officers from the First Precinct sorted through the chaos.

"It actually seemed logical at the time," I told Ben.

"There's a difference between logic and adrenaline, and we ought to get you familiar with that," Ben said.

"It worked," I said, allowing myself a little victory.

"Yes, it did."

"And I think he's still speaking to me," I continued, working hard to make it a statement and not a question.

"Yes, he is," Ben agreed. "Good to see you two back together."

"Yes, it is," I said with a smile. Because as the adrenaline burned off, there was no queasy doubt rumbling in my stomach or musty guilt lingering in my head. I'd been honest and direct with Kyle the entire time, and it felt great. The fact that he smiled reassuringly every time he caught my eye across the frenetic office felt even better.

What felt best of all was locking my apartment door behind us several hours later. "You locking us in or them out?" Kyle asked with a knowing smile.

It would take days for everything to be sorted out, but for the moment, anyway, we had a quiet space, a few free hours, and absolutely no company. Tricia had proclaimed her intention to sleep all weekend, Cassady and Aaron were going to celebrate privately, and the Crowley-Elliott clan was in the process of issuing a statement that stated they hoped their fans would respect their privacy during a difficult time.

"Kyle, I don't know how to thank you," I said quickly, worried that he was going to tell me he couldn't stay long.

"Let me count the ways," he offered, taking my hand and kissing the palm. "And then we'll go through them, one at a time," he continued, tracing each finger lightly with his own while I tried not to tremble. "Because neither one of us is working this weekend."

So we let the voice mail and e-mail accumulate, picking up the phone only to order in, and spent the weekend getting thoroughly and intimately reacquainted—one way at a time.

As magnificent as it was, the real world demanded our presence on Monday morning, which meant Kyle had to go back to his precinct and I had to sit down in the conference room at *Zeitgeist,* the bogus audition letter on the table in front of me and Dorrie across from me. Adrienne's desk had been my first stop, and she'd turned over the key without comment, though I knew Skyler had whispered into more than a few ears. But the word must not have reached Dorrie, because when I sought her out and asked her if we could have a word, she gave me a bright, pleased smile.

The smile had vanished now. Plucking a tissue into a fuzzy

mess, she refused to look me in the eye as she pondered my question. "They wanted another you," she said after a long pause.

"We want a new voice for the column," I said quietly. "Eileen would probably be thrilled by a completely different approach. A fresh start."

Dorrie shook her head defiantly. "But the column's great the way it is."

"It's fun. But you can't have fun with it—with anything—if you're not being yourself." Watching Dorrie maul the tissue, I thought of Adam and Jordan, wrestling with their father's shadow and struggling to find their own voices, fearful that those voices didn't exist or wouldn't be valued. "What were you going to do if you got the gig?"

"I hadn't figured that part out yet," Dorrie said, nose running. "You've written a lot of columns."

"And you didn't think I'd recognize any of them?"

"I thought you'd be flattered by how exactly I'd captured your voice," she said, a subtle tone of pride creeping into her voice.

"In this case, imitation isn't flattery, it's plagiarism, Dorrie."

"Are you going to fire me?"

"That's not my call. I have to discuss it with Henry and Eileen."

"But you want to fire me."

"No, I want to help you find the way to be yourself."

"I'm not sure who that is yet," she said, the pride sliding away again.

"It's a moving target for most of us," I admitted.

But I wanted to dig down and find an opportunity, a teachable moment, in all this because Dorrie seemed like a good person at heart and because I felt guilty that she'd emulated a wreck like me to this degree. And I wanted to be generous, out of superstition if nothing else, because things were working out so well for me.

Right up until the moment I walked into Eileen's office, Dorrie's letter in my hand, and saw the triumphant, cat-that-shredded-the-canary smile on her face. Henry stood beside her, his smile more tempered.

"We were just talking about you!" Eileen said, throwing her arms open to me in a gesture that she may have found warm and welcoming but evoked a Roman empress asking the crowds whether the slave should be executed or set free.

"I'm sorry I didn't get to see either of you at Pillow Friday night," I said. "Things got a little hectic."

"Some of us had the sense to leave when things got 'hectic.' No need for us to again suffer wounds just because you started a war. You never like the simple approach, do you?" Eileen asked, smile still too bright, arms drifting down to her sides.

"Should be quite an article," Henry said genuinely. "Congratulations."

"Thank you. Both. For the opportunity, most of all."

Henry nodded. "You deserve it. Continued good luck."

I had only a moment to register the fact that that sounded as though Henry wouldn't be here for my next article before Eileen said, "Fabulous things are happening for everyone. Did you hear? Henry's moving up and out!"

"Congratulations," I said, offering my hand automatically while I tried desperately to decode the brittleness of Eileen's tone. Was she jealous because Henry was getting a job she wanted, or was she having trouble containing her glee at her vision of what she could accomplish in a Henry-free environment?

"The official announcement is coming later this week, but I ran into Peter Mulcahey at Pillow and he'd already heard, so I was concerned it was leaking out," Henry said.

"With Peter, that's a valid concern," I said. "Are you going over to *Need to Know*?"

"The Publisher is buying it," Henry said, nodding, "and he's asked me to oversee the revamp. Hands-on and all that."

"That's wonderful. I hope you have a great time. We'll miss you," I said, knowing he'd understand that I would miss his leveling influence and, frankly, his support.

"Yes, we will," Eileen trumpeted. "But we'll manage somehow, won't we, Molly? Because The Publisher is looking for a little revamp here at *Zeitgeist* as well, so we're going to have to take a hard look at ourselves and decide exactly where we all fit together in a new and improved *Zeitgeist*."

About to release the lions, Empress Eileen smiled while I tap-danced. "Which brings us to the new advice columnist," I said, bracing myself for Eileen to tell me that I wasn't moving up after all, that with Henry leaving, her new vision included me in my old job.

"I heard we had a little problem," Henry said.

"A misguided applicant," I said, still debating the proper way to handle Dorrie.

"But who do you think gets the job?" Eileen asked.

"I'm proposing a completely new take on the column, in keeping with Eileen's suggestion about looking for things to change. What if we give the column to Skyler and Carlos and let them do a 'he said, she said' approach, which gives our readers dual insight and, as a publication, brings us some male pass-on readership that could elevate our profile?" I was pleased; it sounded almost as good in Eileen's office as it had in the shower earlier that morning when I'd suggested it to Kyle.

Henry grinned. "Wonderful solution. I agree, they had the strongest responses, and this way we don't have to choose between them. I'm so glad to have this decided before I go."

"Decided?" Eileen asked stiffly.

"We agreed the three of us would make the choice," Henry reminded her.

"And of course I agree, it's a delightful solution," Eileen vamped. "I thought we might have to have The Publisher sign off."

"No, he's knee-deep with the new mag. He'll love it. Let's bring in Carlos and Skyler and let them know."

"Wait. What are we going to do about Dorrie?" Eileen asked.

"You're going to need a new assistant," I said quickly, "and I think you have a real opportunity here to reach out and get her on the right track by letting her observe you up close on a daily basis and inspire her to be true to herself, like you always have been."

Henry frowned quizzically, but Eileen beamed. "You're absolutely right. She's clearly looking for a role model, and she'd be much better off with me."

And, I thought, Dorrie does deserve some punishment, and having to sit on Eileen's desk was only fitting.

We called in Carlos and Skyler first to tell them the good news, then brought in Dorrie to explain that she was being given a second chance and a great opportunity. Henry went to assemble everyone in the conference room to make a general announcement, and I stood in Eileen's doorway, savoring the fact that I was walking out of there feeling good about the magazine and about life.

Until Eileen called me back in. "One last thing," she said, coming around her desk and advancing on me. "This is my revamp. Not Henry's and certainly not yours. Do yourself a favor and don't start regarding yourself as irreplaceable around here. Because you're not."

"No one is," I answered simply, and walked away before any of the several emotions colliding in the pit of my stomach could show.

"To the unknown," I said, raising my glass as I sat at a table at Bemelmans that night with Kyle, Cassady, Aaron, and Tricia.

"Too bad she's not the one leaving," Tricia said after we drank. "There's a farewell party I'd love to throw."

"She could be, you never know," Cassady said. "If anyone can outlast her, Molly can."

"There's a lot to be said for the unknown, right, Aaron?" Kyle asked.

"Keeps us both employed," Aaron agreed.

"I was thinking, it makes us appreciate the known even more," Kyle said, squeezing my hand.

He was right. The crucial elements in my life were at this table—the man I loved, my best friends, a new friend marrying into the circle. Instead of dreading the unknown, I should welcome it. "Besides," I said, watching the man walking up behind Tricia, "if you're not open to the unknown, you can never be surprised."

"Hey, mind if I join you?" Jordan asked, putting a gentle hand on Tricia's shoulder as she started in delight. He clinked the ice cubes in the highball glass in his other hand. "I brought my own drink."

Tricia scooted over as Kyle pulled up a chair from the next table, occupied by a couple who were so focused on the argument they were having that we could have pulled over their table and they wouldn't have noticed. "How'd you find us?" Tricia asked.

"I called Kenny to see if he'd spotted you anywhere tonight." Jordan smiled.

I hadn't realized we'd stayed on Kenny's radar, but it was nice to know we'd stayed on Jordan's. Olivia had already promised "full access" while I completed the article, but I wasn't sure how the guys felt about how things had unfolded. "I'm surprised to see you out and about," I said.

“Why should I hide? I didn’t do anything wrong,” he said with a sigh. “And I had to get out. Adam and I have been working all day, and I seriously needed a break.”

“Working on . . . ?” Cassady asked.

“Writing music,” Jordan said. “Together. Kind of a catharsis thing, I think, but we actually . . . I dunno, it’s too soon to tell. Gotta just see how it all plays out.”

An enviable attitude, especially in the face of everything he was going through. But it made sense. Forcing things to happen never works and usually causes bigger problems than you start with. You have to believe that what matters most in life—love, faith, truth—will support you through the rough times and make the good times even more special.

“To letting it all play out,” I toasted, and as they lifted their glasses again, I made a vow then and there to be more patient and trusting and not try to impose my will on the world.

At least until the next story came along.